Tom hit the STOP button. A man in a conservative brown T-shirt and shorts stepped in immediately. Another advantage of time travel is that you can always get to meetings promptly. "Sir?"

"Just what are you trying to pull?" Tom said. "This tape has Conrad getting ready to marry Lady Francine! When I viewed it last week, she talked him into marrying Lambert's daughter."

"But, sir! I edited that tape, and he didn't do either! He went on toward France until an emissary of the duke talked him into returning to Poland!"

"What? If this is a joke, the prankster will spend the next century doing anthropological work on Eskimos!"

"Tom, it's not the sort of thing that would be done as a joke."

"I know. But that means we're seeing a temporal split right here. Two temporal splits!"

"But how could something that happened in the Thirteenth Century affect us, Tom? We're seventy thousand years in their past!"

"I don't know, but it scares the hell out of me!"

By Leo Frankowski
Published by Ballantine Books:

THE ADVENTURES OF CONRAD STARGARD

Book One: The Cross-Time Engineer
Book Two: The High-Tech Knight
Book Three: The Radiant Warrior
Book Four: The Flying Warlord

COPERNICK'S REBELLION

THE FLYING WARLORD

Book Four in the Adventures of
Conrad Stargard

Leo Frankowski

A Del Rey Book

BALLANTINE BOOKS • NEW YORK

DEDICATION

I'd like to thank Phillip C. Jennings for his kind help in proof-reading this series, and for his many valuable suggestions on improving it.

A Del Rey Book
Published by Ballantine Books

Library of Congress Catalog Card Number: 89-90964

ISBN 0-345-32765-9

Manufactured in the United States of America

First Edition: October 1989
Cover Art by Barclay Shaw

We're coming, you Mongols,
We're coming to kill you.
We're coming, you Mongols,
We're coming to die!
And your blood and our blood
Will fertilize meadows,
And our sons will plough them
And grain will grow high!

Krystyana's hymn

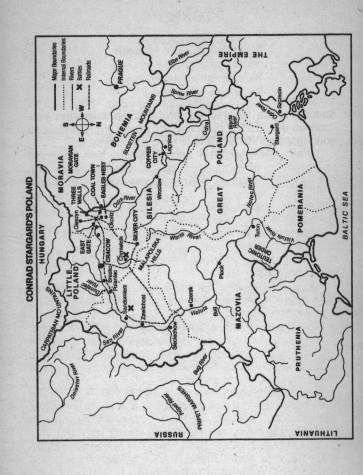

CONRAD STARGARD'S POLAND

Prologue

"WHOOPEE SHIT! . . . It's finally happening," she said. "A hundred years of tracking protohuman migration patterns on the African plain and it's finally over! It feels so good that I almost don't hate your guts anymore!"

"Well, don't get too carried away. You deserved every minute of it for dumping the owner's cousin into the thirteenth century when the guy didn't even know that time travel existed. And you deserve twice that for getting *me* messed up in it. Now get your scrawny body in the box. Time's running short!"

"Eat your heart out! I'll have my old sexy body back, and I'll take bubble baths and while you're eating carrion, I'll gorge for weeks on lobster thermidor and New York cheesecake and—"

He sealed her into the stasis chamber, then watched the readout over the temporal transport canister count down to zero.

The tone sounded and he opened the canister, pulled out his new subordinate without glancing at him, and started to slide his previous superior in. It was *expensive* to hold the canister in 2,548,850 BC, so doctrine was to make the transfer as quickly as possible.

She was almost in when something struck him as being very, very wrong. He took a closer look at the body he had just extracted. He gagged, retched, and vomited on the floor. Then he switched off his boss's stasis field.

"—Cherries Jubilee! Hey! What the hell is this? What am I still doing here? You're holding up the canister, you ass! Do you realize what that costs?"

"So the owner has lots of money but you only have the one life. I figured I didn't hate you that goddamn much."

1

"You're not making any sense; get me out of this time period! I've waited long enough!"

"Anything you say, lady, but take a look at what just came out of the canister and then ask yourself if you really want to get into it."

She stared at him and then at the other stasis chamber.

The body within was shriveled and dried. It was lay-ing on its side, a look of horror on its face. Its fingernails were all ripped off as if the man had tried to claw his way out before his air was exhausted.

"His stasis field must have failed," he said.

"But that's impossible! You know that's impossible! The circuitry for the stasis field is always built *inside* the field itself. Time doesn't exist inside the field, so how could the circuitry possibly have had *time* to fail?"

"Yeah, I know. But I still say that something is screwed up somewhere. The trip here takes six years subjective, and he had maybe two hours of air in the can. But that's not the big question. The biggie is whether or not you want to take the trip back. Me, I wouldn't risk it."

"Well, this chamber that I'm in hasn't failed. Why should it fail just because the other one did?"

"You know better than that, bitch. You're in the same damn chamber he's in. Right after sending you back, I got to send the empty chamber back to yesterday. It makes for a quicker turnaround that way. But I ran a self-check on it last night and it checked out perfect. So make up your mind. You're costing the owner a million bucks a second."

"Screw the owner," she said, squirming out of the chamber. "I'm not going anywhere till I see a live body crawl out of this thing!"

"Then help me get this dead one into your chamber. We gotta let the people uptime know what the problem is and we don't have much time to do it. Getting the body should be explanation enough!"

"Why not just ship him in the one he came in?"

He got the surprisingly light corpse into the other canister. "Lady, your big problem is that you're dumb."

He sent the canister back uptime and waited for a reply.

He waited for a long, long time.

Chapter One

^^^^^^^^^^^^^^^^^^

FROM THE DIARY OF TADAOS KOLPINSKI

My people was always boatmen on the Vistula. My father was a boatman and his father before him, and my great-grandfather was one, too. I still would be, except I lost my boat a few years back. I would have lost my life with it, if it hadn't been for Baron Conrad Stargard.

I was maybe the first man to meet him in Poland, next to the priest, Abbot Ignacy at the Franciscan Monastery in Cracow. I was stuck on the rocks on the upper Dunajeç with no one but a worthless little Goliard poet to help get me off. It was the poet's fault that we were hung up in the first place, since the twit rowed to port when I yelled starboard, but that's all water down the river. It was late in the season, and the weather was cold. Another day, and the river would be froze over and I'd lose my boat and cargo, all I owned, and maybe my life, too.

Then along comes this priest and with him was Sir Conrad. He was a giant of a man, a head and a half taller than I am, and I'm no shorty. He was pretty smart, and after I'd hired them two, we got the boat free in jig time with a line bent around a rock upriver, following Sir Conrad's directions. Never saw the like of it.

He told me he was an Englishman, but I never believed it. He didn't talk like no Englishman and he'd never seen an English longbow!

Now me, I'm a master of the English longbow. There's no one no where who can shoot farther or straighter or better than me, and that's no drunkard's boast. It's a gift, I tell you, and many's the time I've hit a buck square in the head at two hundred yards from a moving boat. I did it in front of Sir Conrad, and he helped me eat the venison.

And if you don't believe me, you meet me down at the practice butts some time, and I'll show you what shooting is all about. Only you better be ready to bet money.

We got that load to Cracow and I paid off my crew, me spending the night aboard to ward off thieves. Good thing, too, because three of them tried to rob me that night and kill me, besides. I was asleep, but at just the right time Sir Conrad shouts me awake, while he was holding a candle to me.

I tell you there was three of the bastards on my boat, coming at me with their knives drawn! I killed the first one with a steering oar, broke it clean over his head and his head broke with it. I threw the broken end at the second one and when he raised his arms to ward the blow, I caught him in the gut with my own knife, just as slick as you please.

The third one, he tried to get away, but in that kind of business, where you're a stranger in town, you best not leave no witnesses! Any thief would have a dozen friends swear that he was an honest man and *I* was the murderer.

So I bent my longbow and caught the bastard in the throat as he ran along the shore. Nailed him square to a tree, I did, and he stuck there, wiggling some.

Sir Conrad, he had his own funny knife out, that one that bends in the middle, but I wouldn't let him finish the thief. After all, it was *me* they was trying to rob and kill, so the honors was mine. Anyway, that was a good arrow, and I didn't want the fletching messed up. I cut the thief's throat and saved my arrow, and I guess Sir Conrad, he was a little mad because he wouldn't help me slide the three bodies into the river current to get rid of them. He even threatened to call out the guard!

But I got him calmed down just fine and he went back to the inn where he was staying at. That was the second time he saved me, because if them thieves had of caught me asleep, I'd be a dead man, and my cargo gone besides.

Well, I got me a good price for my cargo of grain and spent the winter in Cracow with a widow of my acquaintance.

The next summer a friar brought me this letter. He

was the same kid what used to be a Goliard poet and worked for me the last fall. He read it to me, and it was from Sir Conrad and it had Count Lambert's seal on it. They wanted me to come to Okoitz and teach the peasants there how to shoot the longbow. I was sort of tempted because I'd heard of beautiful things about Okoitz. They said that Count Lambert had all the peasant girls trained to jump into the bed of any knight that wanted them, and if Sir Conrad could qualify for them privileges, then why not me as well? At least I could dicker for it, if they really wanted me that bad, and they must have, since they wrote that letter on real calfskin vellum. Not that I was about to give up my boat and the Vistula, you know, but it might make a fine way to spend a winter.

But just then I had a contract to deliver a load of iron bars to Turon, and two other ones to buy grain on the upper Dunajeç and sell it in Cracow. I didn't have the time to find someone who could write me a letter to Sir Conrad, so I told the friar, him what brought me the letter, that I'd reply to Sir Conrad when I got back, in a few weeks, like.

That trip went just fine until I was heading down the Dunajeç again. The water was high, so I was working the boat alone, and I saw a buck at the water's edge in the same place where I'd bagged two other ones before, where a game trail comes down to the water. I was out of meat, so I shot that buck square in the head and pulled for shore to get it aboard before I got caught poaching.

Only it wasn't a buck I shot! It was a stuffed dummy with a deer skin on it, and the baron's men, they had me surrounded before I knew what was happening. They stole my boat and cargo, "confiscated" it, they called it, and I never did see it again. They would have hung me except I had that letter, written on good calfskin vellum it was, with Count Lambert's seal on it.

The baron said he wasn't about to offend a lord as high as Count Lambert, not without finding out what that man would pay for my life. They was all eating and drinking while I was tied up in front of them, and every round of wine they drank, they'd decide on a higher price for my ransom. By the time they was near dead drunk, they had this priest write up a letter to Count Lambert saying that if he didn't come up with four thousand pence in six weeks, they'd hang me for poaching, and I knew I was a dead man. I'd never seen that much money in one spot in my whole life, and the count didn't even know me. Who'd spend a fortune to save a man they'd never even met?

So they chained me with shackles riveted around my wrists and ankles and threw me into this tiny cell in the basement, with barely room to lay down. The only food I got was some table scraps every third day or so and they was stingy with the water. They wouldn't even give me a pot to piss in, and I had to piss and shit on the floor of my cell. But that whole castle stank so bad that they didn't even notice the stench I added. In a month's time, I was covered with my own shit, and being hung didn't seem like such a bad thing after all. At least then I could stop smelling myself!

Then along comes Sir Conrad, all decked out in red velvet and gold trim, with good armor under it. There was another knight with him, Sir Vladimir, and two of the prettiest girls you've ever seen, Annastashia and Krystyana. He paid out four thousand pence in silver coin and got my bow and arrows back, too, but I had no such luck with my boat and cargo.

A blacksmith knocked the shackles off me and it was strange to stand there in the bright sun with clean air to breathe, trying to make myself understand that I was going to get to live again.

Sir Conrad said I owed him four thousand pence, and I'd pay it off by working for him at three pence a day, the same pay that I'd given him the last fall. That was five years pay, even if I saved every penny of it, and many's the time I wished I'd paid him the six pence a day he'd asked for in the first place, instead of dickering him and the priest down to something reasonable.

They all stayed upwind of me until we got to an inn, and the innkeeper wouldn't let me inside until they'd given me a bath in the courtyard. They burned my clothes and I had to make do with a set of Sir Conrad's with the cuffs rolled up.

So we headed north and west, and when we got to Cracow, the ferryboat there had been changed at Sir Conrad's suggestion. It had a long rope running upstream to a big tree on the bank, and by adjusting that rope, the ferry master could take the ferry back and forth without needing any oarsmen!

I'd known Sir Conrad was smart, but this amazed me. I was still staring at it when we was attacked by a band of unemployed oarsmen. They blamed Sir Conrad for robbing their jobs, and maybe they was right. Sir Conrad, he got knocked off his horse by a rock that hit him square in the head, but Sir Vladimir, he went out and started smashing them oarsmen, and darned if Sir Conrad's mare didn't go out there and help him with the job. That horse is spooky, smarter than a lot of men I've hired. Sir Conrad says she's people, and he even pays her a wage for her work, swearing her in just like she was a vassal, but she scares me sometimes. It just ain't natural.

I got my bow bent, but I noticed that Sir Vladimir was using the flat of his sword on the oarsmen, so I didn't kill nobody either. I just nailed a few of their arms to some trees and buildings, me being that good a shot.

Once Sir Conrad got his wits back, he talked to the oarsmen and said that if any of them couldn't find work in Cracow, well, they could come to his lands at Three Walls and get work there. Most of them took him up on it, too. So did a lot of others that never was oarsmen, but it wasn't my place to say nothing. Why should I cost a man his job?

Sir Vladimir, he led the party right up to Wawel Castle, and all the pages and grooms scurried around like our party was real important. I got put up in the servants' quarters, of course, not being quality folk, but it wasn't bad. Them castle servants eat good, and I was still a month behind on my eating.

Besides filling me up on food, them servants filled me in on what was happening. They said that Sir Conrad got on the right side of Count Lambert by building all sorts of machines for him, and the count gave Sir Conrad a huge tract of land in the mountains near Cieszyn. Sir Conrad was building a city there when he heard I was in trouble and he got into a cesspool of trouble hisself on the way to get me.

They said he met a band of Teutonic Knights what were taking a gross of young heathen slaves to the markets in Constantinople, and Sir Conrad wouldn't allow them to do it. He said they was molesting children, so him and Sir Vladimir chopped up them seven guards and took the children back to Three Walls.

The trouble was that them Teutonic Knights, or Crossmen they're called, are the biggest and orneriest band of fighting men within a thousand miles, and they wasn't about to let Sir Conrad get away with robbing them. There was going to be a trial by combat, and Sir Conrad was going to get hisself killed, sure as sin. Nobody beats a Crossman champion in a fair fight, and mostly they don't fight fair.

I tell you that if you ever want to know something, you just ask a palace servant. They know everything that's happening, which is probably the reason that Sir Conrad won't have any. Lots of people works for him, you understand, but he gets up and gets his own meals just like everybody else.

We went to Okoitz, and I could see why Count Lambert was so impressed with Sir Conrad. There was a huge windmill, taller than a church steeple, and it sawed wood, worked hammers, and did all sorts of things, and there was this big cloth factory chock-filled with the damndest machines you ever saw, making cloth by the mile.

It was also filled with the finest collection of pretty girls in the world, and didn't none of them wear much. They was all crowding around Count Lambert and Sir Conrad, hoping to get their butts patted or their tits pinched. Not that any of them would pay any attention to the likes of me. I wasn't a knight and they didn't have time for us common trash.

Then, like there wasn't a gross of pretty girls after his body, and the Crossmen wasn't going to kill him, Sir Conrad invents a flying toy called a kite, and spends a week building them. He's a very strange man, that one.

Then we went to Three Walls and I got put to work, mostly doing guard duty at night. It wasn't so bad, since Sir Conrad let me hunt all I wanted, just so that everything I shot went into the pot, which was fine by me. I ate my share of it, and so did Sir Conrad. One of his rules was everybody ate the same, and there was always plenty of it. I respected him for that, even though a lot of the others just thought he was crazy.

At first, there wasn't much at Three Walls but a big sawmill and some temporary shacks, but they got some fine buildings up real quick before the snow flew, and since Sir Conrad planned it all, you just know they was full of odd things.

The strangest were the bathrooms, where they had flush toilets and hot showers and more copper pipes than you ever seen in your life. And some damn fine scenery, since the girls used the same showers we did. Not that any of the young ones would have much to do with me, no, they was all wanting a real knight and maybe even Sir Conrad.

But I found me another sensible widow and just sort of moved in with her. Nobody said anything about it and in a few weeks somebody else was using my bunk in the bachelors' quarters, and that was fine, too.

Come time for Sir Conrad's trial by combat, everybody in Three Walls went to Okoitz to watch it. I got to talking with Sir Vladimir and Friar Roman—him what used to be the Goliard poet—along with Ilya, the blacksmith. We all allowed as how it was a rotten shame that a fine man like Sir Conrad was going to get hisself killed, and especially by them filthy German Crossmen.

And we came up with a plan to do something about it. The friar had a painting kit with some gold leaf in it. He was going to cover some of my arrows with gold, and the blacksmith, he had some steel arrowheads that could cut any armor. I was going to be up on top of the windmill, and if Sir Conrad got into trouble, I planned to shoot me the Crossman champion. Once I did that, and golden arrows came down out of the sky to punish the evildoers, the others would be in the crowd shouting "An Act of God!", "A miracle!", and such like nonsense, since who'd look for the perpetrator of a miracle? How could they punish me or Sir Conrad for an Act of God?

When the time came, we was all ready. Sir Conrad got hisself bashed out of the saddle on the first pass, and the Crossman, he came around to finish him off. I let fly and then hid myself, but somehow I must have missed him clean because when I looked up, him and Sir Conrad was locked in a close fight. Since I missed once, I was afraid that the weight of the gold leaf was throwing off my aim, and I didn't shoot for fear of hitting Sir Conrad. Just as well, because Sir Conrad kicked the Crossman's smelly arse! He played with the bastard, first throwing away his shield and then killing him with his bare hands!

Then when the fight was over and I was getting ready
to climb down, four more Crossmen charged onto the
tourney field at Sir Conrad. I had my bow bent real
quick and let four arrows fly as fast as you can blink!
This time, I watched them fly through the low clouds and
come out again to hit every one of them Crossmen
square in the heart! I tell you I got four out of four, and
every one of them straight in at three hundred yards! I
killed every one of them fouling bastards and their empty
horses ran past Sir Conrad on either side.

Then, right according to plan, everybody was shouting "A miracle!" and "An Act of God!" The blacksmith
ran out on the field, to be the first one there to recover
my arrows, since we figured that nobody would believe
God using gold-covered arrows. God would use real
solid gold if He used anything. It was best to get rid of
the evidence.

But when Ilya tried to pull out the first arrow, it bent
in his hand! It really was real solid pure gold!

I got religion about then, saying my prayers every
night like the priest taught me and going to mass every
morning. I did that for about a month and then was my
old self again, or pretty near. Only I don't make jokes
about the stupid priests anymore and I try to watch my
language, except when the shitheads push me too hard.

So Sir Conrad lived and them kids all grew up proper
at Three Walls instead of being slaves to the Mussulmen.
And nobody thought to catch me for killing them Crossmen, if it was me that shot them and not God. It was
some damn fine shooting, Whoever did it.

So we all went back to Three Walls, right after Sir
Vladimir married Annastashia. I went back to the
Widow Bromski and spent most of the next four or five
years hunting and standing guard, except for a few side
trips with Sir Conrad. Well, besides that I got me a fine
education at the school Sir Conrad set up, but I guess
that shows up in my writing.

They was always building something new at Three
Walls, and some of it was pretty exciting, especially the
steam engines. In my off-hours I got to looking at them
and talking to anybody what knew much about it. I tried
to get Sir Conrad to transfer me to one of the machining
sections, but he wouldn't do it. He said he had plenty of

good men who could run a lathe, but only one man who could shoot like me.

After that, about the only thing that happened that was worth talking about was once when we was all going to a new site that Sir Conrad got from Duke Henryk to open up a copper mine. We got word that there was a bunch of foreigners in Toszek, just a mile up the road, that was murdering people and burning women at the stake! Naturally, we went right there, and Sir Conrad and another knight went in to arrest the bastards—there must have been five dozen of them—while I got up on a shed to back them up with my longbow.

Well, these foreigners, some kind of Spaniards they was, they didn't want to be arrested so naturally a fight got started. All our workers got into it and I let fly with all the arrows I had, a dozen and a half of them. I only missed but once, when the fletching let loose on an old arrow, but that one time was when a soldier was coming at Sir Conrad and all I shot was some priest standing behind him. Sir Conrad's horse killed the bastard, kicked him square in the face and killed him dead, but like I said, that's a spooky horse!

I felt bad about missing, since Sir Conrad had saved my life three times, and up till then I'd only saved his once, but he wasn't mad about it. Like I said, he was a fine man.

We took prisoner such of them as we didn't kill and we divvied up the booty and I got three months pay out of it, besides a fine sword and a knife. Ask me and I'll show them to you sometimes.

Then they had a trial where everybody could speak their piece, and the foreigners, they said that they was only killing witches, and after that we hung the bastards. I never heard of nobody hunting witches from that time on.

So it wasn't so bad, working for Sir Conrad, but I got to yearning for the river. Being a boatman gets into your liver after a while, and when you been doing it for four or six generations, it sticks heavy in your blood. When I was close to working off my debt, I went to Sir Conrad to talk about it, or rather I made an appointment to see him with Natalia, his secretary. He was a busy man. And he wasn't "Sir" Conrad any more. Count Lambert had bumped him up to "Baron" now.

I was hoping that he'd stake me to a boat and cargo, or maybe let me work a few more years at the same rate so I could buy my own, but he had other ideas.

He said that he was going to build a fleet of the finest riverboats ever seen, and every one of them powered by one of his steam engines. They'd each carry a dozen times the cargo of any boat now on the rivers, and they'd go six times faster, upstream or down!

I asked what would happen to the other boatmen on the river and he said that we'd have to hire them, but he needed a good man to be boss, a man he trusted and a man who could speak the language of the other boatmen. Then he asked me if I was interested in the job.

I near fell off my chair! Hell yes, I was interested! Me running all the boats on the Vistula! Damn right I was interested!

He said good, he wanted me. And it wasn't only the Vistula. There was more cargo to be hauled on the Odra than on the Vistula, what with his installations at Copper City near Legnica and Coaltown north of Kolzie. On top of that, these boats wouldn't only be just for cargo. They'd be armored to stop any arrow and armed with weapons he didn't want to talk about just yet. He said the Mongols were coming in a few years and they would try to kill everybody, but we would stop them, and we would do it with the riverboats if that was possible. If that failed, he had an army building at the Warrior's School, and that would be the second line of defense. But the men on the boats would have to be warriors too, so I would be in the first class through, now that they was almost finished training the instructors.

Now that took me back a peg or five. I'd heard a lot of stories about that school and wasn't none of them good. It was supposed to be a secret, but everybody knew that three-quarters of the men who started didn't live through it and I told Baron Conrad so.

He said that I'd been listening to a lot of old wives' tales. That while only a quarter of the first class graduated, only one in six had actually died. Most of the rest had been washed out for injuries, or physical or mental problems, and anyway the next class would not have it so hard. They were projecting a fifty percent graduation rate. On top of that, everybody who worked for Baron Conrad would soon have to go through the school, so I might as well get it over with, before I got any older. Younger men had a better survival rate.

I said I didn't like them words "survival rate," but Baron Conrad said he only meant the ratio of men graduating, and nobody wants to live forever, anyhow.

I said it was my Christian duty to try, but Baron Conrad, he told me that it was still a secret, but that all of that first class was going to be knighted, and the next one was, too. He told me to think about all them pretty young girls I saw in the shower room every day and to think about the old widow I was living with. Yeah, I guess he knew about it.

So I thought about them eager young smiles and the Widow Bromski's scowling face, and about them bouncing young tits and her sagging dugs and that's what done me in.

Chapter Two

‎ΛΛΛΛΛΛΛΛΛΛΛΛΛΛΛΛΛΛ

FROM THE DIARY OF CONRAD STARGARD

The weather was so beautiful that Krystyana and Sir Piotr had elected to have their wedding ceremony, complete with church service and reception, held outside. Since Sir Piotr was the local boy who had made good, the priest and everyone else went along with it.

And of course, since everything had to be done as ceremoniously as possible, the mass went on for over an hour and I had some time to get some thinking done. I was working on my next four-year plan.

Yes, I know that socialists are supposed to write five-year plans, but in less than four years the Mongols were going to invade, and there didn't seem to be any sane reason to plan much beyond that. If we could lick the Mongols, we'd have a whole lifetime to plan things. If not, well what was the point? We'd all be dead.

For the last five years, I had been working mostly at getting our industrial base going. We now had a productive cloth factory and a sugar refinery here at Okoitz, and a copper-mining, smelting, and machining installation at Copper City, that Duke Henryk owned. More than a dozen of Count Lambert's other barons and knights had various light industries going at their manors, mostly to keep their peasants busy during the winters. Some of them were my vendors, making boots and uniforms for my future army.

At the Franciscan monastery in Cracow, we had a paper-making plant, a printshop, and a book bindery. And besides books, they were also producing a monthly magazine.

I had three new towns of my own running. There was

Three Walls, where we were making iron, steel, coke, cement, bricks, and other ceramics, and machinery, plus several hundred different consumer products. It also had a major carpentry shop, set up for mass production, and a valley filled with Moslem refugees that functioned as an R&D center and a gunpowder works. There was Coaltown, where we were making coke, bricks, glass, and chemicals. And there was Silver City, in the Malopolska Hills, where we mined and refined lead and zinc.

Silver City got its name when my sales manager, Boris Novacek, refused to let me call zinc by its rightful name. He said that a zinc was a musical instrument, and that it was stupid to use the same word on a metal. He wanted to call it "silver" and pass it off as the real thing, but I wouldn't let him do it. We compromised on "Polish Silver," and the name stuck.

In addition to the factories and mines, a major agricultural revolution was taking place, mostly because of the seeds I'd brought back with me, but also because of the farm machinery I'd introduced.

Understand that none of these installations was really up to twentieth-century standards. At best, some of it was up to nineteenth-century standards. Everything was primitive and on a small scale. Most of the work was still being done by hand, and the most useful and cost-effective piece of farm machinery I'd introduced was the wheelbarrow. Well, the new steel plows worked well, and the McCormick-style reapers sold well even if they were too expensive. A whole village had to club up to buy one.

Nonetheless, worker productivity was four times what it had been when I'd arrived, and things were constantly getting better. The infant mortality rate was way down, too, because of the sanitation measures I'd introduced. Of course, the birth rate hadn't changed to any noticeable degree, so the place was crawling with rug rats, but what the heck. There was plenty of room for them. There was an underpopulated world out there.

Eagle Nest was nominally an aircraft development center, but I completely doubted if a bunch of twelve-year-old boys could really develop practical aviation. I'd helped build it to keep my liege lord happy and because in the long run, it was actually an engineering school, which we needed.

Lastly, I had the new Warrior's School ready to go, and my corps of instructors trained. My army was to have three branches.

The first branch would be made up of my existing factory workers. They would all have to go through an abbreviated basic-training period of six months and then train one day a week after that. The problem was that I would have to send the managers through first, since we couldn't have a situation where the subordinates were knighted and the managers were commoners. Discipline would vanish! There wasn't time to send the managers out in small bunches, so there was nothing for it but to send them all at once, which involved running the factories with untrained, temporary managers. It was scary, but I didn't see any way around it. Everybody in the top two layers was told to pick a man from below and teach him how to do his job in ten weeks. Only thirty-five men were leaving, but they were my *best* thirty-five men. There were screams and moans from all quarters, but I got my way.

Furthermore, all new hires, women as well as men, had to go through the six-month training period before they could start work. I required the women to be trained because when we went off to war, I planned to take every able-bodied man with me. The women would have to "man" the wall guns and other defenses without us. And this meant setting up a training program for the wives of my managers as well.

Then there were the river defenses. If the weather was right, and the rivers weren't frozen, we just might be able to stop the Mongols at the Vistula, or even at the Bug. We already had good steam engines and a carpentry shop set up for mass production. Steamboats should be a fairly straightforward proposition. The troops manning them would be hired from among existing riverboat men and then put through the full-year basic-training program. Then, after that, they'd have to learn about fighting from a steamboat on the job.

The regular army would be a full-time group based on the training instructors I already had. Besides training everybody else, they had to multiply their own numbers by at least six each year for the next three years, and then twice more in the last year to get us an army big enough to do the job. And those were absolute minimums. Anything less than fifty thousand men would just get us all killed. The production quotas for the factories were set up for a hundred fifty thousand.

From an economic standpoint, land transport was even more important than river transport. All of the roads were so bad that it was almost impossible to get a cart over them. Almost all goods were transported by caravan mule, and the best of them could only carry a quarter ton. They could only do thirty miles a day and had to be loaded and unloaded twice a day at that. But on level ground, on a steel track and steel wheels with good bearings, a mule should be able to tow two dozen times what it could carry on its back.

But more important than economics was the fact that my army was being trained to fight with war carts. Swivel guns mounted in big carts would fire over the heads of the pikemen towing the cart. I had to get the troops to the battlefields quickly and in reasonably good shape. It was time to build railroads.

And if I was going to build a transport system, I was going to build it right from the beginning. All the railroad tracks would be wide gauge and that gauge would be absolutely standardized. And we would containerize right from the start. Our war carts were six yards long, two yards wide and a yard and a half high. That would be our standard container size. All chests and barrels would be sized to fit neatly within the container, and anything nonstandard would get charged double rates, at least. The four wheels on a war cart were two yards high and mounted on casters, and each could be locked either fore and aft or to the side. Fore and aft, the center of the wheels were two yards apart, so that was the standard track gauge, and future carts would have flanged wheels to keep them on the track. If they tore up the ground when going cross country, tough.

Then we needed maps, and there weren't any. How a medieval general ever commanded troops without adequate maps was beyond me, and I didn't intend to learn. I'd had the machine shop make up some crude but usable theodolites (they didn't have a telescope on them, just iron sights like on a gun) and I had a good mathematician, Sir Piotr, to put in charge of the project. He could train others.

And we needed radios. Integrated circuits, transistors, and even *tubes* were well beyond us, and would be for years. I'd been able to muddle my way through a lot of things because I was too ignorant to know what I was getting into. With electronics, I knew what the problems would be, and they frightened me! Where would I get the rare-earth oxides needed to make a decent cathode? How would I develop alloys with the same temperature coefficients as our glass to take wires into the tube without shattering it? How could I possibly get a good enough vacuum?

But working radios were invented long before there were tubes. They used spark-gap transmitters and coherers to pick up the signals, and with enough work, I thought I could get one going. With radios, I could effectively double our speed, since I wouldn't have to send a runner to convey every order. Speed was the one area where the Mongols would be our undoubted superiors. Those shaggy ponies could move!

Radios were an absolute first priority.

The mass ended and we all walked over to the reception area. I stood in line to kiss the bride, even though I had done it all-too-many times before. Cilicia kissed the groom full on the mouth and warmly, probably because she too was glad to see Krystyana married off. As we went to the sideboard to get a couple of glasses of mead, my liege lord came up.

"Ah, Baron Conrad! You seem to be enjoying yourself!" Count Lambert said. Cilicia remained silent around my lord. They didn't get along.

"I might as well, my lord, seeing as how I'm footing the bill for the wedding feast," I said.

"And the dowry as well, I suppose?"

"Of course, my lord. After all, I've had three children by Krystyana and it seems the least I could do. I'm just glad that the kids will have a proper father."

"Indeed. I'm surprised that the Church hasn't come down on you for it."

"I'm sure that they are keeping careful notes, my lord. The inquisition concerning me is still up in the air."

"That's not all that's up there! I trust you've looked up sometime in the last hour?"

I hadn't, but I did so now. There was this thirteenth-century sailplane circling overhead.

"I guess I must have been thinking about something

else, my lord. There must be quite a thermal above the town."

"Quite. It's doubtless helped by the way every fire in the town is burning bright on a warm, calm day. You don't think that's cheating, do you?"

"I guess not, my lord. We never qualified what it had to do to stay up, only that it had to fly for two hours. It looks like it's climbing. The wager is yours."

"Good! Then where is my aircraft engine?"

"Still in my head, my lord, but I'll get working on it as soon as I get back to Three Walls. Perhaps I can deliver something to you in a few months."

"It will take that long? The boys were hoping to get started immediately!"

"It will take at least that long, my lord. Do you realize what you're asking? It's not just designing and building the mechanical parts, though that's going to be hard enough! I have no idea how we'll go about machining a crankshaft on one of our lathes! There's a lubrication system to worry about and a carburetion system. And how am I to make a spark coil with nothing but beeswax and paper for insulators? And spark plugs! Thermal expansion problems alone could kill us right there! And—"

"You will solve it, Baron Conrad. You always have before. Shall we say by the Harvest Festival, then?"

"My lord, I will work on it diligently, but I cannot promise results by any fixed date. There's the problem with fuel. I *think* we can use wood alcohol, but—"

"We'll discuss it again on the Feast of Our Lady of the Harvest. Oh, yes. There was another thing I wanted to talk over with you. When first you came here, you showed us the *zipper* things that fastened your clothes and equipage together. You distinctly said that you could show my workmen the way of making them. Well, almost six years have gone by and you still haven't done it. I want you to start on that as well."

"My lord, don't we have more important things to worry about than zippers? In less than four years, the Mongols will be arriving. There are all sorts of things that need doing if we are to survive that."

"Indeed? Like what? You are training some very good infantry, and you should have plenty of them in time. As to the cavalry, well, our Polish knights are always ready. All the more so once you have them in plate armor. But

I've seen your stamping presses work, and they'll have no difficulty getting the job done. As to the air force, if you can build the engines you promised, the boys and I can do the rest. What more remains to be done?"

"Plenty, my lord. Remember the binoculars I gave you on the first day we met?"

"Of course! Marvelous things! I keep them in my chambers."

"Well, I think we may be able to produce something similar called a telescope. It will be bulkier and will be used over only one eye, but it should do the job. What if I could have enough of them made so that you could give one to every Polish baron, count, and duke before the battle? What would that do for your fame?"

"I like it, Baron Conrad, and I would even pay the cost of it all, in cloth of course."

"Then I'll put a team to working at it, my lord. It would help if I could borrow those binoculars back for a week or two."

"Take them for as long as you need them. But what does that have to do with zippers and Mongols?"

"I'm just trying to say that we have a lot more to do. Now let me tell you about railroads. . . ."

The conversation went on for hours while the party went on around us. The upshot of it was that Lambert would provide the land to run a line from Coaltown to the Vistula, and from Three Walls north to the line, along with two square miles of land along the Vistula where I would build a fort and a riverboat assembly factory. The fort would be at Count Lambert's expense, in cloth, and he would be in nominal command, but I would see to the manning of it, since the people there would be working at the riverboat factory and the railyard. I would build the track at my expense, and all my goods, and the duke's, would travel on the line free. Others could use it by paying a toll to Lambert, but they'd have to rent railroad cars from me. After that, we'd run a line from the east end of the line to Silver City, and that part of it on Count Lambert's land would be managed on the same basis as the rest.

Medieval business deals were always complicated, especially when Count Lambert was in something like his current mood. Actually, I didn't care who owned what, so long as the job got done. As to the division of the profits, well, I'd have to keep my liege lord happy in any event. After that, the accountants all worked for me so he would be rewarded as I saw fit!

"Done, Baron Conrad! This has been a good day's work! I feel right about it. But I still think that when the Mongols arrive, we should be dressed in our best, so do get to work on that zipper machine, won't you? At your own expense, of course."

With that, he got up and walked away and I started thinking about how one would go about building a zipper-making machine.

Interlude One

I HIT the STOP button.

"Tom, something's been bothering me since you mentioned it a few days ago."

"And what is troubling you, my son?"

"Well, you said that you found out about Conrad's trip to the Middle Ages when you went to the Battle of Chmielnick during the Mongol invasion. You said that the battle you saw had a different outcome than what's written up in the history books. And you said that the investigation teams you sent out came back duplicated. Why weren't *you* duplicated as well?"

"Well, *I was*! It was strange, meeting myself. Not because running into yourself is all that odd. With time travel, we do that all the time. But protocol is that the senior self always talks first, and the two of us just stood there, each waiting for the other to speak first, since neither of us remembered being there before. It was quite a while before I asked him why he didn't say something. Eventually, we figured out what happened. Being a sensible person, both of me, I decided to timeshare the management of the place with my other half. We flipped a coin and I got it for this century and he gets it for the next."

"Good Lord!"

"Well, what else could I do? Fight myself? I suppose it would have been more complicated had I been married, but after a bit of youthful insanity, like Conrad, I'm not the marrying kind."

He hit the START button.

Chapter Three

FROM THE DIARY OF CONRAD STARGARD

Part of my deal with Count Lambert was that I would spend two days a month looking over the projects we had going at Okoitz, so I couldn't go back to Three Walls immediately. I checked the windmills and went down the coal mine. I looked over the progress made on Count Lambert's new castle, which was now more than half built, and spent more time than was necessary in the cloth factory, mostly because all the girls working there wanted to talk to me about something or another. Mostly, they were just trying to get me interested in themselves, and since I was still pretty seriously involved with Cilicia, they were out of luck. None the less, it's fun being pursued by scantily clad young ladies, even when you don't intend being caught, so I ended up spending half of both days there. Cilicia spent her time teaching dancing to the ladies of the town, charging all the traffic could bear.

Then it was back to Three Walls, where I got a half dozen research teams going on the new projects. My usual approach to research was to set up a team of two young men, apprentices, generally, along with one older craftsman. The rule was that they had to try out everybody's ideas, and the older man was not allowed to squelch the dumb ideas that the kids came up with. I reviewed the progress with each team every week or two and threw in my own thoughts, and usually something workable resulted. On really important things, I'd set up two competing teams and let them work independently. The reward for all this, besides their pay, was in the form of cash bonuses if they were successful and the fact that if the new product went into production, the men on the research team were the obvious people to manage the new factory, so promotions were in order.

The railroads and the steamboats were just a matter of design and build, with little real research required at first. Sir Piotr's first survey job was for the railroad track.

Yashoo was sent with a crew to the new lands, which we called East Gate, to build a boat-assembly building and the foundry got busy making cast-iron railroad track. The construction crews were scheduled to go through the Warrior's school in the winter, when there wasn't much else for them to do anyhow.

We didn't have the machinery necessary to roll steel track, and with the comparatively light loads that our track would be handling, malleable cast iron was good enough. Cast iron also had the advantage of being not worth stealing. A blacksmith couldn't make anything out of it. If he tried heating it and beating on it with a hammer, it just crumbled. This fact, coupled with Anna's outstanding ability to sniff out thieves, reduced our theft problem to almost zero.

I was almost tempted to try to build a telegraph again, but not quite. There was no way that I could make copper not worth stealing, and the Mongols would probably be smart enough to cut our lines once the invasion started, so its military advantage would be nil.

Our rolling stock consisted of small flatcars big enough to carry a single container, with a load limit of ten tons. A tenth the size of modern cars, they were huge by the standards of the thirteenth century. They would all be horse or mule drawn, since our line would be only thirty miles long. There wasn't any need for greater speed and the mules already existed. Locomotives were for the future.

Sketching up the boats and the railroad took less than a week, since I had a staff of draftsmen (and draftswomen) now. The aircraft engine was something else.

My first thought had been to make an air-cooled single cylinder two-cycle engine, the sort that is used on lawnmowers, but I got to worrying about balancing it. Static balancing would be no great problem, but dynamic balancing without any sort of test equipment seemed impossible. The thought of vibrations tearing one of our frail wood-and-canvas planes to shreds in midair bothered me.

I went to a two-opposed cylinder design, where both pistons went out at the same time. If every part was identical to its opposite part, it all should balance perfectly. I hoped.

Lubrication? All we had was various animal fats and imported olive oil. I designed a pressurized lube system, knowing that it would be contaminated with the wood alcohol I hoped to use. After that, we would just have to try different mixtures and burn out engines until we found something that worked reasonably well.

Carburetion? All I could do was to sketch up what I think I saw in a textbook fifteen years ago and hope.

Ignition? I put one research team to work on a magneto system and another on the battery-and-coil type and again I hoped.

Then there were the mechanical parts. The engine had to be as light as possible, which meant that I needed the best possible strength-to-weight ratio. Sad to say, our best cast steel was weaker than ordinary cast bronze. Bronze was expensive, since it was made, in part, of tin that had to be imported from England, but hang the expense. I'd get it out of Count Lambert somehow. Everything on that engine was bronze except for the bearings (another research group), the cylinder liners, and the piston rings. These last two were cast iron, just like on many modern engines.

As more and more problems were encountered, more research teams were set up. Did we have a ceramic that had a coefficient of expansion similar to some metal we already had, so we could make a spark plug that didn't shatter when the engine heated up? Get the machinists to make spark plug jackets out of as many metals as they had, and for each type, have the potters mold in all their different types of clays and try to fire them. Could we insulate wires with some sort of varnish? Put a team of alchemists on it!

But many of the problems had to be solved sequentially, rather than in parallel. We couldn't test bearing materials without a working engine, nor could we work on lubricants or carburetion or propellers. The first big snag was ignition, and the problem there was the lack of a decent electrical insulator for the spark coil. The damn things kept shorting out.

While this was going on, there were innumerable problems with the factories, since the entire upper management, everybody above the foreman level, was out playing soldier. And besides Three Walls, I still had to keep tabs on all the other installations, which were also running without their best men and women.

Then there was the problem of the barony that I had just been given. It was previously owned by my enemies, the Jaraslavs. These men had hated everything about me and as a result, they had refused to allow any of my innovations on their lands. Because of this, the barony was the most backward in the duchy. The spring crops were already planted when I got the place, so not much could be done in that direction until next year, but there were a lot of other things that needed doing.

The school system had to be extended into it. That meant more work for Father Thomas, who ran the schools, but not much for me. Along with the schools went our distribution system and the mails. Boris's job. Teaching the farmers about the new crops and machines? I managed to "borrow" two dozen of Count Lambert's more mature peasants, men with grown sons who would just as soon take over the family farm. I made these men my bailiffs and assigned farmland to them scattered over the barony, along with a complete set of the newest farm equipment, with the understanding that they had to teach their new neighbors about the new stuff.

Understand that none of these were trivial jobs. That barony was *big*! There were four thousand three hundred peasant families living on it. No wonder Baron Stefan had been able to ride around with solid gold trim on his armor!

As to the fifty-odd knights and their squires that were sworn to Baron Stefan, I pointed out to them that their previous liege lord had been killed in a fair fight when he was fully armed and on horseback. And that this deed had been done by scrawny and naked little Piotr, one of my students at the Warrior's school. If they wanted to swear to *me*, they had to go to the school, too. And there was a school for their wives as well.

Those who had manors still kept them, but it was

many years before they could do more than occasionally visit. They were in the army now!

All told, it was a rough summer and fall.

In the middle of this, my alchemist, a heretical Moslem named Zoltan Varanian, came to me with a vast grin on his face. He wanted to show me something in the valley I had set aside for the use of his people. He took me to a cave in the hills, which had centuries of bat droppings on the floor.

"You see?" he said. "We will no longer have to haul shit up here to make into your gunpowder, my lord! On this very floor is sufficient to make nine hundred tons of gunpowder! I have calculated it!"

This was extremely good news. Getting enough manure to meet the gunpowder quotas was a problem, and the peasants complained that we were taking the only thing they had to fertilize their fields. Furthermore, the manufacturing process for gunpowder was one of our major secrets, as were the ingredients that went into it. Having an internal supply of saltpeter eliminated one possible security leak. On top of that, why couldn't bat droppings be used as fertilizer? There were a lot of bat caves around.

We still had a problem with the sulfur needed, and were importing it from Hungary in the form of cinnabar, mercuric sulfide. We were just storing the mercury, except for a little that was used in thermometers, but it would find a use someday.

The annoying thing was that Poland has vast deposits of sulfur, but they are so far down that we couldn't get to them without some sophisticated drilling equipment that we hadn't had time to develop. Many of the ores we were mining were sulfides, and in roasting them, we were able to recover the sulfur dioxide and convert it to usable sulfuric acid. But taking sulfuric acid back to sulfur is harder than getting toothpaste back into the tube! As Zoltan put it, "Can the child be put back into the mother?" For the foreseeable future, we were stuck with imported sulfur.

I gave Zoltan my hearty congratulations, and two dozen huge bolts of Count Lambert's cloth as a bonus.

By fall, the team working on the zipper was successful, since all they had to do was duplicate the zipper on my sleeping bag, and this mollified Count Lambert somewhat, but the boys at Eagle Nest were disappointed with me. They had done their part and I had failed to do mine. I finally invited the entire senior class to Three Walls so that they could see the problems we were having with the aircraft engine and try their hands at solving some of them.

And the little bastards did!

A fourteen-year-old kid came up with an incredibly simple and efficient ignition system. Our cigarette lighters made a spark, didn't they? They worked on the principle of hitting a quartz crystal, didn't they?

So he made a spark plug with a hefty quartz crystal inside of it, which was struck by a little hammer connected by a linkage to the crankshaft. It didn't need insulation for the wires because there weren't any wires!

So we named the system after him, calling it the Skrzynecki ignition, and threw a party in his honor. What troubled me about it was the fact that I should have thought of that one myself. After all, I was the one who had designed our lighters in the first place. I just had to put it down to a mental blind spot.

It took a few months to beat down the other problems, but by Christmas we had an engine that could run for six hours without an overhaul and that was good enough for starters.

By spring they had six powered aircraft flying. It is astounding what a bunch of motivated kids can come up with!

Of course, the same electrical problems that plagued the engine also troubled the radio. To make a spark-gap transmitter, you have to have a spark. So I used a variation on the Skrzynecki ignition to power the transmitter. To transmit, somebody had to turn the crank so that a dozen little wooden hammers beat on a big quartz crystal, but that was no big problem.

Waxed paper and gold foil (the only really thin metal available) made a usable capacitor, a large, carefully made air core coil of bare wire served for a choke, and a long bare copper wire served as an antenna.

The receiver had a similar antenna connected with an identical coil and capacitor. This in turn went to a coherer, which was little more than a glass tube with iron filings in it. If a signal was picked up, the iron filings slightly welded themselves together and the resistance through them went way down. This let a low voltage current go through a relay which went "click" and tapped the coherer, shaking loose the iron filings to wait for another signal. It was a year and a half getting a pair of transceivers working that could send and receive over two dozen miles, and they weren't very dependable, requiring constant fiddling on the part of the operators, but they were good enough. We went into production with them.

About then, I somehow found time to polish up the books I had been writing. Over the years, I had tried to write down everything I could remember about science and modern technology, and over time these scattered notes had turned themselves into about two dozen books. Or perhaps I should say pamphlets, since none of them was more than three dozen pages long, and in fact the longest of them was the poetry I had remembered.

One was called *Concerning Optics*. Everything I knew in twenty-nine pages. Another was *Power Transmission*, eighteen pages. It was frustrating! Here was everything I remembered from seventeen years of formal education, and a lot of reading besides, all in one short stack of papers! Even then, some of them wouldn't be useful here for many years, and books like *Computer Design*, *Programming* and *Semiconductors* were filed for future publication. But *Bridges*, and *Canals, Locks, and Dams* could aid contemporary builders, and there was no reason to withhold the information. I got the stack over to Father Ignacy and ordered six thousand copies of each, with woodcut illustrations. He was awestruck, but said he'd start having it done.

Around Christmas, Sir Piotr brought me copies of his first maps, the first accurate maps ever done of my own lands. He was an amazingly good mathematician, and after some years of tutoring on my part, he was starting to pull ahead of me. Certainly, his books on arithmetic, algebra, and trigonometry were better than mine, and we published his instead of what I'd done. He himself, with the help of the accountants that used to work with him, had written a book of trig tables, and had worked out the techniques necessary for accurate mapmaking. Those got into print as well, and we paid decent royalties.

There was a compass rose on the map, so naturally I turned it so that the arrow pointed up and I could read the words. I stared at the representation of the land that I had been riding over for years and I couldn't make heads or tails of it.

"Sir Piotr, there's something very wrong here. This isn't my land."

"But of course it is, my lord. I could hardly make a mistake like surveying the wrong property."

"But . . . you've got Sir Miesko's manor south of Three Walls. It's north of us!"

"Right, my lord. It's north of us."

"Then why do you have it at the bottom of the map?"

"Because I put south at the top of the map, my lord."

"You put *south* at the top of a map?"

"Yes, my lord. I worried a bit about that, since of course it's traditional to put east at the top—"

"*East*, for God's sake?"

"Of course, my lord. But I knew you'd want things done in a sensible and rational manner, so naturally south goes at the top."

"Naturally. Would you please go over your reasons for that conclusion?" I'm not sure whether it was caused by graduating from the Warrior's School, being knighted, or marrying Krystyana, but Piotr just didn't get intimidated anymore.

"Happy to, my lord. Your prime referent has always been your clock. All of our angles are measured as though they were the time of day it is when the fat hand is at that angle. At least that was the system you taught me. The fat hand corresponds to the position of the sun when the clock is south of the viewer, and all of your clocks are always mounted on a south wall for that reason. Therefore, all of the angles shown on the map correspond to the normal clock if the map is placed up next to the clock. Since the map corresponds to the land, and the land, looking south, has the more southerly portions appearing to be higher, this just naturally puts south at the top of the map. In addition, everybody knows that the mountains are to the south of us, and the plains and the sea are to the north. The mountains are higher, so naturally they go at the top."

I had to stare at it for a while and think about it, but in the end I had to admit that his way was more consistent. It was more consistent to read our angles clockwise rather than counterclockwise, as it is done in the modern world, so we did it that way.

In the modern world, electricity flows from negative to positive. It happened that way because Ben Franklin knew that something was flowing, but he guessed wrong about the direction. Since I was starting out fresh, I corrected Ben's error. Our electrons were positive.

The controls on the aircraft worked the opposite of those on twentieth-century planes, because the boys started out flying hang gliders. With the usual control stick, if you want to go down, you push the lever away from you, but on a hang glider, which steers by the shift in body weight, to go down you must pull on the stick to pull your body forward. So when they started making gliders with control surfaces, it was natural for them to make it so that you pulled the stick to go down. Exactly the same thing happened with turning left and right. Sensible, but the opposite of what I was used to.

And on the riverboats, the same damn thing happened. I'd installed a conventional ship's wheel, but Tadaos had insisted on reworking the steering apparatus so it would be more "natural" for him. He was used to steering with a tiller bar, where to go to the right, you push the bar to the left. "Natural" for him was to move the top of the wheel to the left to make the boat go to the right. I had to do it his way or fire him, and just then I didn't have a replacement.

Yes, I know we were all Polish, but is that any reason why everything has to come out backward?

Chapter Four

FROM THE DIARY OF TADAOS KOLPINSKI

Well, they dang nearly killed me, but they didn't.

They shaved me naked and yelled and screamed and ran me up and down mountains and cliffs, and ropes, and all the while singing damn fool songs and blowing on horns and beating stupid drums. They got me up every day before dawn to swear the same dang oath, like I didn't remember it from the last two hundred mornings we'd said it, and then came at me with pikes and swords and axes, and they made me do the same to the others. They made me walk funny and talk funny and smile when they was shouting at me.

You see, one of the twelve things we was always to be was cheerful, and I think that was the hardest of the bunch. I finally figured out that if I squinted my eyes and gritted my teeth at them, I could usually make them think I was smiling.

Worst yet, they made me go the first six months of it without getting drunk or laid.

Sometimes, I think it was that last that kept me going, knowing that once I got out of this hell, all those pretty little girls would be waiting for Sir Tadaos to service them. I lived for that, and like I said, I nearly died for it.

A lot of men did die in that training, but not in my platoon. I guess I was lucky in that I was put in with the baron's managers for the first six months, and not many of them men washed out. I mean that they could all read and write already, and they was mostly pretty sensible. A few got hurt pretty bad on the cliffs, but even they graduated. I thought that I was going to graduate with them, but no, the day before the rest went through the

32

firewalking ordeal and the vigil, they told me that I was scheduled for the whole year-long program. I went and talked to Sir Vladimir about that, since he ran the school and I knew him pretty well. Hell, once he let me use him for target practice, but that's another story.

Anyhow, he said that there was nothing he could do about it since the baron, he had put it in writing and that was that. But he did give me a pass to go to Three Walls for three days, so I could get proper drunk and visit the Widow Bromski. Seeing her again after spending six months dreaming about those sweet young things, well, it helped to get drunk first. I'd worn my armor coming in, but I guess I didn't fool anybody. Certainly not any of the girls. They must have some kind of secret code about that sort of thing. But at least I got good and blasted with the girls at the Pink Dragon Inn. Course, that's a look-but-don't touch sort of place, but I tell you it's well worth the looking.

So I went back to Hell, and this time they put me in with the baron's new knights, them what he got after little Piotr killed Baron Stefan and Conrad stepped into the old baron's shoes. They was pretty standoffish at first, but then one day Sir Vladimir called me "Squire Tadaos" in public, and those knights and squires loosened up some.

I guess I did learn something there. I got to be real good with a sword, one of those long skinny ones you wear over your left shoulder. I could hold my own with an axe or a pike, though I don't much like a pike, and I found out I was near as good a shot with one of them swivel guns as I was with my bow. I could outshoot anybody, the instructors included.

So at last came the day when we was to graduate. They made a big to-do about it, but me, I was just glad it was over. The others was worried about walking on fire, but not me. If Piotr and all them managers could do it, I knew I wouldn't have no trouble, and I didn't.

Look here. Every man in the world has snuffed a candle with his fingers without burning hisself, and walking on coals is just the same thing in a bigger way. Anyhow, I did burn myself a little, though I didn't feel nothing at the time.

Naturally, I had brains enough to go through it all with a straight face, not wanting to be dropped this late in the thing. I know when to keep my mouth shut.

After that, there was some hocus-pocus about sitting up all night and seeing if we had halos in the morning. I guess I never been much of a religious man, except once there, and that didn't last long. But I learned long ago that if you play the game and look nice, there's a whole lot less trouble. So we waited up all night and the sun come up and didn't none of us have a halo showing on the fog. There wasn't even no fog!

So this priest, he says that one of us must not be in a state of grace, and that we'd have to pray all day and try it again tomorrow. We was all pretty disappointed.

Them knights, they all took it real serious and did some real soul-searching, so naturally I had to look like I was doing the same. But any man with half the brains of a cow should be able to figure out that you can't see your shadow on the fog, halo or no halo, when there wasn't no fog in the first place!

So we stayed up the whole day in prayer, and the next night in vigil and again there wasn't no fog. I thought some of them knights was going to die right there from the humiliation of it. They figured God was rejecting them for their sins, and of course, I couldn't tell them no different.

So a third day and night went by without no sleep and in the middle of the night, Baron Conrad came by. He hadn't been there the other two nights, and I figured he knew when it'd be foggy. I always knew that man was smart.

So we finally got fog and saw our shadows in it. What they got so excited about was something I'd seen a hundred times before, only looking into green water instead of fog. Sort of these rays of light seem to come out of the head of your shadow. Every man on the river has seen it, them with brains enough to look down, and fog is just another kind of water, isn't it?

But it wasn't my place to say nothing, so I got in line with the others and was knighted and sworn in and became Sir Tadaos Kolpinski.

We slept in that day and threw a party that night with the help of some beautiful young girls from the cloth factory at Okoitz. The next day, they gave me a full purse of silver and lent me a horse, so I gave one of them girls a lift back, because Okoitz was the place I intended to spend my month's leave.

I had a month off, and after the first day, I just sent the horse back to the baron, cause I wasn't going no-wheres else. That place is even better than the stories they tell about it! They not only had the prettiest and the eagerest girls in the world, they had two shifts of them! You could stand there smiling in your red-and-white dress uniform, with all your brass and boots polished, watching them as they paraded out after the end of their work day, and none of them wearing much of anything. Then when you saw one that suited you, you just smiled and asked her if she wanted to have a beer with you, and never one of them turned me down.

Then in the morning, when you'd eaten and drunk and fornicated all night, you walked her back to the factory and there'd be the night shift coming off work, rubbing the limelights out of their pretty eyes and wondering what they'd do with themselves all the lonely day.

I'd just spent a year in Hell, but now I was in Heaven!

This went on for three weeks, when one night I was sitting in the inn with two of the prettiest girls in Okoitz. Good friends and roommates they was, and I'd had the both of them before, one at a time, and that night I couldn't decide between them so I took them both, and they said that sounded like fun.

They was both wearing about what the waitresses at the inn wear and, that's to say, nearly nothing. They said it was the new style at Wroclaw, and I sure didn't make no argument about their tits hanging out. Not that theirs really hung, you understand, being of the young, conical variety.

We was all laughing and talking when Baron Conrad comes up. I asked him if I could buy him a beer, or maybe a mead would be more fitting for one of his ex-alted rank. He said it had been a hot day, and if I was buying beer, he was drinking it. Course, he never had to pay for his drinks anyway, seeing as how he owned this Pink Dragon Inn and fifty others besides, but it felt good playing host to my liege lord. He downed it quick and bought the next round for the table, just like he was a normal man and all.

Then he got down to business. He said that I was going to have to cut my leave short. It seems that the first steamboat was all built ahead of schedule, and if I figured to be its captain, I'd better be in East Gate tomorrow by noon.

Course, I wouldn't of missed that boat for all the girls in Okoitz, now that I'd had three weeks of them. But I figured that it was worthwhile complaining about it, since the baron might sweeten the pot a bit to get me there. It's the squeaky oarlock that gets the oil.

So I said that it would be hard, tearing myself away from these poor girls, leaving them to God knew what sad fate.

So the baron, he says that if I was worried about their futures, why, I could marry them if I wanted to.

I said I couldn't marry them both and he said I could if I was of a mind to. Hadn't I read the manual and rules of the Radiant Warriors?

Well, they'd given me this little printed book just as I left, but I hadn't read nothing and I had to admit it. So the baron says that any knight in our order had the right to have a servant, with his wife's permission. And a servant of ours had all the rights of a wife, so it was the same thing, except for the church ceremony, of course.

Well, that sort of flabbergasted me, and I said I didn't know which one I should marry. I don't rightly know if he was serious or not, but he says that if I couldn't decide, I should let the girls do it. Let them flip a coin, he says.

Before I can blink twice, the girls are grinning and nodding at each other. One of them digs a silver penny out of my purse and flips it in the air. The other calls "crowns," and that was the way that I proposed to Alona. I never had a word to say about it.

Course, the girls were both jabbering now, working out the details. If I had to go to East Gate tomorrow, why, Alona's village was only a half mile off the new railroad. She could come with me and I could speak to her father and post banns at the village church, because that's where she wanted to be married. Then Petrushka would be her bridesmaid and right after the ceremony, she'd become the servant.

All this was fine by Petrushka, so the girls had it all settled while me and Baron Conrad never said a word.

Then the girls left in a hurry to tell all their friends and I was left staring at the baron. I think that if I hadn't been drinking and fornicating for three weeks, I might have had enough sense to shout "NO!", but I had been and I didn't. The baron, he just seemed amused and said that under the circumstances I didn't have to get to East Gate until tomorrow *night*.

But looking back on it all, I tell you that if I had been sensible that night, I would have made the biggest mistake of my life. Them girls was everything a reasonable man could want, and we've been mostly happy together.

So the next morning, I rented us two horses, one with a sidesaddle since Alona didn't figure it was smart wearing the Wroclaw styles home, but had on a nice wool dress she'd made. We got there before noon and I talked to her old man and the priest and we settled everything real quick, since I didn't much care about the dowry and all, what with me making eight pennies a day now. Then I left her with her folks to visit for a day or two and got to East Gate before dark.

They had limelights up around the dock area, so I went out to look at my new boat right after supper, and she was a beauty! She was painted red and white, with gold and black trim, and a big white Piast eagle was painted on her side, just like the one on the back of the dress uniform. She looked more like a castle than a boat, what with her tall, flat armored sides, and there was crenelations all around the top and turrets at all four corners.

I swear I loved that boat more than the girls I was going to marry.

She was huge, fully three dozen yards long and ten wide. She was two and a half stories tall and armored with steel thick enough to stop any arrow but one of mine! She could carry sixty tons of cargo in six containers, and had fourteen cabins for passengers as well, plus five more for the crew. Yet the night guard told me that she only drew a half a yard of water with a full load!

I went down to the engine room and who do I find there but Baron Conrad hisself. I told him this boat of his was the finest looking thing I'd ever seen, both my girls included, and he said he was glad I thought so, but I better not let them hear that. Then he showed me all over that engine. It had a tubular boiler that ran at two dozen atmospheres, and a sealed condenser below the waterline so we got full power from it. It had a separate distillery run off waste heat, with its own condenser to make distilled water for the main boiler, so he didn't figure we'd ever have a fouling problem. It had two big double expansion cylinders that turned a paddle wheel that was two stories tall. There was a kitchen that could feed a whole company of men. There was even a bathroom with hot showers!

Then he got into the armament. We carried twelve swivel guns aboard, plus four steam-powered guns in the corner turrets he called peashooters. These fired ball bearings at the rate of three gross rounds a minute, one after another. And there was two steam projectors, Halmans, he called them, that could throw three pounds of death at the enemy. And during wartime, the boat was set up to carry a full company of men with all their equipment, including their war carts!

Then he told me I better get some sleep, because we was going to take her out in the morning.

Chapter Five

^^^^^^^^^^^^^^^^^^^^

FROM THE DIARY OF CONRAD STARGARD

We took the steamboat out with a skeleton crew: an engine operator, a fireman, Tadaos and myself, plus a dozen of the carpenters and machinists who had helped build her. And of course I brought Anna along, since she didn't like being far from me, and her senses were better than a human's. There was always the chance that she would spot something wrong before the rest of us did.

One of the watertight compartments below deck leaked a bit, but that was not serious. There were two dozen of them, and it could have been holed without endangering the boat. There were no other hitches, except for Tadaos' problems with the steering wheel. Once, when he wasn't sure if the water ahead was deep enough, we sent a man out ahead of the boat, walking. As long as the water stayed above the guy's knees, we were safe!

I'd planned to just take her a few miles downriver and return, but with things going so well, we went all the way to Cracow. We took up half the dock and drew quite a crowd, so I told Tadaos to speak with the riverboat men and try to talk them into joining the army. We were advertising in the magazine, but most of these men couldn't read.

I rode Anna up to Wawel Castle to pay my respects to the duke and see if he wanted a ride. Duke Henryk the Bearded was even more important to me than Count Lambert, and without the duke's support, I couldn't have accomplished a tenth of what I had. On the way there, Anna gestured that something was wrong, but she didn't know what it was.

The guard at the castle gate looked glum, but he recognized us and let us in. I didn't find out what was the trouble until I asked the marshal, the man in charge of the stables, where I could find the duke.

"Young Duke Henryk is in his chambers, my lord, but I wouldn't bother him just now."

"*Young Duke Henryk*? What are you talking about? The duke is over seventy!" I said.

"You hadn't heard, my lord? Duke Henryk the Bearded was killed last night. Duke Henryk the Pious now rules."

"Good God in Heaven! How did it happen?"

"It was one of his own guards that killed him, my lord, a Sir Frederick. Shot him with a filthy crossbow while he was asleep. The other guards chopped up Sir Frederick, killed him on the spot, so I don't guess we'll ever find out why he did it."

I left Anna with the marshal and went to young Henryk's chambers. Actually, he was ten years older than I was, but he still might want someone to talk to, and I knew the man fairly well. In any event, I could hardly leave the castle at a time like this without his permission. There was a crowd around his closed door, but just as I got there, the door opened and the new duke came out. He was wearing an army uniform.

"Ah, Baron Conrad. You got here quickly."

"In truth, your grace, I didn't hear the news until I arrived."

"Your grace?" he mused. "Yes, I guess I am that now. I've been going over my late father's private papers. I want to talk to you alone. The rest of you, please tell everyone that I will want to see every noble in the throne room in two hours, but for now, disperse. Come in, Baron Conrad."

"Thank you, your grace. May I say how sorry I am about your father's death?"

"No sorrier than I am, I assure you. But things must go on if I am not to waste the work he spent his life on."

"Have you any idea why Sir Frederick would do such a thing, your grace?"

He thought a moment. "My father was often rude to the man, but there must have been more to it than that. My father made many enemies. He had to knock a lot of heads together to get the lords of both Little and Great Poland to swear allegiance to him. There are a lot of young hotheads out there who thought that they would inherit petty dukedoms and who now find themselves only becoming counts or even barons. Doubtless one of them got to Sir Frederick somehow. But which one? I doubt that we'll ever know. But I tell you this—every noble on my lands is going to swear allegiance to me, and those who don't are going to *wish they had!*"

"Whoever did it might come after you next, your grace. Perhaps you could use a special sort of body-guard. I'm sure you've heard many stories about my horse, Anna. The truth is that she's not really a horse. She's almost as intelligent as a man. She's absolutely loyal and she's saved my life many times. The first of her children are of age now, and I'd like you to have one of them, sort of a permanent loan. The young ones are identical to their mother, and might save your life."

"Can they run like she does?"

"Yes, your grace."

"Then I'll take one. But that's not what I wanted to talk to you about. My father's secret letters to me say some astounding things about you. Are you really from the future?"

"Yes, your grace. I was born in the twentieth century."

"And you don't know how you got here?"

"Not really, your grace. I think it had something to do with an inn I slept in, but that inn is gone now. Certainly my own people never had a time machine."

"But you were Polish, and a sworn officer in the military."

"I *am* Polish, your grace, and once an officer, always an officer."

"Yes, yes. Then your knowledge of the Tartar invasion is one of simple historical fact?"

"Yes, your grace. But in truth, I am no longer sure just what a historical fact is. In my history, at this time there was nothing like the factories or railroads or aircraft or steamboats that I have built here. My being here has changed things, and I have no idea whether or how these changes will affect other things. In my time, the Mongols invaded Poland in late February and early

March of 1241. Two major battles were fought, one at Chmielnick on March seventh, and another at Legnica two weeks later. We lost both battles."

"But you don't know if these things are fixed by fate?"

"No, your grace, I don't. I'm praying that they are not. It is my intent to defeat the Mongols and kill them all."

"I see. Well, you may rest assured that the 'Mongols,' as you persist in calling them, are indeed coming. They are already invading southeastern Russia. We just got word that the city of Vladimir has fallen. They said it had been larger than Cracow. But it's gone now, with almost every man, woman, and child slaughtered. The Mongols even killed every animal—why, I do not know."

"Perhaps they simply enjoy killing, your grace."

"I see. You were definitely not sent here by anyone?"

"Not to my knowledge, your grace, but I got here somehow. Someone must have done it."

"Well. I'll expect you and any of your knights that you have with you to swear fealty to me this afternoon. Tell me, if you hadn't heard of my father's death, why did you come here today?"

"It seems trivial now, your grace, but we just got the first riverboat working. It's tied up at the docks here in Cracow. I came to see if your father wanted to ride it."

"Perhaps tomorrow I might have time to inspect it. For now, good day, Baron Conrad."

I scrounged up some writing materials, wrote some quick letters, and then went down to see Anna.

I met Lady Francine in the courtyard. She had been the old duke's companion (Paramour? Assistant? Toy?) for some years, and we had been friends for even longer. Perhaps next to Cilicia, she was the most beautiful woman in Poland. I gave her my condolences and invited her to join me on my errand.

"I would love to, Baron Conrad. But do not be so downhearted," she said with her thick French accent as we walked to the stables. "The old duke had a long full life, and he died without pain, yes? How many others have done the same?" She was wearing a most modest dress that covered her from wrists to chin to ankles, a far cry from the miniskirt and topless styles the old duke preferred.

"I suppose you're right. That's a most attractive dress, my lady."

"It is the style that will be worn at court from now on, I am afraid. Everyone knows the young duke's displeasure with the styles preferred by his father."

"Perhaps it's just as well, my lady. The bare-breasted style was lovely on you and on a few other young women, but on the battle-scarred spinsters who were wearing them, well, perhaps it's all for the best."

"My only regret is that the bare styles had to arrive in the wintertime, and these cover-it-all things must needs be worn now that summer is finally here. If only the old duke could have lived five months longer!" She smiled at her own audacity.

"Still, he'll be missed."

"All too true."

"But what about you, my lady. What is to happen to you?"

"Indeed, I do not know. I am not in want. Much to the contrary, for I had little chance to spend my excellent income. Also, the duke saw fit to elevate me to the peerage. I am a countess now, with a large estate near Wroclaw. But as to what I will do, I do not know."

"Don't worry, my lady. The most beautiful woman in Poland will not be left alone for long."

"Oh, the boys are already flocking around, but only boys. Not men like you."

I was saved by our arrival at Anna's stall.

"Anna, I have some errands for you to run." I threw on her saddle and cinched it down. "This letter is for Tadaos down at the boat. He is to come here right away, so give him a lift up here, drop him off at the gate, and then be on your way. This one is for the people at East Gate, since they have to be worrying about us. And this one is for your servant, Kotcha. If you haven't heard yet, the old duke was killed. I think that the young duke would be a lot safer if one of your daughters was with him. Do you think one of them would like that?"

Anna nodded YES.

I put the letters under her saddle where she could get at each of them individually. "Oh, yes. This last letter is for anyone silly enough to try to stop you. On your way, girl."

Anna sped out of the stables and past a startled guard. I waved to the man so he would know that nothing was wrong.

"Such an amazing beast!" Lady Francine said.

"Not a beast at all, my lady. Anna's people."

"Still, would that I had such a mount."

"Well, Anna's not exactly for sale."

"But you said that she had children."

"She does. But I also said she was people and you didn't believe me. One doesn't sell children, my lady."

"Well, I never offered any money, my lord."

"Sorry. It's just that I feel protective toward her. Everybody tries to treat her like a dumb animal and I don't like to see her feelings hurt."

"You always take so much upon yourself, Conrad. You cannot change the whole world."

"It's strange, my lady, but you know?—I really think I can. But while I can't give you Anna, I can give you a lift. After the funeral, if you want transportation back to your estate, I can provide a steamboat to East Gate and a railroad to Coaltown. Or you could stay a while at Three Walls if you like."

"Much of my last stay there was enjoyable, my lord. Perhaps I shall get a job again as a waitress at your inn, yes? I still qualify."

That was her way of telling me that she was still a virgin. Well, the duke was a very old man. But while I enjoyed the tentative way she was offering herself to me, I had the feeling that she wanted much more than a casual affair. And the whole idea of marriage *scares me shitless*!

I was saved again when a page called us to the throne room. We got there just as Sir Tadaos came puffing in.

"Your uniform's a mess, Sir Tadaos. It's filthy! Don't you know that you are about to swear fealty to the new duke?"

"It's not like I had a spare to change into, my lord. I didn't even know we was coming to Cracow! And I was fixing the cabling on the steering wheel, and—"

"Well, there's nothing for it now. We'll have to bluff it through. Come and sit by me and do what I do. My lady?" I said, offering Lady Francine my arm.

And thus it was that I swore fealty to Duke Henryk the Pious of Silesia, Little and Great Poland, and my future king if I had anything to say about it, standing between a filthy subordinate and a woman I was afraid of.

Chapter Six

ANNA CAME back as soon as the city gates were opened the next morning, and with her were all four of her oldest daughters. They said that they all wanted to work for the duke, and figured that he should make the decision between them. Of course they said this in a combination of the sign language we'd worked out and by my playing a game of twenty questions with them.

The funeral was held the next day. Embalming techniques were unknown, and in the summertime, well, these things couldn't be delayed. The old duke was placed in the crypt below Wawel Cathedral.

The morning after, I was trying to talk the kitchen help into scrambling me up some eggs, since nobody else in this century ever ate before late morning and I was partial to a decent breakfast. But word came that the duke would speak to me, so I missed another breakfast.

When I arrived before him, the duke looked up from a stack of parchment. We were producing some decent paper now, but everything official was still being handwritten on real sheepskin parchment, when it wasn't on the even more expensive calfskin vellum.

"Ah, Baron Conrad. Riders have been sent out to every noble in Little Poland, telling of my father's death and my requirement that they all swear allegiance to me. It will be a few days before they start getting here, so I have time to inspect that boat of yours. Also, the marshal tells me that there are now five 'Annas' in the stables, but I suppose you know about that."

"I do, your grace. The children felt that you should choose among them."

"Then let's do it."

At the stables, the duke said, "By God, they *are* identical. How do you tell them apart?"

"I have to ask them who is who, your grace. Anna, please come here by me, and the rest of you get into alphabetical order, so I can introduce you properly."

There was always a crowd around the duke, but this drew a bigger crowd than usual. I noticed Count Lambert's sister-in-law, who was trying to flirt with me as always. Both she and her husband, Count Herman, were of the opinion that people should be respected on the basis of their rank, and only on that basis. To her mind, this made her infinitely desirable, despite the fact that she was ignorant, supercilious, intolerant, married, and shaped like a pear. I ignored her, as was my custom.

I introduced Anna's children, and each bowed properly to Henryk. Everyone was familiar enough with Anna not to be too astounded.

"They're all perfect, and I don't see how one could possibly choose between them. I'd be forced to choose a horse by its saddle. But they're not really horses, are they?"

"No, your grace."

"Well, we must call them something. You keep calling them 'people,' but they're not really like ordinary people either, are they? What say we call them 'Big People'?"

"Well girls, what do you say?"

They all nodded YES, that was fine by them.

"We all seem to think it an excellent term, your grace."

"It's all settled, then. Well, Big People, am I correct in assuming that you all would like to serve me?"

The four sisters nodded YES.

"I see, and I thank you. Baron Conrad, you have offered me the loan of one of these lovely ladies. But what if I was attacked on the road by a superior force? I might then have to run for it, wouldn't I? But I would hate to run if I had to leave my wife or sons behind. In fact, I likely wouldn't do it. Could I prevail upon you? I know you have others like these growing up. Could I have all four?"

"You are a hard man to refuse, your grace. Of course. Since the Big People are willing, you may have the loan of all four."

"And that's another point. Why do you keep saying

'loan'? Many would simply make it a gift."

"Three reasons, your grace. One is the fact that they really are people, which you are already forgetting. I can't give them away because I don't own them. They are sworn to me and I pay them a regular salary, so I can loan out their services. The second is that I want to keep very careful control over who has them. I don't want them abused, and I wouldn't want an enemy to have them. The third is that I want all their fillies returned to me, again so that I can take proper care of them, and keep control over who has them."

"You seem adamant on these points, Baron Conrad."

"I am, your grace. Surely you can see my reasoning."

"I suppose I can. Perhaps I was being greedy. But what if there were enough for all my retainers? For all my knights! Such an army would be unbeatable!"

"Perhaps in time that will be possible, your grace. They reproduce rapidly. Indeed, all five that you see here are expecting, and each will have four fillies. In twenty or thirty years, they could outnumber people, if they wanted to. I assure you, we'll discuss such a mounted force when the time comes. For now, I suggest that we go for a ride. You notice that none of them has a bridle. They don't need them. Also, I'd thank you if you took off your spurs."

"What? Oh, yes. I'd forgotten that."

Two of his knights bent down to remove the duke's spurs, and I noticed Lady Francine join the crowd.

"Baron Conrad, may I join your group?" she asked.

"I'm sorry, my lady, but I believe the duke already has his party chosen."

"But there would be room for me if you put that thing behind your saddle on Anna."

"That thing" was the sidesaddle I'd had made to fit behind a regular saddle so a passenger, Cilicia for the last few years, could sit comfortably. It was sort of a pillion with a foot rest. Kotcha had given each of Anna's children one of my saddles, every single spare one that I kept for my own personal use, and I had the feeling that it would be awkward getting them back. This way, I could at least save the sidesaddle. I gestured to a groom to switch the thing.

"Then I would be delighted to have you riding apillion, my lady."

The duke mounted up along with three of his armed guards. They each carried an oversized shield and they'd had brains enough to remove their spurs.

"We'll go out by way of the Carpenter's Gate, then take the outer road to the docks," the duke announced. "That should let us give the Big People a good run."

I gave Lady Francine a lift into the rear saddle. She was a lot fleshier than Cilicia, but in fact she was lighter, not having the dense, muscular dancer's body that Cilicia has.

Once we were out of the city, I told Anna to go at her best speed, to show the duke what running was. We were soon going at a solid run, doing about the speed that a modern thoroughbred can run, but where an ordinary horse might match our speed with a tiny jockey aboard and for a mile, Anna and her kin could do it with two full-sized people on their backs, and keep it up all day!

Nonetheless, Anna was carrying double and her daughters pulled ahead of her. They were two-gross yards ahead of us when the attack occurred.

Suddenly, an armored man stood up in the bushes a gross yards from the road. He leveled a crossbow at the duke and let fly. The guard to the duke's right, a left-hander who carried his shield on his right arm, had remarkably good reflexes. He raised his shield in time to deflect the bolt high into the air.

But at the same time, two other crossbowmen were raising on the left, hoping to catch the duke's party off guard. They didn't. Those guards were on the ball, and Anna's daughters weren't being slouches, either. They had the duke surrounded, and the guards were holding their shields, not to cover themselves, but to cover the duke! It was as though they considered their own bodies as extensions of their shields. The next two bolts were stopped, one by a shield and one by a guard's arm.

The duke's party continued down the road, not knowing how many assassins they faced. But from my vantage point, I was sure that there were only the three of them. Sad experience had taught me that speed was more important than planning. When in doubt, charge straight in! I signaled Anna to attack the two on the left.

They were franticly trying to rewind their crossbows, hoping to get off a second shot. I don't think they saw us coming. Anna can run very quietly when she wants to, although she says that it's a lot more work. We were only a few dozen yards away when they noticed us. I had my sword out, but I wasn't wearing armor or carrying a shield. Heck, I'd started out dressed for a boatride. A knight is always supposed to be ready for emergencies, but that's often hard to do!

Anna passed to the left of the first man, and I found that he had stuck his sword in the dirt so as to have it near if he needed it in a hurry. He dropped his crossbow and swung his sword at me. I wanted to take prisoners, since these men probably had something to do with the old duke's assassination, but all I could do under the circumstances was to chop down at his sword as hard as I could. My sword went right through the crossbowman's blade, and through his helmet and head as well.

Before I could recover from the blow, Anna was already onto the second man. She just went right over him, trampling him flat. She turned and I saw that there were four hoofprints in the assassin's chest. He had squirted out of his armor like toothpaste from a tube hit by a sledgehammer.

We turned to see the last assassin mounting his horse and leaving.

"Catch him, Anna!" I shouted, but she was already on the way.

"This is so exciting!" Lady Francine shouted.

This shocked me. Would you believe that I had actually forgotten that I had a beautiful woman riding at my back? Worse yet, that I had gone into combat without even considering that I was risking her life!

"My lady!" I yelled, and Anna picked up from my body language that I wanted to stop.

"NO, NO!" Lady Francine shouted. "We must catch him! He must know who had the duke murdered!"

She was right, of course. Her safety and mine were unimportant compared to insuring the young duke's safety. The mystery had to be solved.

Anna picked up speed as she felt my new resolve. The assassin had quite a lead on us, but we caught up with him within half a mile. He ducked into a woods, trying to shake us, but it did him no good.

"We need a prisoner, Anna!" I shouted, as we approached him from the rear. She nodded okay. My thought was to hack off one of the horse's hind legs and then deal with the rider at our leisure. I never had a chance to, since Anna had similar ideas. She broke both of that animal's rear legs with her forehoofs. The horse went down in a heap. The rider flew over its head and stopped abruptly against a big tree trunk.

We dismounted in a hurry. The horse was still alive but the rider was not. He had both a caved-in forehead and a broken neck. One hundred percent overkill.

"Damn! Not a single prisoner."

"Your sword, Conrad! It went right through that knight's sword, and his helm and head as well!"

"Yes, it's quite a blade. I wish I knew how it was made." I bent to search the dead knight, hoping to find some clue to who he was.

Interlude Two

I HIT the STOP button.

"Hey, Tom, how was that sword made?"

"It happens that I am well informed on that subject, seeing as how I invented the process and made that particular sword myself," he said smugly. "First you get a good quality Damascus steel blade, which, by the way, were mostly made in India. Damascus was nothing more than a distribution point. You split the blade in half the hard way, right down the middle, through the edge."

"How do you do that?"

"Simple. You line up a nonlinear temporal field just right, then send one half of the blade a few minutes farther forward in time than the other. This gives you perfectly smooth surfaces, and since you're working in a vacuum, those surfaces are pretty reactive, chemically. Then you put a thin slice of diamond between them, about a hundred angstroms thick. You get that by slicing it off a larger block, using the same temporal cutting technique as you used on the blade. Then you clamp this sandwich together at four thousand PSI for two hundred years in a hard vacuum at room temperature. This welds the pieces together without harming the crystalline structure of the steel. You end up with as perfect a sword as is possible, with a pure diamond edge."

"Uh-huh. Where did you get a block of diamond that big?"

"Simple. You just put a block of graphite somewhere at thirty million PSI and two thousand degrees for twenty thousand years. It's not as though you need a flawless, single crystal."

"Oh. Is that all. I should have known." I hit the START button.

Chapter Seven

^^^^^^^^^^^^^^^^^^^^^^^^^

FROM THE DIARY OF CONRAD STARGARD

Lady Francine was flushed. "That was very... exciting, my lord."

"The first time you've seen combat? Well, try not to let it upset you." I was checking the dead man's pouch. Of course, nobody carried any ID in this age, but there might be something identifiable.

"I am not upset, I am... excited. Take me, my lord. Please."

"What? My lady, you don't know what you're saying. Look. Violence excites a lot of people sexually. It doesn't get me that way, but it's not uncommon. It's nothing to be ashamed of, but don't lose your head." I went over to dispatch the wounded horse, not looking at her.

"I know exactly what I am saying. Take me. Now."

"Here? Lady, besides the violence, you were just bouncing your butt on Anna's hindquarters. That can get you horny, too, but for physical rather than psychological reasons. Anyway, you're a virgin and—" I was still avoiding looking at her. I took out the wounded horse by cutting its head off. Then I checked its saddlebags. Nothing.

"I am a twenty-six-year old virgin and I know exactly what I am doing. Look at me. Please?"

I looked at her. She had stripped down to her slip, and was naked to the waist. Lord, what a magnificent body. I went over to her.

"You know I'm not the marrying kind. I can't promise—"

She put her arms around me. "Do not promise anything, do not say anything, just take me. Do it now."

Well, the woods were fairly secluded and there is a limit as to how many times a normal man can say "no" to a beautiful woman. And if the violence and bouncing had turned her on, well, I have my hot buttons, too. One of my major ones involves holding a beautiful, passionate and nearly naked woman in my arms.

If she wasn't totally rational, well, neither was I. I pushed my own future regrets aside and took her, with a dead horse on one side of us and a dead man on the other. But the taking of a virgin is a time-consuming affair, if one is not to be a total klutz about it, and it was over an hour before we sat up on the woodland moss.

I noticed a knight in the duke's colors sitting a hundred yards from us with his back turned.

Embarrassing as hell. Once we were dressed, I shouted, "Okay! You can turn around now! What are you doing here?"

"My lord, I was sent with others by the duke to see to your safety and come to your aid, though when we found you we thought our assistance might not be welcome. We have reported your safety to the duke, and have your other rewards of combat, that is to say, your booty, packed and ready for transport." His left arm was bandaged, but it didn't seem to bother him.

"Thank you, I suppose. Did you report what we were doing to the duke?"

"It was needful, my lord, since he asked about the delay."

Great. The rumormongers would be going for months over this one. Yet Lady Francine didn't look the least bit embarrassed. She looked as if there were canary feathers on her mouth.

"I take it that the duke is at my boat?"

"Yes, my lord."

"Then we'll be going there now. Clean up the rest of this mess," I said, gesturing to the dead knight and horse. "And then bring it all to the boat. The duke will want to examine it."

"And after that, my lord?"

"After that, you can keep it. Divide the booty up among your fellow guards."

"Thank you, my lord, you are most generous! But then, you have taken a far greater reward for yourself."

"Shut your damn mouth!"

At the boat, the duke was smiling. "Well, Baron Conrad, they tell me that you killed all three would-be assassins, and with a lovely lady at your back, besides!"

"I killed one, your grace. Anna got two, and one of those was an accident. We were trying for a prisoner, but he was killed when his horse went down."

"A prisoner? But who would ransom an assassin? To do so would be to admit one's guilt!"

"I wasn't worried about a ransom, your grace. But the men who were trying to kill you were probably connected to whoever was behind the death of your father."

"Yes, of course. Stupid of me. I think my father's death must have affected me more than I had thought. Well, I shall instruct my guards to try to capture assassins in the future, and if we can't identify the men you killed, I'll have their heads set on poles in the marketplace, across from St. Mary's Church, with a reward posted for any information about them. For now, your excellent Sir Tadaos has shown me around the boat during your absence, and I suggest that we take it out for a ride."

They had the booty on board before Tadaos could get a head of steam up. We went downstream to the limits of the duke's lands, halfway to Sandomierz, and then back past Cracow to East Gate. Lady Francine stayed close to me the whole while, but I stayed close to the duke, so she couldn't speak what was on her mind.

The duke tested all our weaponry himself, and was both impressed and troubled by it. He'd seen the swivel guns before, though this was the first time he'd fired one. The Halman Projectors were essentially steam-powered mortars, of a type that was used on merchant ships during WWII. We fired off a number of dummy rounds and one grenade. The peashooters were turret-mounted steam-powered machine guns. They worked as well on the boat as they had in the shop, with one problem. They drew so much steam that firing a single one of them noticeably slowed the boat. Something would have to be done, but I wasn't sure what.

What troubled the duke was that these weapons could rip up any group of mounted knights, and there wasn't much that conventional forces could do about it. And the duke's power was ultimately based on his knights.

"Good, Baron Conrad. We will need dozens, many dozens of these boats. With them, if the rivers be free of ice, you might stop the Tartars from killing my people. But in so saying, I am chanting the doom of my own kind."

"Not so, your grace. Poland will always need leaders and the land must have a king."

He looked at me strangely. "Yes. But who?"

I got off at East Gate and offered to have Tadaos run the duke back to Cracow. He said he preferred to ride back on his new mounts, and left. One of the guards made quick arrangements with Tadaos with regards to the bodies and booty, and Francine sent a note back with the guard concerning her servants and luggage.

Lady Francine stayed with me and seemed to take it for granted that she would continue to do so.

As soon as we were alone, I said, "I once asked you if you wanted to join my household. You know that offer still stands."

"To join your household? To be one among many?"

"Not so many. Actually, you'd be one among two."

"Two. Do you mean that foreign woman?"

"Cilicia, yes. And you yourself are something of a foreigner here, my lady."

"I had hoped for something better."

"It's all that I have to offer, my lady. I couldn't dump Cilicia. She's heavy with my child. And I've told you that I'm not the marrying kind."

"I must think on it."

Well, she didn't seem to think much, but continued acting as if she owned me. We got back to Three Walls the next day and I introduced her around.

She'd met Cilicia a few dozen times when she was with the old duke, and always they had been cordial, even friendly with each other. Now all that was changed. You could see little lightning bolts flash between the two women, with plenty of fireworks and the occasional atomic blast!

It was an awkward, unpleasant situation, and I did my best to ignore it. I found myself working late in the shops and hoping that the ladies would come to some sort of an accommodation. I tried to be fair, and took them to bed on alternate nights, but their concept of fairness was different from mine. At last, I tried to sit them down together and get them to talk it out, but they both just sat there radiating hate.

After a month, Lady Francine rather stiffly thanked me for a pleasant visit and said that she was leaving for her estate. She stressed that I would always be welcome there, but that she would not be returning to Three Walls.

We gave her a nice sendoff, and I breathed a vast sigh of relief. Having the two most beautiful women in the country was nice, but it was not worth the total absence of domestic tranquility.

I think I must be growing old.

Yet ever after, I could not help but visit the countess at her manor, once or twice a month. And always I stayed the night.

FROM THE DIARY OF TADAOS KOLPINSKI

In the summer of 1238, I married Alona and took Petrushka on as a "servant" as we'd agreed, and we was as happy as three people could be. The captain's cabin on my boat was bigger than a lot of the houses we'd all lived in, so that was no problem, and the girls just naturally took over the kitchens and all, just like the boat was a house.

I even got them both on the payroll, at two pence a day, each.

Most of that summer, while the people at East Gate was building a dozen new boats, we went up and down the Vistula and its tributaries, setting up small depots with the help of Boris Novacek, him with no hands, and his wife, Natasha.

The idea was to have a depot every twelve miles or so along all the rivers, where they'd buy and sell goods, or contract goods for shipment. Every one of these was to have a radio, once we got them, so we'd know when to stop, but for now they just ran up a flag.

'Course, once it started working, every boatman on the river started howling about how we was ruining them, since we was charging half what was usual. I kept telling people that if they could get through the Warrior's School, they could work on the steamboats, and maybe get one for their own. Well, a lot of them went to that school, and more than half of them got through it alive, but we was always pressed for enough good boatmasters.

Yet I don't think we put anybody out of business. We collared the long-run trade, sure, but once we got going, there was just a whole lot more trade going on! The short-run stuff and running up small rivers kept all the boatmen busy enough.

But for me, the best part was the baron's strict orders that we wasn't to pay no tolls! He said that despite the fact that we was engaging in trade, this was a military craft engaged in defending the country. It was owned by a baron and commanded by a knight, and if anybody didn't like it, they could challenge me if they wanted to. Their boat against mine! Didn't nobody take me up on it, though, except maybe once.

There'd be their toll boat out there and I'd come steaming past them just as smooth as you please, and I'd wave at them bastards as I went by.

Even that jackass Baron Przemysl had a toll boat out when we went up the Dunajec. Just like I was ordered, I explained why we wasn't to pay no tolls. 'Course, I had to explain to them that I was the man they jailed for poaching some years back, and suggest to them what I felt about their morals and standards of cleanliness. They got abusive in return, and I decided that this was a sufficient affront to my knightly honor as to constitute a challenge. Anyhow, they wouldn't get out of my way, so I just ran the buggers down and dunked them. 'Course, they was wearing chain mail, and they didn't come back up again, but that was their problem and not mine.

I tell you that it was worth more to do that than all the money I got paid for doing it. No man ever said wrong about Baron Conrad when I was around, or at least not twice!

But there was a lot of petty nobles that wouldn't let us set up depots because of the way we didn't pay no tolls. They didn't bother Boris none. He just spread the word that we was paying to set up our depots this year, but next year we wouldn't. And the year after that, if anybody wanted a depot, they'd have to pay *us*.

And you know, some of them that wouldn't have us at first later on paid us to come. There was profit in having a depot on your land, and in time, a lot of them depots got a Pink Dragon Inn by them, and there was profit in that, too.

Well, come fall, both of my ladies was bulging, and they both had their kids within a week of Christmas. Now, I knew that that was only seven months from the time I met them, but the saying is that a kid takes nine months, except for the first one, which can take any time it wants to. I never said a thing about it to them, since a grown man knows when to keep his mouth shut. I knew when I had a good thing going, and I wasn't going to let a few little months upset it.

But after that, we tried to work it so only one of them got pregnant at a time.

Chapter Eight

▲▲▲▲▲▲▲▲▲▲▲▲▲▲▲▲▲

FROM THE DIARY OF CONRAD STARGARD

By the fall of 1239, all the people who worked for me at any level above the bottom had gone through the Warrior's School, with the exception of a few like Boris Novacek, who had no hands. There was even a four-month winter school for the peasants on my new barony. Three years of it and they could be knighted. But a lot of men didn't make it through, and I had to be fairly brutal about weeding them out. Since they were sworn to me, I couldn't fire them for not passing, but I wouldn't let them stay on in any kind of a managerial capacity, either. Mostly, I just demoted them down to apprentice, no matter what their skill level, and I gave some of them plots of land and let them be peasants. Many took this pretty hard. Some people quit and there were even a few suicides, but I was adamant.

To keep in practice, everybody spent one day a week in military training. Not the same day, of course, since the factories had to keep running full blast if we were going to meet our production quotas.

I would have preferred a system where the men who worked together fought together, but there was just no way we could do that. In the factories, each section had people with specialized skills. If they were all off and in training on the same day, their machines would be idle.

As it was, most work teams had seven men, counting the leader, who was always knighted. The bottom rank was made up mostly of pages and squires. On any one day, five of them would be working, one would be at military exercises and one would be enjoying his day off.

This meant working Sundays, and I got a lot of flak

about it, both from the men and from the Church. I tried to prove to them that what God meant was that they should spend one day a week in prayer and rest, and the original Sabbath was on Saturday, anyhow, but they were still mad at me. We tried juggling schedules, hoping to keep everybody happy, but that didn't work either.

On top of this, virtually every industrial job was worked in two shifts, one days and one nights, and that was another set of headaches.

Finally, I just threw a temper tantrum and said they could do it my way or they could leave. Very few quit.

We tried to keep the training as amusing as possible, with contests, races, and that sort of thing. To a certain extent, we were successful and military sports became the big game on campus. At Three Walls, these drills and games were generally held on the "killing ground" in front of the walls. This was where we held our portion of the yearly Great Hunt, the harvesting of the wild animals on our lands. It was a great alluvial, fan shaped area, almost a mile to the side, and was surrounded by a vast tangle of Japanese roses, fully five yards high and twice that thick. Barbed wire would have been inferior as a military defense!

It wasn't only the men who did military training. The women had their duties as well, concentrating on defending the walls. They got proficient with the swivel guns on the outer wall, as well as with grenades. They didn't work out with the pike or halbred, the usual woman's arms being a little weak to handle these big weapons, but most of them were decent with a rapier.

Lady Krystyana became a master swordswoman, always winning the women's championship and outfencing me most of the time. She seemed to get a special thrill out of scoring on me, I suppose in revenge for all the years I'd spent sticking it to her.

But these exercises were a problem for the night shift, since despite fudging things by an hour or two, most of their training day happened in the dark.

Sir Ilya was my night shift manager at Three Walls. He had wanted this job because his wife was incapable of sleeping in the day, and the arrangement suited him. He just got a bunk in night shift bachelors' quarters and mostly ignored her, despite my orders to the contrary. After a year of being ignored, she ran away with Count

Lambert's blacksmith to places unknown. It was two weeks before Ilya noticed it, and then only when he checked his account at the bank. Not that he tried to find her, or replace her, or even take on a "servant." A bachelor's life suited him.

But despite his marital problems, Ilya took his work seriously, and if military duties were part of his job, he did it. But he did it in his own way.

He figured that what we needed was a special group of men trained to fight at night. He even named them "The Night Fighters." As a group, they worked out the techniques for silent fighting in the dark. I helped them where I could, mostly telling them about commando stuff I'd seen in the movies, but they got good at it. They learned to walk quietly in total darkness, the leader signaling the men behind him with a string they all held in their left hands. They practiced with the knife and with the garrote, their version of which was a steel wire with a couple of wooden spools and a strange, one way slipknot. I think it might have been the world's first disposable weapons system. It only worked once. But since you weren't likely to miss with one, once was enough.

And they played games, just like the day shift, only different. One of their's was "steal the pig." This was played with a live pig, one scheduled for tomorrow's supper, since the pig often did not survive the game. It was played in pitch darkness, and if there was a moon out, they'd play it in a basement. The pig wore a harness around its body which was tied to a pole with a three-yard rope. A lance of seven men was assigned to guard it and another lance was given the task of stealing it. It was played in full armor, and no weapons were allowed except on the pig. After that, anything went! Real class was to steal the pig without the guards knowing it was gone, but decking them all out cold was fair.

Games of this type put a premium on quiet motion, which wasn't easy in regulation plate armor. They naturally got to working on the armor. I told them that we could not possibly make new stamping dies, not this late in the game, so they worked within those limitations. What they came up with was a set of armored coveralls. It used the same pieces as our standard armor, but each piece fit into a sort of pocket sewn in the garment. Baggy when you first put them on, they had zippers up the sides and on all four limbs which snugged them up properly. Where the plate armor couldn't cover, as on the armpits and on the inside of the knees and elbows, pieces of chain mail were sewn in.

One of the beauties of this design was that you could get into it in a hurry. It took a quarter-hour for a man to arm himself with our standard armor. With Night-Fighter armor, it was a matter of a minute.

Another problem with any plate armor was that it didn't breath. Steel is impervious to air. This was no problem in the winter, when we normally wore quilted goose-down long underwear, but in the summer, you could suffocate in there, and cases of heat exhaustion and even heatstroke were all too common.

They worked out a system of forced ventilation. In the summer, you wore a set of thin linen long johns that had zippers all over the place. These zippers matched up with zippers on the inside of the armored coveralls. Since the armor was about a finger's width bigger than you were, all around, the result was a number of separate compartments all over you. The front of your shin was one compartment and the back of it was another. There were valves, simple flaps covering holes, at the knees and ankles, such that cool air could come in at the ankles and go out at the knees. As you walked, you naturally moved around inside this oversized armor, and this motion pumped cool air in the bottom and hot air out the top. Since there were eighteen of these compartments around your body, you stayed reasonably cool. Not like you'd be in a pair of shorts and a T-shirt, but cases of heat exhaustion became rare.

They did talk me into a summer helmet, which resembled a Chinese coolie hat, and we tooled up for that.

Their system was so superior to what we had that I made it the army standard, for the men anyway.

There wasn't much to setting up for the new armor. A number of conventional knights were looking for something for their peasants to do as a winter money-maker, so we set them up sewing armor coveralls.

I'd originally issued the same armor to the women that I had to the men, but the girls didn't like it. It had to be of the same thickness as the men's or it wouldn't be able to stop an arrow, and they said it was too heavy.

Since they would be fighting only from the walls,

where the parapet protected them from the waist down, they soon discarded the leg armor. They said that the gauntlets made it hard to operate a gun, so they got rid of them, too. But the man's sword had only a small hand guard, about what you'd find on a Japanese sword, since the men wore steel gloves. Without authorization, the girls got the shop to tool up a special big hand guard, like they put on a modern épée.

And the standard breastplates. No style at all! Completely without my permission, special tooling was made, *thirty-two expensive dies in all*, just to satisfy them.

Now their breastplates had breasts on them.

And having done that, they thought that it was prettier polished and shiny, so they didn't go the practical coverall route. They'd even come up with a zowie-looking helmet with a Greek-style crest on it when I put my foot down. There was no face guard, and it didn't protect the neck at all, since the girls wanted their hair to show! I ranted and swore that this was a stupid design and a stupider waste of resources. They said, yes, sir. You're right, sir. We'll do it your way, sir.

Then two months later they were all wearing these new helmets!

I never could find out who made the dies, since they knew I would have fired the bastard, and the production schedules on the stamping presses showed no time allotted to the silly things. How they got them made, I don't know, but soon the ladies at all the other installations were in the new outfits, too.

But *you* try holding back a bunch of women when they get a bright idea.

Then to top it all off, the duke saw the ladies' helmets and thought that, gold-plated, they'd be just the thing for a ceremonial guard! I managed to talk him out of it. They wouldn't have fit a man, anyway, a female's head being much smaller than a male's. Darned if I was going to let any more draw dies be made.

Strange to say, despite its obvious advantages, the new coverall armor didn't catch on with the conventional knights.

Of course, during all this time, we'd been selling plate armor at decent prices to anyone who wanted to buy from us. Well, we wouldn't have sold to a Mongol, but none of them applied. But after three years of selling polished plate armor, it was all the rage among the hawking and hunting set. While our troops were discovering camouflage paint, they wanted to shine. There was nothing we could do about it, so we let them have their own way.

Another thing the Night Fighters did was with the swivel guns. They put a big pie plate of a flash suppressor at the muzzle of the gun. This did two things for them. For one thing, it stopped the muzzle flash from blinding the gunner at night. For another, it reflected all of the light forward, and they worked out a system where each gunner fired just after the man to his left. This let him aim by the flash of light caused by the last gun going off. From a distance, it looked like a string of chase lights on a theater marquis, but they got reasonably accurate with the system. Flash suppressors soon became standard for all our swivel guns.

Innovation was the name of the game at Eagle Nest, where a sturdy band of very young men were busily conquering the skies. Actually, they were getting too innovative, and I had to work at converting their efforts from research to production.

They had started out with motorless sailplanes, and their aircraft showed that heritage. The wings were long and thin, the bodies long and sleek. They were all high-winged, since I'd always been aiming at observation craft, and even with motors, they still had to be catapult launched.

This catapult was built on top of an ancient, man-made hill about six dozen yards high, probably some sort of prehistoric defensive structure. The hill was conical, with a flat spot on top about two dozen yards across. We built a low, circular concrete wall, and the catapult rode on this wall, so as to point into the wind. The catapult itself was a wooden ramp, six dozen yards long and angling upward at a half-hour angle. A rope ran from the back of the catapult to a pulley at the front, then back halfway to the center where it went over another pulley and then was attached to a massive concrete weight that was hung over a well we'd dug in the hill.

To launch, a plane was hauled up the hill and loaded onto the catapult. Then four dozen boys walked up to the front of the catapult, grabbed the rope, and hauled it back to the plane. With practice, they got so they could launch a dozen planes an hour this way.

But instead of building a few dozen planes of the best design we had and "fine tuning" them, they wanted to continue designing whole new ones. Part of the problem was that I'd once mentioned that a canard-type plane, with the propeller in back and the elevator forward of the wing was more efficient than the conventional design, but that these planes were too difficult for us to design and fly. The boys took that as a challenge, and Count Lambert was on their side. It took me three temper tantrums, and them four deadly wrecks, before they went into production on a standard, conventional aircraft.

Even with that, crack-ups were so frequent that they rarely had three planes ready to fly at any one time, and the price they willingly paid in lives still gives me nightmares.

Chapter Nine

ABOUT THIS time, we began to notice that there wasn't enough money to go around. I don't mean that we were spending more than we made. Far to the contrary! Our products were being sold all over Europe, and the local currency had become a hodgepodge of pennies, deniers, pfennigs, and what have you, minted in dozens of different places. In theory, all these coins were of the same value, but in fact, their weight and silver content varied all over the map.

But despite this influx of foreign coins, there still wasn't enough to go around. I was converting Poland from a barter economy to a money economy. Peasants who had rarely needed or even seen money in their lives suddenly found that they wanted money to buy the things we sold, and that they could get money by selling their crops, now that the railroads and steamboats were operating and they could get those crops to market. The lack of silver coin was causing a serious deflation, and the prices of things were dropping precipitously.

I, of course, had all kinds of money, and at first I tried to counteract the deflation by raising the pay scales of the people who worked for me. I kept the bottom rate the same, a penny a day, since we always had a waiting list to get in, even with the military-training requirement. But after that, pay doubled with each promotion. There were three grades of nonmanagerial workers, warriors, pages, and squires, earning one, two, and four pence respectively, and from then on, well, a man could get rich working for me.

But it didn't help the deflation a bit. Most of the extra pay was spent in my stores and my inns, or left in my bank. Very little of it got out to the general public.

Then I tried buying things I didn't really need, mostly land. I started buying up land along the rivers because I had some vague ideas of one day building a series of forts along them. But not that much land was for sale, and buying land was not as easy as it would be in the twentieth century. There were all sorts of incumbrances involved, oaths of fealty, requirements of military service, the rights of the peasants living there, strange taxes, and what not. I managed to get out of most of these—but not peasants' rights—with one-time cash payments, yet it did not cure the major problem that I was trying to solve. When I bought land from some nobleman, he usually spent the money to buy the things that my factories were making! He wanted arms and armor, glass windows, and indoor plumbing. The money came right back to me and the deflation continued!

Furthermore, I couldn't resist making the land I'd bought productive and profitable.

Surely, this was a problem that no capitalist ever had to cope with!

Charity work was another matter. With the assistance of Abbot Ignacy and his monks, I worked hard at helping the poor. We set up soup kitchens in the major cities and a large leper colony on an isolated estate that I'd bought. But the engineer in me hates waste, and the waste of human potential is the worst sort.

Many of the poor were that way simply because they could not find honest work, so I gave it to them. I set up nonarmy construction groups to build railroads and bridges. They were supervised by army personnel, of course, since there weren't many trained, technically competent people outside it. We were running tracks as fast as the blast furnaces could cast them, and most of our lines were double-tracked, so we didn't have to worry much about scheduling. With a single-tracked line, you have to make sure that a train isn't coming north before you take yours south. Double tracks can be treated just like a highway.

Some of the poor were children, orphans. We set up an adoption service, and many of these kids were adopted by army families. Some of the poor were old or feeble. In the cities we set up factories that turned out knitted goods, much of which were bought by the army. We always needed socks and underwear.

Undoubtedly, all of this did a great deal of good for the people. I think it made me something of a people's hero. At least they insisted on cheering whenever I was around, though in fact I would have preferred some peace and quiet. And what do you do when children and old women insist on kissing your boot, for God's sake! It was embarrassing. I got to giving a standard speech, thanking them, but saying that I didn't like people yelling at me, and if they wanted to do anything for me, they could pray in church for my soul, which needed it. It didn't help much. Most people would rather yell than pray.

Yet the prices kept on dropping and my coffers stayed full. Even feeding the indigent, we had to buy from the farmers, and the farmers made enough money to buy our plumbing supplies and glass windows. Raising my prices didn't help either. They just bought less, but spent the same amount of money, so I put prices back where they had been.

In the middle of this charity work, Abbot Ignacy became His Excellency Ignacy, Bishop of Cracow, and he stepped lightly from the regular clergy to the secular branch of the Church. How much I had to do with this promotion, I don't know.

Despite his elevation, Bishop Ignacy remained my confessor, and I made a point of seeing him at least once a month. He had traded in his humble monk's robe for the glorious raiment of his new office, but he wore his embroidered silks and velvets with the casualness with which he had treated his old brown smock when we had camped along the river, so many years ago. His new office, in his palace near Wawel Cathedral, was as ornate as a church altar, with brightly painted carved wood encrusting the walls and ceiling, but he had moved one of our standard wooden desks into it, the sort that our cabinet shop turned out by the gross.

"Ah, Conrad! Have you come to confess again? Have I told you how much I like these desks you've designed? What with all the drawers, I can keep everything at hand. I've recommended them to all my priests."

"Uh, yes, no, and thank you, your excellency." I made a mental note to have a special desk made that would match his office, rather than looking like a computer in a church.

"Oh, 'Father' is sufficient when we are alone, Conrad. Did I tell you that there is word on the inquisition the Church is conducting in your regard?"

Ever since arriving in this century, an inquisition had been hanging over my head. The Church was trying to decide if I was an instrument of God, perhaps to be canonized, or an instrument of the devil, to be burned at the stake. I couldn't help being a little anxious about it.

"What has happened, Father?"

"Well, you recall that when first you came to this century, I wrote up all the particulars quite diligently and presented them to my abbot. He, in turn, quickly annotated my report and within the month sent it to this very office. The bishop of that time felt that the matter would best go through the regular branch of the Church, rather than the secular, so he sent it back to my abbot with that recommendation. My abbot then sent it to the home monastery as soon as someone could be found who was going in that direction, and the speed and diligence of all concerned was such that the home monastery in Italy was able to reply back to us within the year."

"Yes, Father, but—"

"But the home monastery was sure that this was a matter for the secular branch, so my abbot sent the report, with notations, back to the Bishop of Cracow. But by this time, you had established yourself in Silesia, which of course is in the Diocese of Wroclaw. The Bishop of Cracow therefore sent the report to the Bishop of Wroclaw, who forwarded it to the Archbishop at Gniezno. From there, it was sent to Rome, with further notations. Rome then replied with a request that the Abbot of the Franciscan monastery here confirm the report. By this time, however, I was that very personage, and having all the facts at my fingertips, as it were, I was quickly able to comply, and provided an update on all your doings."

How could I forget that? After three years, all that had happened was that Father Ignacy had written a letter to himself, and then he had replied to it!

"Yes, Father, but—"

"Now, since all this had transpired within a few years, you can see that the matter was being pushed forward as quickly as possible. But then several years went by in which I heard nothing, so I took it on myself to write a letter of inquiry to Rome. As it turned out, my reply to the report had somehow gone astray somewhere between Gniezno and Rome, no one has any idea what happened to it, and the merchant who carried it was never seen again. Fortunately, the Archbishop of Gniezno had caused to be made a true copy of the entire annotated report for his files. A copy of this was made and again it was sent to Rome. Rome's reply returned through proper channels only a week ago, and it orders that a full inquiry be made by the Bishop of Cracow, who at this time again happens to be me. Of course, I complied immediately, and a full report is again on the way to Rome, through channels, of course."

So Father Ignacy had for a second time answered his own report! And nothing of significance had transpired in seven years! It made me want to scream and pull out my hair! But, with work, I kept my cool.

"So Rome still doesn't know much about me, Father?"

"How can you say that, Conrad? They've seen my reports, haven't they? They also subscribe to the magazine you started and get a copy of it every month! People are learning Polish just to be able to read it! Your books and plumbing supplies are all the rage in Rome, and everyone there has one of your lighters! Of course they know about you!"

I sighed. After Confession, I mentioned that I was going over to the monastery to talk to the artist, Friar Roman.

"Then I've saved you a trip, Conrad. I brought Roman over with me, I think mostly to keep an eye on him. He had been using the wealth he gained from designing church windows to hire young ladies as models, and was posing them most immodestly!"

"In most cultures, your excellency, that would be considered an artist's prerogative."

"Not in *my* church, it isn't! What did you want to see him about?"

"Lithography. It's another printing process, well suited to art work. We have accurate maps of much of Poland now, and I need many copies made of each. I have a new machine almost ready at Three Walls, and I want to teach him how to use it, since it takes an artist."

"Three Walls would be just fine, Conrad. Take him

for as long as you need him. But you keep that boy away from Okoitz! If it was in *my* diocese, there'd be some changes made there, I assure you!"

"Yes, Father."

Friar Roman was delighted to get out from under Bishop Ignacy's thumb, and caught the next boat to Three Walls.

The deflation was still troubling me, and I finally realized that to inflate the economy back to its previous levels, I was going to have to add new money to the system. With the duke's permission, I started making my own coins, with his likeness on one side and a Polish eagle on the other. For some years, we had been refining zinc and calling it "Polish Silver." No one had paid much mind, but the fact was that we were the only people in the world that had this technology. I made it a *secret* technology.

The only problem was that to use zinc for coinage, I had to drastically raise its price. I could sneak it into the brass, since very few people realized that brass was an alloy of copper and zinc. They acted like it was a separate metal. But the price of pure zinc items had to go up and the price of galvanized iron skyrocketed to the point that sales went way down.

I wrote a series of articles for our magazine, explaining the cause of the deflation and what I intended to do about it. My alchemist, Zoltan Varanian, made an analysis of the silver content of each of the six dozen supposedly identical coins that were in circulation, and I published it. The silver content of those coins varied from forty percent down to as little as three percent!

The result was economic chaos for a half year. But at the same time, I came out with a series of zinc coins in various denominations. I rated zinc at one-sixth the value of pure silver, but the whole concept for different denominations was new, and it took some people a while to get used to it. But in our money system, with a few large coins you could buy a horse, and with the smallest, a kid could buy a piece of candy, something that was not possible before.

In one of my magazine articles, I made a serious oath that the content and weight of my coins would be absolutely constant, that we would trade any worn (but not clipped!) coin for a new one, and that we would trade our coins for standard silver coins on demand. "Polish Silver" caught on.

Then we started buying everything in sight! We bought land, we bought furs, we bought amber. We bought land in the Bledowska Desert, built huge granaries there, and set up a constant pricing system for purchases and sales, buying grain by the hundreds of tons! We even bought silver and gold. But mostly we bought land. In a few years, we owned most of the land within five miles of the Vistula, the Odra, and many of their tributaries. Once we had the time, I was going to ring Poland with a line of concrete forts!

But all this land aggravated some of my other problems. Besides being the owner, I had to be the police force and the judge as well. The police force wasn't a big problem, since I had set one up years ago. Whenever one of my bailiffs had a problem he couldn't handle, he called in a detective. And now that these men were partnered with Anna's progeny, their arrest rate was near perfect. The Big People could smell out a thief or a murderer every time.

Most of the other Big People were working carrying the mails, and the speed of mail transport was doubled. After the first few months, we started using them without riders, and except for some astounded travelers, there wasn't a hitch.

But what I needed now was some judges and lawyers, and the man I knew who was most knowledgeable of the law was Sir Miesko. He had been my next door neighbor for years. Well, his manor was six miles away from mine, but that's the way these things went. He was my assistant Master of the Hunt, and in fact ran the thing on all the duke's lands. He got all the furs taken each fall, and this had made him rich. He had once been my biggest vendor, providing food for Three Walls, but now was one of my best customers. He'd built a truly fine castle using my building supplies, and many of the features of my own defensive works, like the combination granary and watchtower, were invented by him.

He'd been a legal clerk, the closest local equivalent to a lawyer, before he was knighted for valor, so I asked him to head up my legal department.

"I'd like to, Baron Conrad, but I just can't. The Great

Hunt takes up a lot of my time, and running my manor takes up more. You know that all of my boys have joined your army instead of helping me out around here, and, well, I'm just not as young as I used to be."

"Damn. I can see your point, though. Okay, if not you, then who? Do you know a truly honest man who knows the law?" I said.

"That's a hard one, Baron. Somehow, the more a man knows about the law, the less he seems inclined to obey it! But yes, one man comes to mind. He's only a few years younger than I am, but he doesn't have my responsibilities. We worked together in my youth, and we've kept in touch. Adam Pulaski, he's your man."

So I got in touch with this Pulaski. I set him up with three younger men, one to act as prosecutor, one to be defender, and one to be court recorder. I sent them out to take over my case load. I had to approve all their actions, of course, and any capital offenses had to be taken to my liege lord, Count Lambert, but they were the start of the army court system.

Before the Mongol invasion, prices were back up to where they had been before I had arrived. After that, we just watched the prices of a dozen common commodities, and if the average price got too low, we brought it back up by making more coins and buying things we didn't need.

Chapter Ten

By the spring of 1240, I knew we'd be ready. The Warrior's School was completed, even though everybody was calling it "Hell" now. The main building was a mile square and six stories tall, surrounding a collection of mess halls, parade grounds, churches, huge warehouses filled to the rafters with military goods, an induction center, and even a synagogue.

I was surprised to find how many Jews I had working for me. The Jews were a new element in thirteenth-century Poland, most of them coming in with the Germans in their peaceful "invasion." There were no racial tensions at the time, mostly because the Christians were rarely aware of the Jews. In fact, most people didn't even know of their existence as a separate religious group, lumping them in with other foreigners.

But most work crews were eager to get them when they could. Jews were perfectly willing to work on Sunday, providing they could get Saturday off, or Friday night in the case of night-shift workers. The vast majority of my people were Catholics, and the more Jews in your crew, the better your chances were of getting Sunday off.

A delegation of rabbis had once come to me, asking if they could set up a ghetto at Three Walls, the way they were being set up in the increasingly German-dominated cities. I wouldn't do it.

I would like to make it clear that these ghettos were not slums where the unfortunate were stuffed to get them out of the way. The ghetto was a portion of the city where Jewish Law, rather than Christian Law, was practiced. In the ghetto, the Jews had their own council, their own schools, their own courts, and what amounted to their own police force. Furthermore, there were special courts to handle problems between Jews and Catholics, and an attempt was made to keep these fair. The ghetto was a privilege that the Jews sought and paid cash for.

In the world I grew up in, and I am becoming convinced that it was a different world than that which I am now living in, the Jews came to Poland at about the same time, and settled in the cities.

There is a natural animosity between city dwellers and rural people. Before the days of movies and television, they lived in such totally different environments that neither comprehended the lifestyle of the other.

Yet each needed the products of the other. The cities needed food and the countrymen needed the manufactured goods of the cities. They traded, but each soon felt that the other was out to cheat him, and so retaliation seemed the sensible thing to do. Once this started to happen, the myth had become truth, a self-fulfilling prophecy.

When this difference in lifestyles was added to differences in language, differences in customs, and differences in religion, these animosities naturally were accentuated. There were even differences in political allegiances, for many cities within the political boundaries of Poland became members of the Hanseatic League, and no longer swore allegiance to the Polish Crown.

And in Silesia, the countrymen were Polish, the nobles were sworn to the German Holy Roman Empire and mostly spoke German, and the cities were allied with the Nordic Hans! And part of each city was yet another separate political entity, the Jewish ghetto! A crazy system, yet it survived for centuries!

The truth is that the Jews in Poland maintained their separate culture for *seven hundred years*! They did not learn Polish, the language of the people around them, but continued speaking German, although in time their language drifted so far from standard German as to become a separate dialect, Yiddish.

The Jews called the people surrounding them *goyim*, cattle, and were sure that these farmers were out to poison them. And indeed, there were unscrupulous farmers who tried to make a quick profit. Not many, but some. The Jews overreacted with a ridiculously strict adherence to the bibilical dietary codes, having a religious leader inspect all food eaten, and cheated a dumb farmer whenever possible.

In the early thirteenth-century Poland, Jewish dietary rules were not nearly as evolved as they became later.

The countrymen became convinced that the Jews stole Christian babies for sacrifice at their religious services. This was of course not true, but a few Jews did engage in kidnapping Christians and selling them as slaves to the Moslems, a thing that Christians generally could not do since the Moslems usually refused to trade with Christians.

Without a basis of mutual understanding, the actions of a few criminals became "what everybody knows."

Having said all this, I must point out that Poland was the best place in Europe for a Jew to be, at least up until World War Two. Everywhere else, it was worse. The Jews were thrown out of England, France, Spain, and many other countries. All their property was confiscated, and many of their people were killed. This never happened in Poland, at least not until Poland itself was conquered by foreign powers. There has always been an official policy of toleration, no matter what most people actually felt.

Separate peoples, hating each other and misunderstanding each other, they lived together because they needed each other.

I wasn't going to let this happen again, at least not on my lands. The Jews were welcome as individuals, as was anybody else. Well, I wouldn't want an Atheist around, but in fact I never ran into anyone who would admit to being one. But if I let the Jews segregate themselves, they would keep to their own German language and their own customs. They never would become part of *us*, and racial tensions would inevitably develop. I let them have the use of some of the common rooms for their own religious services and religious instruction. Where the rabbis were sufficiently educated, we hired them into the school system, and the Jews could always wrangle it so they got Saturday off. But separate housing, separate schools, separate laws, and separate dining facilities were out!

Well, I did have the kitchen staff put up a little sign when something was grossly nonkosher, since many traditional Polish foods were based on blood and others on pork. A Jew would sometimes get violently ill if he found out that he had just eaten *kishka*. Anyway, you only get a little bowl of blood from a duck, and there is no point in wasting *tchanina* on somebody who doesn't appreciate it!

Now, I know that I was at the very same time keeping the Moslems sworn to me segregated from the rest of the country. But it was not my intent that this should be a permanent situation. One day, we would defeat the Mongols and drive them back to where they came from, at which time I meant to help Zoltan Varanian's people resettle their original homeland. And if we didn't beat the Mongols, we'd all be dead anyway, so the problem would solve itself.

Count Lambert's new castle was completed, and he was vastly proud of it. It really was a functional military defensive structure, with thick masonry walls six stories tall, crenelations, machinations, turret towers, and all the rest. It was completely fireproof, with even the floors being made of masonry, rather than the usual wood. It had room for all of his peasants as well as the four-gross young ladies that worked at his cloth factory. Further, he could play host to half the nobility in the duchy and have beds for everybody.

And it had glass windows, indoor plumbing, and steam heat. There were even gaslights in the public areas. There was a church, a granary, huge storerooms, a sauna, and an indoor swimming pool. There was even a system of conduits going to every room, so that when we got electric lights and telephones, these things could be easily installed. The kitchens and dining rooms were such that everybody ate there, and private cooking was frowned on.

I think I was as proud of that building as the count was.

The fort at East Gate was up as well, and it had gone up much quicker, since at Okoitz I had used vaulted construction throughout, but at East Gate I used prefabricated reinforced concrete for the floors and ceilings. Not as pretty, but it sure was cheaper.

I was sure that this fort was impregnable. The outer walls were seven storeys tall and made of thick, reinforced concrete. It was surrounded by six tall towers, which were really storage silos for hay, grain, and coal, but each had a fighting platform on top, and a dunce-cap roof to protect the fighters. These towers were connected to the main fort by underground tunnels. An enemy attacking any point would be in a crossfire from at least two and usually four directions. A two-storey wall (that doubled as a long barn for the mules that pulled the railroad carts) surrounded the entire complex, connecting the towers. It wasn't high enough to stop men with ladders, but it would stop horses and siege equipment.

The ground plan was a symmetrical hexagon, and what with the six surrounding towers and walls, it resembled a snowflake. We ended up calling the design just that, and I got to toying with the idea of someday building hundreds of them.

Let the Mongols try and take this one!

I think that we bragged about it too much, and that this contributed to a major tragedy. But I get ahead of myself.

Three Walls really had three walls now, and the outer one was of sturdy concrete. There were towers above the surrounding cliffs, and all sorts of dirty tricks were built in as defensive measures.

And all my other installations at Coaltown, Silver City, and Copper City were similarly fortified. This was necessary because when we men went off to war, we needed someplace safe for the women, children, and old folks. And it was not only our own dependents that we had to protect, but those of everyone else in Silesia and Little Poland. I calculated that by stacking people in like cordwood, we'd have enough room to save them all. And while they might eat a lot of *kasha*, there would be food enough to feed them all as well.

Except for adding wall guns, I'd left the castle I'd inherited from Baron Stefan alone, and in fact rarely used it. It was well enough designed as a defensive structure, but the moat made it difficult to add a sewage system. The peasants in the immediate area used the castle for weddings and what not and, come the invasion, would retreat to it for safety, but aside from that, I really didn't see much use for it. Maybe someday I'd fill in the moat and put in a septic system.

Eagle Nest, on the other hand, got only a single, sepa-

rate concrete tower, which doubled as a control tower
for the airport. If attacked, the boys could go there and
be safe enough, since the thing was nine stories tall.
There simply weren't enough people there to defend a
wall long enough to surround the entire airport, and
there weren't enough peasants nearby to help them. I
was sorry to do it, but we had to treat the whole wooden
complex as expendable.

The old cities weren't in very good shape either. The
walls around Cracow were only three stories tall, and a
wall that low can be scaled. Wawel Hill was well enough
fortified, but the city below it looked likely to fall if it
was seriously attacked. But try to get those damn merchants to spend a penny they didn't have to! I offered to
sell them guns and to train their people as gunners, all at
cost. They bought only a dozen swivel guns for the
whole city and considered this to be sufficient!

Wroclaw was in similar shape, and Legnica! Legnica
still had *wooden walls*!

We didn't have room enough inside our fortifications
for the farm animals, so doctrine was for the animals to
be released to try their luck in the woods. At least the
wolves were pretty much eradicated now, what with the
Great Hunts and all. A program of branding was under-
way, so that the animals could be returned to their
owners after the invasion.

We had a similar program going to identify people.
My own troops had dog tags, of course, but we enlarged
the program to include the conventional knights as well.
The service was free, and most of them took us up on it.
If they fell in battle, we could at least mark their graves.

The radios were working, although they weren't all
that dependable. They weighed two-gross pounds each
and had a range of only thirty miles and that only in good
weather. A lightning storm within fifty miles could
drown them out, and they required endless fiddling by
the operator. Nonetheless, we'd gone into production,
and produced them by the thousands. There was one on
every steamboat and one at each depot. Every Pink
Dragon Inn had its radio, and there were four at each of
our major installations. In addition, one war cart in six
had a radio, so each company could keep in touch. Get-

ting enough trained operators was a huge problem, but people were being trained as fast as sets were being built. Most of them were still pretty slow, but we kept them in practice.

With only nine months to go before the Mongol invasion, Zoltan came to me with a new device. Our swivel guns used brass cartridges. They were breech-loading and clip-fed. But after years of fruitless effort, the alchemists had been unable to come up with a dependable primer to detonate the black powder in the shell. What we were using was a firecracker wick on the back of each shell that was lit by an alcohol burner near the breech. It was a clumsy alternative, but it was the best we could do.

Zoltan presented me with a new cartridge and a new gun to fire it. Each cartridge had what amounted to a spark plug in the base, and the bolt of the gun contained a piezoelectric crystal to provide the spark.

This was the same system that we had been using for years on our lighters, and the same system that the boys at Eagle Nest used on their aircraft engines, and the same system we used on the spark-gap radios. And for years, it hadn't occurred to me or anyone else until now to use it to ignite gunpowder!

In truth, I had to take the blame for this one myself. I had made gunpowder a secret thing, something you weren't supposed to think about. I had kept Zoltan working on chemical projects and generally away from the Christians working on almost everything else. Secrecy is hell on innovations, and it was all my fault.

To make things worse, there was no time to convert the tens of thousands of swivel guns we had already made. We would have to meet the Mongols with obsolete equipment.

I designed a simple, single-shot pistol to use the new cartridges, and a few hundred of them were made in time, for use by officers. It had a breaking action like a shotgun, and had the general appearance of an old-style dueling pistol. I also designed a submachine gun along the lines of the Sten gun, but only prototypes were made. There just wasn't time!

Then we got word that Kiev had fallen, the walls had been stormed, and the armies slaughtered. The tales we heard from the few survivors were ghastly. They told of old people tortured, young women raped, and children hunted down in the streets for sport.

No one doubted that we were next on the list.

FROM THE DIARY OF TADAOS KOLPINSKI

I was Komander Tadaos now, and making sixty-four pence a day! It makes me wish my father could have lived long enough to see it! I had eighteen boats on the Vistula, and twenty-two on the Odra.

'Course, only three of those Odra boats was real fighting boats, two operating above Wroclaw and one below it. The rest were low, skinny things that could make it under the bridges at Wroclaw. There weren't any bridges on the Vistula, nor were there any on any of the tributaries that you could get a fighting boat up, but those Wroclaw bridges was a pain!

We could build new bridges wide and tall enough. Baron Conrad's book on them showed just how. But the damn city father (mothers, the lot of them) wouldn't hear of tearing their old ones down.

I figured that with twelve barrels of gunpowder, we could do in one of the bridges some dark and stormy night and claim it was lightning, an Act of God, but the baron wouldn't let me do it. He said it would take thirty barrels, easy, and the rubble would likely block the channel. And he said that the duke wouldn't like it, so that ended it.

But someday, I was going to find a way of getting me them thirty barrels and trying it!

All the boats was way overmanned, since we had to train crews for the new boats being built. Come spring, I was to have three dozen on the Vistula alone. What's more, we had a gas generator on all our fighting boats now, and limelights on top of the turrets. These lights had big reflectors that turned with the gun below them, and we could run and fight in the dark, so we needed night crews as well as those for the day.

We had flamethrowers now, too. These was a big barrel of pitch and wood alcohol in the bow with sort of a fire hose on the end. There was a lighter built in it, and when we put steam pressure to the barrel, we could squirt fire for six dozen yards! 'Course, it only worked for about a minute, but that was a lot.

We was always doing target practice, mostly with the Halmans and the peashooters, since they didn't use no gunpowder and was cheap to shoot. The peashooters didn't draw nearly the steam now that they used to, and I was pretty proud of that, since it was my doing. I came up with a valve that shut off the steam, just for an instant, while a new ball was dropping into the chamber. It was a little like the valve the baron designed for the bottom of the Halmans, which let loose a blast of steam when the round hit the bottom, only sort of backward. Anyway, the baron, he was tickled red over it cause now we could fire all four peashooters at once and still power the boat. I got two thousand pence as a bonus and they named that valve after me.

But like I was saying, there was a target range set up about every two miles on the rivers, and we used them. These targets was set up by young boys after the baron wrote a magazine article asking them to do it. They was pretty good at coming up with interesting things to shoot at, since they wanted us to do all the shooting we could. See, the ball bearings used by the peashooters and the dummy rounds from the Halmans was all reusable. After we'd go by, the kids would be out there digging them up so they could turn them in for the reward on them. Since we gave them about a quarter of what it would cost to make new ones, everybody came out pretty good.

Then somebody found out that the Halmans could shoot a potato about as well as a dummy round, and we got to shelling the other steamboats as they went by. The baron told us to stop before somebody got hurt, but everybody on deck was required to wear armor, and no potato ever hurt an armored man. Why, after coming out of a Halman, they was half cooked, anyway. And moving targets was more interesting, so that order sort of got misplaced.

I was having a row with my wives. They both got pregnant at the same time again, which they'd agreed not to do, and I was finding myself having to do without. Can you believe that? Two wives and still going horny?

Well, they said it was as much my fault as theirs, it taking two to accomplish anything, but you know how women like to come up with excuses. Then they said that at least this time, they'd both be mine, and I hit the ceiling! I said that the first two was mine, and I'd wallop anybody who said different!

Then I said that what with my rank and all, I was allowed a wife and four servants, and I was going to Okoitz to find me another one. They said that it took their permission, too, and they had to pass on any girl I picked. So we left two of the kids with a family at East Gate and we took one of the passenger carts to Okoitz the next time we had a few days off.

Well, you know I found me a pretty and willing girl in just no time at all, and so did they. The trouble was that they wasn't the same girl, and we had us another row about it. Finally we compromised and I took the both of the new girls on. But that's going to be the end of it, unless all four of them get pregnant simultaneous. If they do that on me, well, I'm still allowed one more, and after that I'll just have to get me some more rank.

Chapter Eleven

^^^^^^^^^^^^^^^^^^^^^^^

FROM THE DIARY OF CONRAD STARGARD

There were Mongols in Cracow, but they weren't invading just yet. This was a diplomatic party, and the duke wanted me and some of my people there to advise him.

We'd had plenty of warning about their coming, since they were spotted at one of our depots on the River Bug. The operator there got out a radio message fast, and she was bright enough to warn away the steamboats in the area. I don't think they saw any of the planes, either.

I knew that it was important to make as brave a show as possible, but at the same time I didn't want them to see everything we had. Word went out on the radio that the steamboats and airplanes were to avoid the Mongols, the guns were to be taken down and hidden, and that the radios themselves were not to be talked about.

I'd never publicized the radios, but I knew that scattered around as they had to be, there was no way of keeping their existence a secret. Operating principles were something else, but since few people knew them anyway, I wasn't worried.

In fact, I needn't have worried at all, since people who did hear about them didn't believe it. They'd believe in a steamboat because they saw it, and the same was true with the airplanes, which still had people running outdoors and pointing upward whenever one went over, but a machine that made sparks and talked to people miles away? . . . Nawww. . . .

I wanted the Mongols to be afraid of us, but for the wrong reasons. There wouldn't be enough of Anna's mature children to make a difference in the invasion. Oh, they'd stand night guard duty and run messages, but there would only be thirty-three adult Big People by the time of the battle, and that wasn't enough to tip the scales.

Still, if I could make the Mongols worry about fighting a highly mobile cavalry force, they might conduct their strategy accordingly, and that couldn't do us any harm. Mobility was where we were weakest.

I collected all the Big People I could, twenty of them counting Anna, along with some of my main people, and rode to Cracow. I brought Sir Vladimir, Sir Piotr, and the Banki brothers, among others.

I brought Cilicia along, and I had the others bring their wives. We came in civilian clothes and without armor, my idea being to lend the occasion as little dignity as possible.

We arrived in the early morning, just hours ahead of the Mongol delegation. Duke Henryk met with me and asked me to do the bulk of the talking at the preliminary meeting, since I apparently knew more about the Mongols than anybody else.

"Just stand on the dais by my left hand, Baron Conrad. Should I want to talk to them directly, I shall signal you. But talk as you see fit."

A number of counts were up there as well, sort of an honor guard. The throne room was filled with gawkers, but all of my own people were there as well. This was supposed to be just a formal meeting, with further negotiations to be held in private. At least that was what the duke thought. I had somewhat different ideas, and the Mongols were way out in left field!

The Mongol ambassador entered with twenty warriors at his back. Surprisingly, he spoke very good Polish.

"I have come—"

"A moment," Duke Henryk said. "First off, who are you? Are you a Mongol?"

"No. I am a Tartar."

The duke gave me a smug look, but the ambassador continued.

"I am a Tartar but the great Ogotai Kakhan is a Mongol. They are slightly different tribes, like your Silesians and Mazovians."

"Thank you for clearing that up. Now, you were saying?"

"I have come to accept your submission to my lord, Batu Khan, and to the great Ogotai Kakhan, Lord of All the World!" He was bowlegged and he stank, but you couldn't accuse him of not coming to the point. His head was shaved, leaving ridiculous tufts of hair on his forehead and behind his ears, but then military organizations generally adopt funny haircuts. He wore gaudy silk brocades that might once have been attractive, but now were grease-stained and filthy.

Yet he wasn't at all what I had expected. He didn't look like a Mongol! He did not have slanty, black eyes. They were green and Caucasoid. His skin, under the dirt, looked to be white, rather than yellow, and his hair was not black. It was red! And none of his men were "Mongoloid" either.

Rather than answer the man, the duke glanced at me, so I said, "That's quite a statement. Why should we want to do such a thing?"

"Why? You will do it because you want to live!"

"We've been doing a pretty good job of living without the khan. Why should we want that to change?" He wasn't using any honorifics on me, so I didn't see why I should use them on him.

"You talk like a fool or a crazy man! All men must submit to the kakhan!"

"*I'm* a crazy man? I hope you realize that your last few statements sound like those of a rampant megalomaniac. But I repeat my question. Why should we want to do something as silly as bowing down to your kaka?"

"That's *kakhan*, you fool, and you will submit or our swords will take all your heads!" He drew his sword for emphasis. Apparently, he felt that I wasn't playing my role properly.

"Oh. With swords like that? May I see it?" He handed it to me. It was good Damascus steel, better than what most of the conventional knights carried. But I couldn't let him get one up on us.

"A pretty handle," I said. "Where did you steal it?"

"I won that blade at the Battle of Samarkand, when the fools there refused submission."

"Well, that's a bit far to go. Mine only has an iron hilt. May I test them?"

"Destroy your blade if you want!"

I drew my own sword. Setting the tip of his blade to

the marble floor, I shaved a thin wire of steel off the edge of his sword.

"The edge is soft," I said, throwing the wire to him. Then I put my blade tip to the floor, edge up, and swung at it with his. His blade was cut in two. "The shank was weak. Next time, don't steal a sword because of its flashy mountings." I tossed the pieces back to him.

The emissary was livid. This was not going as planned. "It is not weapons that win, it is the men behind the weapons!"

"You know, I've been saying that for years. That's why I know that we have nothing to fear from you people."

"The kakhan has the finest army in the world!"

"He has a bunch of undisciplined goat herders, suitable only for murdering helpless women and children. True warriors need not fear them."

"Undisciplined? You lie! Choose three of my men."

"If you wish. That one, that one, and that one." I'd picked the three most gaudily dressed of his entourage, and I think I picked right. I must have singled out someone pretty important, since a trickle of sweat went down the ambassador's cheek. I could see him weighing the loss of face against the loss of someone special. Face lost out.

"The first man you picked is Subotai Bahadur. He, like me, is sworn to report to Batu Khan. You must pick another."

"As you like. How about that pretty little guy on the end?" I later found out that this man was the ambassador's son, but the father didn't bat an eye.

He spoke briefly to the three men in what must have been Mongolian. Then he said, "I have just ordered these men to cut their own throats, as a demonstration of their loyalty and obedience to the kakhan!"

And those three men did it! One after another, they stepped forward, said some sort of prayer, drew their belt knives, and cut their own throats! There were gasps of horror and disbelief from the audience. I glanced at the duke and he looked a little pale.

If word of this got around, Polish morale would suffer. I couldn't let them outdo us, but I wasn't going to see if any of *my* men felt suicidal! So I laughed at him.

"Well, don't feel too bad about it," I said. "We have

crazy people in this country, too. Of course, we try not to show them off in public when company is calling, but I suppose that customs differ. How about that one? Would he cut his throat, too?"

"Any true Mongol would obey orders!"

"Then let's see it!"

And damned if he didn't order it and the poor bastard ended up bleeding on the floor along with the others.

"And how about that one?" I said.

"What are you trying to do?" screamed the ambassador.

"Well, I figured that if we could get every Mongol to cut his fool throat, we wouldn't have to fight a war next spring." The room exploded in laughter.

"Were I not forbidden by my lord Batu to fight, I would kill you here and now!"

"It wouldn't be much of a fight, especially since you don't have a sword anymore. Why, any of our women could beat any of your fools with a sword. Even little Krystyana over there could take on any one of you, and she's had six children."

"Could I, my lord? Could I really fight him?" Krystyana said as she eagerly stepped out from the crowd. She was in court dress and so of course was unarmed, but she had borrowed her husband's sword with such vigor that Sir Piotr had a thin trickle of blood running down from his left ear.

"Well, I was just talking, Lady Krystyana. This is a diplomatic meeting, and not the place for a fight."

"Ah! You make a foolish boast and then you try to wiggle out of it! I say that you must back up your boast!"

"I suppose, if you insist. Sir Piotr, what do you say about this? She's your wife, after all."

"My lord, when she's in this mood, I've found it's best to let her have her own way."

"Very well then, pick your best swordsman," I said to the ambassador.

"Let the lady choose her own executioner," he said with a greasy smile.

"I want *that* one," Krystyana said. "He's wearing the most gold, and I get it when I win, don't I?"

"To the victor goes the spoils, my lady," I said.

"Good! Of course, I can't fight in *this* silly outfit!" She said, as she stripped her clothes off. The Mongols were all wearing armor and she was proposing to fight naked!

At this time, Poland didn't have a nudity taboo, so a naked lady wasn't all that unheard of, but the duke had let it be known that he wanted a complete coverup in his own court, and thus far, no one had ever dared defy him. I glanced at the duke again, but he just looked up at the coffered ceiling.

The Mongol acted as if he was just going to walk up and murder her. Krystyana parried his blow easily and gave him a horizontal cut on the forehead.

This startled the man, and he started hacking in earnest. It got him nowhere. He might have been good at saber fighting on horseback, but his footwork was almost nonexistent. The parries used on horseback are different from those used on foot, and are slower, since on a horse you have the animal's neck between your legs and it gets in the way.

But mostly, he'd never seen a rapier before, whereas Krystyana had often fought rapier against saber. She'd beaten me that way quite a few times.

So she played with him. She added a vertical cut to the one horizontal one on his forehead, making a perfect Christian cross. Then she put a cross on each cheek, and during all this had not taken a cut herself.

She was making the Mongol look like a buffoon, which was wonderful. She was savvy enough to realize that we had to take people's minds off the dead bodies on the floor.

The crowd was going wild, and the ambassador was turning livid purple.

"She's making a Christian out of him!" Piotr yelled.

"Does that count as a Baptism?" somebody shouted.

"No! That's Extreme Unction!" another wit called back.

"Krystyana, didn't your mother tell you not to play with your food?" yelled someone else.

She was working at cutting the Mongol's armor off when I said, "I think you've made your point, Lady Krystyana. Kill him and be done with it."

"Yes, my lord. On the count of four! One!...Two! ...Three!..."

And she skewered him, straight through the heart, on the count of four. Then she bowed to the duke and to the crowd, picked up her clothes, and retired. The applause rocked the castle!

I turned to the ambassador. "With regards to your request for submission, the answer is no."

"And who are you, to say this thing? What is your name and station?"

"I am Baron Conrad Stargard."

"What! I have been talking to a mere baron?"

"Surely you didn't expect our duke to dirty his lips by talking to such as you? I'm the lowest ranking man up here!"

The Mongols turned and left, leaving their dead on the floor.

The duke stood and motioned for me to follow. Once we were alone in his privy chamber, he turned and glared at me.

"Damn you, Conrad! I asked you to conduct a preliminary interview, not to set policy for me!"

"Yes, your grace. I guess I sort of got carried away."

"You 'sort of got carried away'? Were my father still on the throne, you would be carried away in a *coffin*!"

"Yes, your grace."

"'Yes, your grace!' Is that all you can say?"

"Well, your grace, what other outcome could there have been? Surely you never considered submitting to them! You know what has happened to every other people that has done that. They make insatiable demands, require hostages, and ruinous tribute! Poland under the Mongols would be a living hell until they killed us all! Then it would be a dead one!"

"I know, I know. But there was no need to make them mad! You've told me that their plan is to simultaneously attack both Poland and Hungary. After what you've done, they just might come at us alone with all their forces! King Bela can put two knights in the field for every one that Poland can, and I include Sandomierz, Mazovia, and the Teutonic Knights as being with us!"

"Then maybe I've done some good, your grace. If I've made them mad enough, they'll go straight back to Batu Khan without talking to the other Polish powers. There was always the chance that they could have split us up, or talked some of the others into being neutral."

"That would never have happened, Baron. We may

not be united, but we Poles would always stand together against a foreign aggressor."

"I hope you're right, your grace. But the Crossmen aren't Poles, they're Germans who have no great love for us. The Duke of Mazovia is a fourteen-year-old boy! Who can tell about a child?"

"Perhaps the Teutonic Knights are a cipher, but if the Duke of Mazovia's youth causes problems, they will be in the other direction, entirely. He might rashly charge into certain slaughter, but he won't prove a coward."

"Yes, your grace."

"As to the Mongols, well, we'll talk to them again tomorrow."

At this point, a page knocked, entered and announced that the Mongol party had left Wawel Hill.

"Damn!" the duke said. "Baron Conrad, go after them and see what you can do about extending the negotiations."

"Yes, your grace," I said, fully intending to do just the opposite.

I had had my people dress, not in armor or even dress uniforms, but in civilian court garb, and our embroidered velvets shone in all the colors of the rainbow and then some. Some of the colors that Piotr wore had to be unique!

Since we were all riding Big People, we caught up with the Mongols within the hour.

"Hello, ambassador. You left without your honor guard!" I said.

"More of your insolence, Baron Conrad? You call this bunch of fops an honor guard? Why, none of you are in armor and half of you are women!"

"What's more, they're our better half. Why should we need armor in our own country? None of our people would harm us and these woods were cleansed of wolves years ago. Haven't you ever been in a civilized country before?"

"I've seen silly fools before, riding sleek horses."

"Speaking of which, can those little ponies of yours run? What say we race, say from here to the River Bug."

His men had four spare mounts each and he could see that we didn't have any. He said, "Are you suggesting a wager, Baron?"

"Why not? Shall we say a bag of gold to the winner?"

He insisted on seeing my gold, but we made the bet. We soon left them in our dust. When we were about six miles ahead of them, we stopped by a brook and broke out a picnic supper. We were well into it before the Mongols caught up with us, their horses lathered with sweat.

"Care to join us, ambassador?" Krystyana shouted and waved. "There are plenty of leftovers!"

"A Mongol eats in the saddle!" The ambassador was not amused. They rode on.

We passed them again a while later, and I slowed down to chat. "I notice that you have changed horses already. Surely those little things can't be tired yet!"

"Changing horses is the custom of my people," he said stiffly.

"As you like," I said, "but it's obvious that this is not a fair contest. We'll try to make it more even."

With that, Anna and I went to the front of his column, circled ahead of it, ran back to the end, then back to the front again, literally running circles around them. The others in my party joined in the fun, laughing and shouting while the Mongols galloped stoically forward.

Toward dusk, we again left them behind, and when they caught up with us, we had a big campfire going, and Cilicia was dancing for us around it. Piotr and two of the Bankis were playing recorders and the rest of us were keeping time by beating on saddles and swords. A glass bottle of wine was being passed around. I was stretched out with my back to a tree.

Cilicia timed it such that they got a good eyeful of her magnificent nude body, then ended the dance by falling naked into my arms.

"Again you work to humiliate me," the ambassador said. "What manner of devil's spawn are you riding?"

"These? Why, they're just ordinary Christian horses. In fact, these are all just mares. We keep the stallions for battle, when you really need something big and fast. Haven't you seen good horses before?" I asked.

"We have fought Christians before. All the Russias do homage to us! But they did not have such animals as these!"

"Oh. Well, those were Orthodox Christians. We're Catholics. There's a difference."

"Your false gods have nothing to do with your horses!"

"Don't tell them that! They might get mad. They're all very religious," I said.

"Bah! They might be fast, but they would never last through a campaign. Sleek horses like those must eat grain! They'd starve if they had to travel across the steppes!"

"Well, we have a lot of grain for them to eat, but in fact they prefer fresh grass when they can get it. And in a pinch, they can eat darned nearly anything. Anna! Come here, girl!"

The ambassador looked astounded as Anna came up.

"Anna, this man doesn't think that you can get along without grain. Would you please eat that tree for him?"

Anna looked at the pine tree I'd pointed to, winced, and made an expression of a bad taste in her mouth. Then she looked wistfully at a young apple tree near by.

"Oh, okay. Eat the apple tree instead."

Before the dumbfounded Mongols, Anna and a few of her daughters ate that tree right down to the ground, biting off chunks of wood and chewing them up.

"Well," I said, "this has been a pleasant diversion, but we didn't bring our camping gear with us. There's an inn a dozen or so miles up the road, right on the River Bug. We'll wait for you there and collect on the bet."

"Mongols prefer to sleep under the stars!"

"Suit yourselves. You're welcome to the fire, but be sure to put it out when you leave. Forest fires, you know."

The Big People came when we called them. We saddled up while Cilicia put her clothes back on and galloped off into the pitch-dark night. Big People have the most amazing eyesight. They really can see in the dark.

It was another of my Pink Dragon Inns, one I hadn't visited before. The innkeeper promised to wake me when the Mongols arrived, but they never came. Later the next day we got word that they crossed over into Russia a few miles upstream.

"They cheated on their bet!" Sir Vladimir said.

"Don't worry," Sir Piotr said. "We'll collect in the spring."

Chapter Twelve

▲▲▲▲▲▲▲▲▲▲▲▲▲▲▲▲▲▲▲▲

ALL THE factories were idle and no one manned the machines. The mines were no longer functioning and the furnaces were cold. The farms no longer had farmers and the countryside looked abandoned.

Right on schedule. The winter of the war was coming and almost every able-bodied young man in southern Poland was training for combat. Our propaganda, appeals, and sometimes outright orders had borne fruit, and from all the lands controlled by the duke came a hundred thirty thousand new men to Hell. In a few weeks, a square mile of nearly empty buildings became the most populous city in Europe. Every skilled man I had was needed to train the new troops, and if we lacked some piece of military equipment, we would just have to do without it. There was no time to build more.

Squires and pages found themselves knighted and training their own lances of six men each. Knights were now knight banners and even captains, and above that we were hard-pressed to keep the command situation from becoming chaos.

Hell itself was chaotic, or at least it must have seemed so to the new men that arrived. There were big signs everywhere, but half of the new people couldn't read, and there was no time to teach them. We even got to painting some men's barracks number on their sleeve so that they could compare it with the numbers over the doors to find their bunks.

But somehow, arms and armor were issued and fitted, men were fed, and training went ahead full blast. There was very little skull work in the training schedule now; the men were not taught to read and write, and there was little mention made of strategy and tactics. We already had all the leaders that we were going to get, and we had only four months to train the men who would do most of the actual fighting.

It was drill and drill and drill, with pike and axe and gun. Even the sword was deemphasized, since it takes years to make a swordsman. The new troops were issued axes as a secondary weapon. Most of these farmboys already knew how to use an axe.

And amid all this work, doing something that none of us had ever done before, dealing with six times as many people as we had ever handled before, trying to keep track of millions of details without the aid of a computer or even a decent bureaucracy, my liege lord, Count Lambert came visiting.

"Baron Conrad, there is a very serious matter that I wish to speak to you about."

"Yes, my lord?" Shit. A brand new steamboat had just sunk the first time it slid down the ways, six tons of battle-axes had been found to be improperly heat-treated, and we seemed to be out of size-five shin guards. What did *he* want?

"Can we speak privately?"

"Of course, my lord." I led the way back to my private office, leaving Piotr to track down the fifty-five cases of missing maps.

"It's my daughter, Baron Conrad. She's come to Poland, and I'm worried about her."

"Your daughter, my lord? I'd forgotten that you had one. Well, except for the children that you've gotten off your peasant girls—but I gather you aren't talking about one of them."

"No, no, of course not. I mean my real daughter, the child of my deceased wife."

"I'm sorry, my lord, but I hadn't even heard that your wife had died."

"I suppose that we can allow for the fact that you've been inordinately busy lately, and of course you never met the woman. She lived with her relatives in Hungary for her last eleven years, and of course our daughter was with her. But now that she is dead, my child has returned to me."

This sudden outbreak of parental love surprised me. I'd never known the count to get sentimental about anything before, and his habits with the girls at Okoitz were such that he must have fathered *hundreds* of children. Oh, he always made sure that the girl was married off properly, and with a decent dowry, but his interest always stopped at that point. Why bring the problem to me?

"I suppose that will make for some changes in your household, my lord, but I can assure you that children add a lot to a home. She'll doubtless be a great comfort to you as you grow older." Just smooth it all over with honeyed oatmeal, I thought. Sometimes that works.

"Well, there is that, but don't you see? She's not exactly a child anymore. She's a young woman! She's fourteen years old and it's my duty to find her a proper husband."

"That's certainly fine, Christian thinking, my lord, but why discuss it with an old, confirmed bachelor like me? Better you should go talk to all of your female relatives and have them be on the lookout for a suitable young man."

"You know that most of those old bitches don't like me, Conrad, and anyway, I know the man I'd want for my heir."

That was the first time in nine years that he had called me just "Conrad." I was beginning to get a very bad feeling about this conversation.

"What's this talk about an heir, my lord? You're barely over forty and you come from a long-lived family. Why, you'll probably live longer than your uncle the old duke did!"

"Lately, I have had a premonition of death. I feel it strongly, and I am worried." He shook his head.

"We're all concerned about the invasion, my lord. Any of us could fall in battle, but a knight doesn't worry about that sort of thing, does he? Anyway, if you've come for my advice about your daughter, it's to let the girl pick her own future husband. She'll be a lot happier that way, and it will vastly increase your domestic tranquility."

"But I didn't come for your advice, Conrad. I came for your consent!"

"My consent, my lord?"

"To marriage, of course!"

"To marriage!" I stood. For the first time in twenty years, my voice broke and it came out like a squeak.

"Of course! What do you think I'm talking about? I want you to be my son-in-law! I want you to marry my only child and be my heir."

"But, but I'm just not the marrying kind! The whole institution frightens me! No, no, my lord. I would never make a decent son-in-law! You'd learn to hate me. So would she!"

"Nonsense, my boy. Why, you and I have gotten along for years with never a cross word. All the women around seem to love you. Why should my daughter be any different?"

"What's this 'my boy' business? I'm only two years younger than you! I'm an old man! You shouldn't saddle your daughter with an old man! She'll end up being a young widow, and you know all the trouble they get into!"

"Again, nonsense! You're as healthy a man as I've ever met, and any woman with any brains about her prefers a mature man to a young stripling."

"They didn't when *I* was a stripling!"

"Well, that simply proves your prowess! None of your ladies are complaining, are they?"

"It's not a matter of my ladies, my lord. For years now, I've been satisfied with just one, Cilicia. She's heavy with our second child now. I couldn't possibly leave her."

"Well, you wouldn't have to leave her, just sort of get her out of the way for a while. Anyway, I know full well that you haven't been absolutely faithful to her. You manage to get to Countess Francine's manor at least once a month."

"She's an old friend."

"And a close one, no doubt. But that's all one to me. Just keep up appearances, and you'll hear no complaints from your father-in-law."

"My lord, I've never even met your daughter."

"So? She's a normal, healthy girl. She has all the standard features. What more can be said? And she'll learn Polish soon enough, so that's no problem."

"She doesn't even speak Polish! Well, I don't speak any Hungarian! What do we do? Invite an interpreter to bed with us?"

"Mind your manners, Conrad. This is my own flesh and blood we're talking about."

"There are hundreds of girls that are your own flesh and blood! And all the rest of them can at least speak the language! Why don't you make me marry one of them?"

"Conrad! Control yourself! If this goes on, you shall anger me."

"See what a lousy son-in-law I'd make? We had an excellent relationship until it was torn asunder by the mere mention of marriage! Find another man, my lord. I don't want to get married!"

"That's your final word, then?"

"Yes, my lord, it is."

"Well then. It has certainly been a pleasure having you for a vassal, and the experience has been vastly profitable. Tell me, where were you planning to go next?"

"My lord, what are you talking about? You can't fire me like a bricklayer who's finished his job! We made an oath together, and that oath gives you no right to force me into marriage."

"True. We made an oath. Do you remember it? It was Christmas time, almost nine years ago. True, I don't have the right to force marriage on you, but you made one strange addition to the standard oath, which at the time I thought inconsequential, but now it comes into the fore. You swore fealty to me for only nine years! Those nine years will be up in three weeks, at which time our agreement is off! So I wish you well. Be sure and fill your saddlebags before you leave. Take a few carts of gold with you if you wish. But I am not minded to renew my oath with one who would so crassly insult my own daughter as to refuse her hand in marriage."

I was dumbstruck. I *had* put that in my oath! At the time, I wasn't sure whether I could get technology going in this century or not, and if I couldn't I wanted to have the right to be somewhere else than in the middle of a Mongol massacre, where one more dead body wouldn't have done Poland much good. I had left myself a coward's way out and now I was paying for it!

"But—but the army, the boats, the aircraft! I'm needed here now more than ever! You can't do this! Not to me nor to Poland."

"Wrong, Baron. Or at least 'baron' for the next three weeks. I can do it and I intend to do it. Sir Vladimir can handle the army properly, I'm sure, and Sir Tadaos can do what's right with the steamboats. And the aircraft? Well, I'm already in charge there!"

"Well, I won't stand for it! I'll go talk to the duke about this!"

"Feel free, but I've already discussed the matter with him. You know that he has long been displeased with you concerning the way that you have consistently lived in sin since coming here. He thinks that you should get married and that my daughter would be an excellent match. He has already given his blessings on the union!"

"But my lifestyle is a good deal more moral than yours!"

"True, at least by any sensible standard. But I am a mere backwoods count, whereas you have made yourself into a hero. Heroes have to live upright lives! After all, the youth of Poland looks to you for guidance! Myself, I think where you went wrong was all the charity work. You should have left those wretches alone."

"But this is filthy, rotten blackmail!"

"Yes, it is, isn't it. Shall we say the day after Christmas for the wedding? The Bishop of Wroclaw has already given dispensation for the posting of the banns."

"Damn you, Lambert! God damn you straight to hell and the devil!"

I stormed out of my office, pushing aside a startled secretary who was standing in the doorway. I went down to the stables, threw a saddle on Anna and charged back to Three Walls. I told the stable girl, Kotcha, to put Anna's best saddle and barding on her and went up to my room.

I put on my best armor, not my efficient Night-Fighter suit, but the fancy, engraved, gold-plated stuff they'd given me for Christmas a few years back. I threw my wolfskin cloak over my shoulders and went down to the strong room. I came back up with my saddlebags filled with gold. To hell with the silver, the gold would do. It was all that I could carry, anyhow.

Then I headed down the trail, or railroad track now, and at the first intersection I headed not east, toward the Mongols, but west, toward France! I'd heard a lot of nice things about France. Maybe I could even learn the language.

Nine years in a country that punishes a man for helping the poor! Well, to hell with them! To hell with them all.

We rode like thunder for hours and Anna never let up. She didn't know where we were going or why, but I wanted to go and that was enough for her. The one good friend I had.

Darkness was closing in as we rode by the trail to Countess Francine's manor. Well, it was a bit cold for camping out, and I hadn't brought my old camping gear along, anyway. Maybe Francine would like a lift back to France.

She was a countess while I was only a baron, despite the fact that her county was much smaller than my barony. She only had six knights subordinate to her, yet she was my superior in status. Because of this, she absolutely refused to use my title or her own when we were together, and got unhappy when I used them myself. I think she thought I really gave a damn about that sort of thing.

Her watchman must have called her, because the drawbridge was lowering as we approached, and she stood just behind it, waiting.

"You come gaily clad, my friend!" she said as she warmly embraced my cold armor.

"It seemed like a good idea, if I was going to France."

"France! But you must come inside and tell me all about it!"

A marshal came up to take care of Anna, but I slung the heavy saddlebags over my own shoulder. I just wasn't very trusting anymore.

At supper, Francine got the whole story out of me.

"So you charged away like a hero in a fireside tale, without even a change of underwear." She giggled. "Oh, you poor little dumpling."

"Well, I don't think it's the least bit funny."

"Of course it is not, darling. It is horrible. You have been rudely treated by a man that you have done everything for. You have a perfect right to be angry, but if Lambert has made himself your enemy, then you must fight him! You have done great things here and you must not let them be stolen from you!

"The truth is that I really don't give a damn anymore."

"You have just worked too hard for too long and have treated it all too seriously," she said.

"Call it a long vacation, then. Say, fifty years or so. France still seems like a great idea. Would you like me to give you a lift there?"

"To ride with my knight and hero back to my home-land? Oh, Conrad, what a romantic thought! But France is not Poland and if you did not marry me, people would call me a strumpet! Would you let them do that to your poor damsel?"

"And so I would have to do the very thing I was running away from. You're pretty good at popping bal-loons."

"And someday you must tell me what a balloon is, but not right now. Think! If you do not care about your wealth or position, what of the people who are depending on you? What of the noble Sir Vladimir? What of earnest little Sir Piotr? And Lady Krystyana. I know you loved her once. Has that love turned to such hate that you would abandon her to the Tartars?"

"No. I guess not."

"Then you must stay in Poland and find a way to re-solve your problem with Lambert. We must plan our strategy! We must confound your liege lord and defeat him!"

"Well, I can hardly go out and fight the man."

"Of course not. You have a hundred fifty thousand fighting men and he does not have a hundred fifty, yes? How could there be a fight? You could massacre him if you wished, but that would be immoral. No. You must use a woman's arts of persuasion and intrigue, and I am the woman to help you with this. First, you must realize that you have many friends in the very highest places. The Bishop of Cracow is your friend and confessor, yes? And the duke himself is a member of your order of Radi-ant Warriors. And you have me. I spent many years by the side of the old duke. I know where all the bodies were buried and was privy to all of the old duke's se-crets."

"All? You mean . . ."

"Yes, all. Even about you. An old man will always tell everything to an adoring young woman."

"Then . . . tell me what you know about me."

She glanced around to see that the servants were out

of the room, then said quietly, "I know that you have come to us from the far future in some way that even you do not understand. Is that enough?"

"It's way too much. You shouldn't have been told."

"But I was. Don't worry, darling, your secret is safe with me. I swear that you are the only person I have ever told it to, and ever will."

"And it doesn't bother you?"

"It is passing strange, but I love you still."

"Well. You mentioned strategy. What do you think we should do?" I asked.

"First we must speak to the duke. We must do this right away, before Count Lambert has a chance to see him again. We must find out where he stands on your marriage to Jadwiga, and—"

"Who?"

"Jadwiga. Oh, you dumpling! You do not even know the name of the girl they are trying to marry you to?"

"The count never mentioned it."

"Well, now you know. Knowing the young duke as I do, it is quite possible that he really does want you to get married. He is such a prude about some things! Has he ever mentioned it to you?"

"I'm afraid so. Quite a number of times, as a matter of fact."

"Then you just might have to get married."

"What!"

"Hush, dear. It is not the end of the world. You have been living with Cilicia for many years now, yes? Nothing need change if you were married to her. It could be done quietly, a few minutes with a priest. Is that so bad?"

"I can't marry Cilicia. We couldn't have a Christian wedding because she refuses to become a Christian! Believe me, I've been trying to convert her since we first met. And even if I was willing to become her brand of Moslem, which I'm not, her father has some sort of complicated theological reason why I couldn't join their church, or whatever they call it. The whole thing is simply impossible!"

"Then marry me. You have been coming here every few weeks for years. That would satisfy me, if I could get no better. Nothing need change, darling."

"But . . ."

"Then think on it. Come love, we must be up before gray dawn to ride to Cracow and see the duke. Let us go to bed."

Even after a vigorous bout of lovemaking, I had a hard time getting to sleep that night. Francine was asleep with her head on my arm, her back to my stomach, spoon fashion. I was careful not to wake her, but I needed a good think.

Okay, I told myself. You've got this phobia. Nothing to be ashamed of. Lots of people have phobias.

You've got to stay in Poland and fight this invasion. That's a given. A lot of good people are counting on you. You can't let them down. You've made promises and you have to live with them.

Is that what really scares you about marriage? The fact that it's a lifetime promise, without any way out if you were wrong? But you've made so many other promises, and you can't get out of them, either. You didn't go into a cold funk when you swore to Lambert, did you? Oh, you let yourself have a coward's way out, but that's one of the things you're regretting now, isn't it?

But if you're going to stay, you've somehow got to placate Lambert *and* the duke. Lambert isn't going to let up, you know. Once he gets an idea into his head, he's like a bulldog clamped down on a bull's snout. As long as there is any chance that you will marry his daughter, he'll be in there conniving a way to force you to do it.

And the duke. He wants everybody to live a fine, conventional and Christian life, just like in all the stories the priests like to tell. He would have had Lambert back with his wife years ago if she hadn't been out of the country and the duke's jurisdiction, that's sure. If you were married, you'd have the duke solidly on your side against Lambert. What's more, once you were married, Lambert would give up on his plans for you and his daughter. He's a bulldog, but he's not stupid.

So getting married is the rational thing to do at this point. It solves all the conflicting problems of duty, morality, your boss, and your boss's boss.

So why aren't you rational about it? Because you're scared shitless, that's why! All this business you keep telling yourself and everybody else about rationality and the scientific method is just a hypocritical ball of lies!

Underneath, you're just a wad of primeval fears, a caveman huddled around his campfire, afraid of the dark, a whining neurotic desperately in need of professional help!

Well, maybe not that last, but you sure need help. Look, would it really be so bad? This woman in your arms, is she so bad? She's beautiful. She's easily the best looking Christian you've seen since you got here. She's mature, well educated, and damned intelligent. What's more, she wants to marry you, and you damn well know you'll never get a better offer. You're almost living with her now. Is she really asking so much? One little church ceremony? It could be over in minutes, in some obscure little village church.

Five minutes. It could be over in five minutes. You're man enough to stand up to that, aren't you? It would solve your problems with both Lambert and the duke, and would make a very nice lady very happy. Like she said, it would make no difference in your lifestyle. Nothing need change at all. You could do that, couldn't you?

Yeah, I thought, I suppose I could. But just a little ceremony.

Francine snuggled even closer in my arms.

In her sleep, she murmured, "I am so glad that it is settled." Then she was quiet once more.

I don't like it when things like that happen.

In the morning we both sort of half awoke and calmly, warmly I was inside of her again.

"Francine, do you really want to marry me?"

"Of course, darling, with all my heart!"

"Then let's do it."

This brought on a smile and a squeal and a hug and a kiss that quite literally took my breath away, followed, naturally, by far more enthusiastic lovemaking.

Later, she said. "You really want this? I have not done anything unfair to get you?"

"Yes, I want you, and your magnificent body is a most unfair enticement."

"Good. I did not want you to think you were forced. But if you are going ahead freely, there is something that I must tell you."

"What?"

"That you are going to be a papa again, and this time, I am going to be the mama!"

I should be getting used to this sort of thing, but I'm not.

Interlude Three

^^^^^^^^^^^^^^^^^^^^^^^

TOM HIT the STOP button.

"What the hell goes on here!" he shouted.

"What are you talking about?" I asked.

"I'll show you!" He pushed the intercom button. "I want the asshole who edited this tape front and center, here and now!"

A man dressed in a conservative brown T-shirt and shorts stepped in immediately. Another advantage of time travel is that you always have time to get to meetings promptly.

"Sir?" the man said.

"Just what are you trying to pull?"

"Sir? What are you talking about?"

"This tape! It has Conrad getting ready to marry Lady Francine! When I viewed it last week, she talked him into marrying Lambert's daughter. If this is some kind of joke, mister, I don't like your sense of humor!"

"But sir! I edited that tape, and he didn't do either one of those things! He went on toward France until an emissary of the duke caught up with him in Worms and talked him into returning to Poland!"

"What?" Tom thought a minute. "If this is a joke, the prankster will spend the next century doing anthropological work on Eskimos! But right now, I want you to get your staff together and find out who the joker is. I want to see how this version comes out, but I'll see you and your people in two hours. Now get out!"

The man bolted out the door.

"Tom, I don't think he fudged it," I said. "I mean, he would have to have found actors who were exact doubles for Francine and Conrad. He would have to build

107

perfect sets and backgrounds. It's not the sort of thing that would be done as a joke!"

"I know. But the alternative is frightening. It means that we are seeing a temporal split right here. Two temporal splits!"

"But how could something that happened in the thirteenth century effect us? We're seventy thousand years in their past!"

"I don't know, but it scares the shit out of me!"

He hit the START button.

Chapter Thirteen

▲▲▲▲▲▲▲▲▲▲▲▲▲▲▲▲▲▲▲▲▲▲▲▲

FROM THE DIARY OF CONRAD STARGARD

Anna carried us both through the day, and that night in Cracow, the duke granted us an immediate private audience.

"Baron Conrad. I'm glad you're here. I was about to send men out in search of you. But the matter which we must discuss, well, are you sure that you want the Countess Francine present?"

"Quite sure, your Grace."

"Very well, then. What is this business between you and Count Lambert's daughter? Dalliance with peasant girls and heathens is bad enough. Trifling with the peerage is something else!"

"Your Grace, I have never met the count's daughter! I have never seen her, let alone touched her. I had forgotten that she even existed until Count Lambert told me yesterday that she is in Poland!"

"Then what's this business of his insisting that you marry her?"

"I don't know, your Grace. I was shocked by his demands. He said that you had approved the marriage."

"Well, he asked me if I would approve such a marriage, and of course I said I would do so. You know that I would be delighted to see you married. This business of your cohabitating with an infidel Moslem is shameful, and your fornications with my ward are even worse!"

"Your ward?"

"Countess Francine here, of course! She's not married and she has no family in the country, so she must have a guardian, and who else but a duke could be guardian to a countess? Use your head, man. It's complicated by the fact that she was my father's friend and is quite capable of taking care of herself, but nonetheless I am personally responsible for her before God, and you have been bedding her!"

"That is the other matter that I would like to discuss with you, your Grace. The Countess Francine and I would like to be married."

For the first time, the duke relaxed and smiled. "And is this your wish as well, Countess?"

"With all my heart, your Grace."

"Then with all mine, you have my approval. But back to the matter at hand. My impression was that you, Conrad, had been the instigator of the marriage proceedings between yourself and Jadwiga. I mean, that's the usual thing! If two people wish to get married, they talk to the girl's father, and if there is a major inheritance involved, the father talks to his liege. I thought that in approving Lambert's request, I was granting *your* wishes!"

"I swear I knew nothing of it, your Grace."

"Well. For now, I'll take your word for it, but if you're lying to me, I'll see you hung! All I know of this is that your secretary, Lady Natalia, came to me this morning and reported your conversation with Count Lambert *verbatim*. She even had it in writing, though I could scarcely believe it! Does she always do things like this?"

He tossed a sheaf of papers at me. I quickly scanned it.

"She has a remarkable memory, your Grace. The door was open and I guess we were pretty loud. But this is what was said, word for word."

"She also told me that you had taken all your ready gold and had headed west without explaining to anyone. She was deathly worried about you."

"I'm sorry I upset her, your Grace. I was pretty upset myself."

"As I suppose I would have been in your position. This business of only swearing for nine years. I suppose that's true?"

"Yes, your Grace. At the time, I didn't know how long I would want to stay."

"I see. But later, when you were enlarged to a barony, you must have sworn again to Lambert. Was there any time limit made in that oath?"

"No, your Grace."

"Then the second oath supercedes the first. Count Lambert had no right to threaten you with escheating your lands. Also, if you are to marry Countess Francine, you must be enlarged to her county. That is to say, you must swear fealty to me as my count, though you will also remain Count Lambert's baron. You will be his subordinate, yet his equal in status. As to Lambert, you will have no further problems with him, I assure you. He and I will have a serious talk! For the rest, see a priest, or perhaps the Bishop of Cracow, since he's a friend of yours, and post proper banns. Your oath of fealty can be taken at the wedding."

"Yes, your Grace, although we had thought that just a simple ceremony—"

"What! My ward being married in a back chapel like an eloping peasant? I wouldn't hear of it! You shall be married in Wawel Cathedral before all the nobility of the land and I shall give the bride away! Now be off with you both and, uh, separate bedrooms until the wedding, right?"

The next morning, Bishop Ignacy was as pleased about the wedding as the duke, and the date was set for three days after Twelfth Night. Francine stayed on in Cracow to help with the arrangements, but I still had a war to get ready for.

Word of my engagement had gotten to Hell before me, and I had to put up with a lot of stupid cheering, but I soon got things back to business.

"The steamboat that sank has been brought back up," Natalia reported. "And the boatyard says they'll have it fixed in a month. Sir Ilya has taken over the problem of those axeheads. He says that he was tempering axeheads over wood fires nine years ago and he can still do it. They found three containers of size-five shin guards labeled size one, so that's all right, and one of the cooks from mess hall eleventeen brought over the fifty-five cases of maps and wanted to know how he was supposed to cook them so that even a grunt could eat it. They got delivered to him in the same container as the seven cases of applesauce he'd ordered."

"So problems are being solved," I said.

"Yes sir. But there are eighty thousand rounds of swivel gun ammunition that were cast oversize and won't fit in the chambers. Coherers—is that how you

pronounce it?—coherers for the radios have been breaking faster than expected and we're almost out of spares,
and six thousand sets of goose-down underwear were
found to be stuffed with chicken feathers. They say
they're too scratchy to wear."

"So things are back to normal," I said. "And Natalia
—thank you. Thank you for everything."

That night I went back to Three Walls. Cilicia had
already left, gone back to her father in the valley I had
given his people. Well, all right, I'd miss her, but she
had to do what she had to do. She'd taken our boy with
her and that was not all right. He was my son and by
God he'd be raised a Christian, and that went double for
the one in the cooker.

But then I cooled down and decided that this was not
the time to push it. Maybe Cilicia would come back.
Maybe we'd all be killed in the invasion. And maybe the
horse would sing.

Later. We'd see about it later.

For now, there were mass maneuvers with the war
carts.

I think I was dreading my wedding more than the
Mongol invasion. It was not a pleasant Christmas, in part
because of my worries, but mostly because we really
didn't celebrate it. We held a High Mass in the morning
and served a better than average dinner, then spent the
afternoon in training. There were complaints from all
quarters, but we couldn't waste the time. Furthermore,
the men couldn't have their families with them, and I
would rather have them mad than maudlin.

My wedding preparations went on without me. Countess Francine wrote me constantly and visited me twice at
Hell to keep me updated, although she insisted on sleeping alone. These wedding customs are ridiculous! With
both Cilicia and Francine unavailable, sexual frustration
was added to all my other problems. After a week, Natalia got together with Krystyana, who had taken over
food preparation at Hell. They started sending me young
peasant girls on the theory that I shouldn't go to waste.
Bless them.

Despite the war preparations, the duke was planning
to make my wedding the major social event of the year!
Every count and baron under the duke was expected to

attend, and the dukes of Sandomierz and Mazovia were coming along with their peerages. This when we should have been sharpening our swords!

But there was nothing I could do about it.

Years ago, I had mentioned cutting gemstones to my Moslem jeweler, and now he gave me a faceted stone that I think was diamond. It wasn't as sparkling as a modern gem, but maybe that was because the jeweler didn't have all the angles exactly right. At least it cut glass. I had it set in a gold ring and Countess Francine was pleased with it, but nobody had ever heard of an engagement ring before. It started a new fad.

The day approached and I left for Cracow with my best three-dozen men and their ladies. We got there to find out that the heralds had taken over the seating arrangements in the cathedral and there was room for only barons and better. My own party wouldn't be able to attend!

I went to the duke with the problem and he swore me in as count a day early. Then I swore in my whole party as barons! I even swore in Novacek, who had never been knighted! Damn all heralds, anyway.

Word was that this was to be a military wedding, and all were to be dressed in their best armor. Well, I had my gold stuff and my best man, Baron Vladimir, had managed to scrounge up a similar set, as it turned out, from Count Lambert. But most of my people had only Night-Fighter armor, efficient but not decorative. They did what they could, bleaching it white and adding bright red baldrics. They certainly stood out among the polished plate.

For me, well, it was like I had agreed to have my leg amputated with an axe, and then the doctors decided to do it with a grinding wheel instead.

Somehow, I survived the ceremony.

Why is it that men smile at a wedding and women cry?

Afterward, there was a reception that filled most of the rooms in Wawel Castle. I was trying to be agreeable to a crowd of people that I hardly knew when Count Lambert came up.

"May I offer you my congratulations, Count Conrad, as well as my apologies? I realize now how crass and crude I was to handle that matter in the way I did. Can you forgive me?"

"Of course, my lord. At least I think I still address you that way. There is nothing to forgive. We were both overwrought and the less said now the better."

"I quite agree. And as to your form of address, my friend, well, you can call me anything you like but a coward. I think that equals speech would be most appropriate, don't you think so, Conrad?"

"That sounds good to me, Lambert." I smiled, though I knew our relationship would never again be the same.

Finally, things settled down enough so that Francine and I could sneak off and enjoy our first night together in a month and a half.

Early the next morning, Duke Henryk called the visiting dukes and all counts present to a council of war, and I finally saw why attendance at this event had been mandatory. The wedding had been a cover for the council.

Besides the Polish nobility, the Grand Master of the Teutonic Order was there with a dozen of his masters. There was bad blood between the Crossmen and me, so they had not attended the wedding. There was also a representative from the Knights Hospitalers, as well as nobles from both King Louis IX of France and Emperor Frederic II of Germany. Duke Henryk had been doing his homework.

After an opening prayer, Duke Henryk introduced the envoy from the King of France. Speaking through an interpreter, this marquis pledged the support of France to our cause, and said that already, three thousand lances of French knights were coming to our aid, a total of about nine thousand men, a third of them nobles, a third squires, and a third crossbow men.

The emperor's envoy made a similar statement, promising half again as many men as the French, as well as supplies for the French forces as they crossed the Holy Roman Empire.

You could see the mood of the room lightening. The Polish knights wouldn't have to fight alone! We had powerful friends coming to our aid!

Duke Henryk spoke of strong contingents of Spanish, English, and Italian knights coming to Poland as well. He had been in communication with King Bela of Hungary and Tzar Ivan Asen II of the Bulgarian Empire. Since these two empires were threatened with invasion at the same time as Poland, he could not in good conscience ask them for aid. But they had agreed that should any of the three powers defeat the Mongols in its own country, that power would then go to the aid of the others.

With emperors and kings accounted for, the Knights Hospitalers stood and promised six hundred knights to our aid, which was almost all that they had.

The Teutonic Knights promised only five hundred, saying that their men were on the frontiers as well, and they could not leave those borders undefended. All present knew that was bullshit. The Crossmen had over three thousand men and the Pruthenians against whom 2500 were supposed to be guarding were no serious danger. At worst, they might do a little cattle-raiding and, what with all the animals running free, they could take their pick without hurting anybody. I got madder when I found out that to get even this little help out of the Crossmen, the duke had had to promise to rescind his father's ban on their order in Silesia. I'd nearly gotten killed getting them thrown out! There was nothing I could do about it now, but someday I was going to get those bastards.

Duke Boleslaw V of Mazovia stood and pledged every man he had, about sixteen thousand of them. In the history books, he's called "the chaste" or "the bashful," depending on whether the particular historian liked him or not. The nickname had to do with his love life, not his fighting. At fifteen, he looked to be a hell-raiser.

The Duke of Sandomierz followed suit, pledging twelve thousand men. Knighthood was not really well established in Sandomierz and Mazovia. The men fought in family groups rather than in feudal levies, and the concept of nobility was somewhat different. Not that it mattered much right now.

Duke Henryk announced that from Silesia, Great and Little Poland, he would lead twenty-nine thousand men into battle, over half of whom were knighted, and that he did not include in this total the infantry that I was training.

I was the only mere count who spoke at that council. I said that they all knew about the arms and armor that my men had made. Indeed, most of those present were wearing our products. They knew about the steamboats, but were surprised to learn that there would be three dozen of them on the Vistula alone. The aircraft were well known, and I spoke a bit on the advantages of aerial reconnaissance, until the duke motioned for me to hurry it up.

Then I announced the radios and told what they could do. I don't think anybody believed me! They'd all heard tales about my Warrior's School, but when I said that we would march out with a hundred fifty thousand fighting men, there were looks of stupid disbelief and a few people laughed. They simply didn't think in terms that large.

I was red-faced when I stepped down.

Nonetheless, there was a feeling of buoyancy and confidence in the room. We had the men, we had the power, we had allies coming in from all of Christendom!

Then Duke Henryk announced his battle plan and things started to fall apart. He said that all the foreign contingents, most of which were already on the way, would be gathering at Legnica, and that the rest of us should meet them there. We could then have a single, strong, unified army with which to advance eastward toward the Mongols.

The knights of Little Poland, Sandomierz, and Mazovia were not the least bit pleased by this plan! It meant that they would have to march hundreds of miles west, wait for the foreigners to arrive, and then march back again! And while this was going on, their own lands would be completely at the mercy of the Mongol invaders with no one to defend them!

Young Duke Boleslaw was the first on his feet, shouting. "Henryk, do you expect me to abandon my own duchy, my own people, to go off to your estates to defend your lands? Because if you do, you're crazy! My lands, and those of Sandomierz and Little Poland are in front of yours! The Tartars must go through us before they can touch your precious lands! It is *you* who should come and support *us*!"

Duke Henryk was on his feet. "We *will* come in your support! But don't you see that we must come *together*? If every man stands and defends his own manor, the Tartars will chew us up one by one in little bites! If we join together in a single army, we will be invincible! The choice of Legnica as a rallying point is the result of simple geography. It is the center point of all the knights who will be fighting on our side, the center of gravity, as Count Conrad would call it. Yes, it is on my lands, but it has to be on somebody's lands! Further, arrangements have already been made to feed and house the vast number of fighting men who will be gathering. Can any of you provide such a thing? Can Sandomierz or Plock feed so many men?"

"Merchants will come," Duke Boleslaw said. "They always do! I say that I will defend eastern Poland with my life! I will not run back for three hundred miles while my people are murdered! I will defend, and if you and your foreigners can come up in time to help me, I will be forever grateful to you. But if you are late, may God have mercy on you, because no one else will!"

And with that bit of bombast, the kid stomped out of the room, followed by all the men of Mazovia. After a few awkward moments, the Duke of Sandomierz stood and followed him, and in a few minutes, the hall was half empty. Even those men from Little Poland, men from the Cracow area who were personally sworn to Duke Henryk, had left. To them, the decision to be made was between abandoning their lands and peoples, or abandoning their oath to their duke. And they had made it. Even many still in the room seemed uncertain.

"Well," the duke said. "It seems that we must fight without them. But at least you men are with me, and Count Conrad's men outnumber by far all those that have left."

I had to stand. "Your grace, don't you see that I can't bring all my men to Legnica, either? I have a major force in my boats on the Vistula. I cannot bring those boats overland to the Odra. They must be used in eastern Poland or not be used at all! The aircraft will be far more useful than you now realize, but we only have one airport! That airport is near Okoitz, which is east of Legnica, and if it is overrun, the planes are useless! My infantry needs the railroads to travel quickly. We have built extensive tracks along the Vistula and through the Malapolska Hills, the area that we will need to defend first. If we can win there, western Poland is safe. But the railroad net is thin in western Poland and nonexistent in many areas. We haven't had time to expand it yet. My men can not effectively fight in western Poland!"

"So. You, too, Conrad?"

"Your grace, I am not abandoning you, but don't you realize what the radios and the rails mean? It is not necessary for all of us to be in the same spot for us to be together! With good communications, we can work in concert even though we are hundreds of miles apart."

"Count Conrad, I don't understand what you're saying. But what I do know is that every man true to me will join me at Legnica before the first of March!"

With that he got up and left, and the council of war was never called again. Instead of one Polish Army, there were now three of them. Those in the east under Duke Boleslaw, those in the west under Duke Henryk, and those men sworn to me. We were in pieces before the Mongols had even arrived.

Chapter Fourteen

▲▲▲▲▲▲▲▲▲▲▲▲▲▲▲▲▲▲▲▲▲

THERE WASN'T much time for marital bliss. Not with the war just weeks away. Francine moved into Hell with me, but that was only temporary. The place for her when it started was Three Walls, only she didn't see it that way. She had visions of herself being a female power behind the throne.

We were arguing about that one night in bed. "Look, love. Three Walls is my home. It's where I normally live and work. It's also my biggest installation, and my best defended. On top of all that, it's the one farthest back. Before the Mongols dare attack it, they must first destroy East Gate. Then they must take out Sir Miesko's formidable manor, as well as Hell, or they have an enemy at their rear. They'd even be well advised to destroy Okoitz before they tried to take Three Walls. It's a matter of simple geography."

"Geography, yes. But not politics. It would be best if I were in Cracow. There I can do you some good."

"I don't need you to do me any good. I need you to be alive. You will have a much better chance of staying that way at Three Walls."

"You have no feeling for the politics of the situation."

"I don't give a damn about the politics of the situation! The city walls at Cracow are made of old crumbly bricks. They are only three stories high, and they are defended by only two dozen guns. Do you know what came into the office today? An order from the city fathers of Cracow for two thousand swivel guns, to be shipped immediately! They should have placed that order two years ago! Then it could have been filled! Now, I could fill it only by stripping the guns from the walls of other cities, and I won't do it!"

119

"You see? If you had understood the politics there, you could have sold them those guns at the time, yes?"

"It's not that I *wanted* to sell them the guns! I've never made a penny selling arms and armor! It's just that the city is weak and the people there don't have much chance if they're attacked. You are going to Three Walls. I am your husband and you will obey me in this!"

"What happened to letting each other live our own lives?"

"I'm still for it! But you have to be alive before you can live! Now shut up and go to sleep. I have other things to worry about."

"What other things, my darling?"

"Treason, for one. There is no way that I can obey the duke and retreat to Legnica. That move would destroy the usefulness of everything that I've done here. I must disobey him."

"So. This must be?"

"Absolutely. There is no way around it. I wish I could obey him, and after the war I hope he still wants me for a vassal, but his battle plan is Just Plain Awful."

"Then perhaps I should be going to Legnica, yes?"

"No! You are not going anywhere but Three Walls. And I, well, I'm going to Okoitz in the morning."

"And why do you go to Lambert, whom you do not like anymore?"

"I go there to add conspiracy to my treason, and compound it with sowing disaffection among the duke's loyal men. If I'm going to send out the riverboats to hold the Vistula, and maybe even the Bug, I'm going to need the aircraft to help patrol the area and watch for the enemy. Lambert is in solid control of the boys at Eagle Nest, so I have to talk him into joining me."

"And you say that you do not care for politics."

"I don't. And I'm sure not looking forward to tomorrow's meeting."

At Okoitz, Lambert was effusive.

"Ah, my dear Conrad! It's so good to see you again! I trust you've come for your usual monthly visit. I want you to look over our defenses here one more time. Those old women you sent to teach my girls how to defend the place seem to know what they're about, but defense is really a man's business, what?"

"I'd be happy to go over the defenses, my lord, but there's another matter to be discussed."

"Now, what's this 'my lord' nonsense? I thought we agreed to treat each other as equals, as brothers, even!"

"Sorry, Lambert. Just habit, I suppose."

"Good! Now, what was this other matter?"

"Treason."

"Dog's blood! Whose?"

"Mine. Maybe yours as well."

"What the devil are you talking about?"

"I'm talking about the duke's battle plan. You were at the council of war. You saw what happened, and you heard what I had to say. It still goes. If I follow the duke's plan, everything I've done here is wasted. Poland will fall and most of us, the duke included, will likely be killed. I'm going to have to disobey him."

"I see. But you've always had an obligation to a Higher Power."

"What do you mean?" I said.

"Prester John, of course! I figured out who sent you here long ago. The greatest Christian king of all, Prester John."

Good lord! Lambert told me about this fantasy of his nine years ago, but he hadn't mentioned it since, so I'd hoped he'd forgotten about it. Yet my oath to Father Ignacy still stood, and I couldn't tell him the truth of the matter.

"You are silent," Lambert continued. "Well, I understand your problem and your oath of silence. But to answer your implied question, I'd say that your duty to your king takes precedence over your later oath to the duke, so you are safe on moral grounds. As to the practical considerations, well, if your strategy is right and the duke's is wrong, then you will be a hero and there won't be much he can do to you. If the duke's strategy is right and yours is wrong, then you are likely to die on the battlefield, and again there won't be anything he can do to you. Offhand, I'd say that your treason is a safe one."

As safe as a tomb, I thought.

"Thank you, but I didn't come here for your moral support. I came here for your physical support. My boats are going to need your aircraft to show them where the enemy is concentrating. Can I count on your help here, though it be treason on your part?"

"You can count on my help and that of the boys from Eagle Nest. We'll be up there, you may be sure! But how would that be treason to the duke? My oath to him requires that I send him so many knights in the time of his need. I shall do so, and then some, for I now have more men than my oath requires, despite the loss of those knights that once served Baron Jaraslav and now serve you. In truth, since you are arming all of my knights and squires and my barons, and I need only provide training and a horse, in the last six years we have been able to more than double the number of knights that serve me. I was wise to accept your offer, you see.

"And while my oath does not require it, I have told him that we shall be watching the enemy from above, and reporting their movements to him, and this, too, I shall do. If we also tell your boats what we tell the duke, how is that treason? It's just the sensible thing to do. We're all fighting the same enemy, after all!"

"You have relieved my mind, Lambert."

"If you say so. Myself, I can't imagine how you thought I could have done otherwise! Now then, shall we see to my defenses? And afterward, you shall have supper here with me and my daughter, and you shall see what you missed out on!"

FROM THE DIARY OF TADAOS KOLPINKSI

In the last week of February, the ice on the Vistula was breaking up some, but it wasn't gone. Like usual, it'd drift downstream and jam up at some turn, then more ice would pile on top, then that night, sure as Hell for a Heathen, it would turn cold again and the whole damn thing would freeze solid.

I had three boats on the river and we was loaded with bombs, something new we wasn't sure would work. They was big iron barrels filled with gunpowder and weighted so's they'd just barely sink. There was a slow fuse in a bottle in one side, and the idea was when you came to a jam, you lit one, screwed down the cap, and got it over the side before it blew up in your face. It was supposed to drift with the current under the jam while you was paddling backward under full steam.

Sometimes it worked. Sometimes it drifted too far or

not far enough. Once it blew and took the whole damn boat with it.

At least I think that was what happened. Nobody from *The Pride of Bytom* lived to tell about it. We just heard the blast around the bend, and when my own *Muddling Through* got there, well, there wasn't much left. Every barrel in her must have blown with the first one.

But we was pushing the ice downriver, and not that much was coming from upstream behind us. Once we got past Cracow, I ordered the other boats out, so's we could at least patrol what was clear. They went down their ways without a hitch and each loaded up with six war carts and a full company of warriors.

We continued north with the *Hotspur*, blowing ice and sometimes getting a shot at a Mongol patrol, until we got to the River Bug. It was froze solid and there was nothing we could do about it. We was out of bombs then, and there wasn't no way we could work upstream, anyhow. I'd hoped to save maybe three dozen of them bombs for another project I had in mind, but there was no way to do it, what with the loss of *The Pride of Bytom* and all. We couldn't get up the Dunajeç either, so all of Poland west of the Vistula was left open to the enemy.

But we did what we could, damn it! What else *can* a man do?

The other boats was running into bigger patrols and we turned back to pick up our troops at East Gate. It took a while. Doctrine was to give refugees a lift across the river when we weren't actually in a fight, and we had to stop and ferry God knows how many thousands of people across.

The planes was up and flying whenever the weather was decent, and they'd tell us about refugees and Mongol patrols. They had these big arrows with a long red ribbon on them that they'd drop right on your deck. They'd stick right in the wood and it was amazing they never killed nobody. But there'd be a message in the arrowhead that wasn't hardly ever wrong. Them flyboys was okay.

In two places we found river ferries that we put into service and to hell with their owners. They was both of the long rope kind that Count Conrad invented years ago. In both places I put two of my men ashore to work them, since a civilian couldn't be trusted not to run. Not one of those four men lived. They stuck to their jobs till they was all killed. Let me tell you their names. They were Ivan Torunski and his brother Wladyclaw, and John Sobinski and Vlad Tchernic. Good men, every one of them.

That was all we could do for them refugees, though. Lift them across and give them a map showing where they was and where the safe forts was. Maybe some of them made it alive.

We'd been telling people for years that noncombatants should evacuate by the first of February, handed out leaflets and wrote magazine articles, but the fools wouldn't move until they was burned out and half of them was dead. But you can't let a kid die just 'cause his folks are dumb!

Then half the idiots would want to ferry their cow across, too, when there wasn't hardly room for the people! But doctrine was to leave the animals for the Mongols to eat, cause if they couldn't get animals, them bastards would eat humans!

Our own people was out of there long before that. The inns and depots was long closed down except for the radios. The baron had called for volunteers to man the forward radios so we would know where the enemy was. Almost all of those people, half of them women, stayed at their posts. Sometimes there was some last words, sometimes not. Usually we found out that a site had been taken when the radio went off the air.

When we got to East Gate, Count Conrad was waiting for us.

FROM THE DIARY OF CONRAD STARGARD

On the last day of February, we seemed to be ready. We had to be, for we were moving out at dawn. The new troops hadn't been given the graduation ceremony that all the other classes had gotten. There was simply no way that we could have scheduled that many men to do the hillside vigil. The halo effect didn't happen that often in the wintertime, and anyway, these men weren't being knighted. With only four months of training, and all of it physical training, they just weren't ready for it.

But every one of them was armored and armed, and

they knew how to use those arms. Their equipment had been inspected hundreds of times, as had the contents of their war carts. They had spares, bedding, food for a month, and a ton of ammunition in each cart.

That afternoon, people were running to me with scores of last minute problems, things that should have been done earlier, or things that should have been done without my knowledge. I think that everyone else's nerves were about as shot as mine, and they all wanted stroking. Well, I wanted it too, and I wasn't getting it either. I was growling at people.

At this point I got a surprise visit by two priests. They spoke Italian and Latin. I spoke Polish and Modern English. I don't even understand how they got in to see me, but I had them sit in the outer office and had a runner find Father Thomas Aquinas. Maybe he could figure out what they wanted.

Fifteen trivial problems later I was getting ready to start chewing holes in my desk. At this point Father Thomas came in.

"It's the Inquisition," he said. "Was there an inquisition being held concerning you?"

Good God in Heaven! Nine and a half years had gone by since the thing had started, and they had to pick today of all days to show up.

"Yes," I said, "but it concerns something that happened long ago. Ask them what I can do for them."

They talked a while in hesitant Latin, their arms stiffly at their sides. Then they seemed to discover that they all spoke Italian and the conversation speeded up considerably, and their arms started waving. They brought out a thick sheaf of parchment, but wouldn't let Father Thomas see it. They handed it to me. I looked it over. It was all in Latin.

"They want you to read this and say if it is the truth," the Father said.

"Tell them that I'm sorry, but I don't speak Latin. I don't read it or write it, either."

They looked sheepishly at each other as Father Thomas translated what I had said. There was more conversation, and I finally got the idea that they weren't allowed to tell Father Thomas what the case was about. They couldn't tell it to the interpreter and they couldn't speak my language. And it hadn't occurred to the silly twits until now that they might have a problem!

They argued between themselves for quite a while, mostly in what had to be unfinished questions, for there were a lot of pregnant silences and glaring eyes. I didn't know whether to laugh or to cry, but I figured that either one could get me into trouble, so I just hung in there. Finally, they came up with what they thought was a suitable question, but maybe it didn't translate well.

"What do you think is the truth of the matter in which you might think we are talking of?"

I had to puzzle that out a bit. Then I said, "If this is concerning the matter that I think it might be about, I regret to inform you that I made a solemn oath to Father Ignacy, who is now the Bishop of Cracow, in which I vowed to discuss the matter with absolutely no one. I therefore can't answer what I think might be your question."

I had to repeat that three times before Father Thomas dared make a stab at translating it. Even then, they talked a long time in Italian before they got back to me.

Father Thomas looked at me and said, "I think what they want to ask you is 'What should we do now?'"

"Tell them that they should talk the matter over with his excellency, the Bishop of Cracow. Draw them a nice map. Use small words and big letters. Point them on the road and wish them well."

"Yes, sir."

The clergy left and I got back to work. With any luck, the twits would run into a Mongol patrol and the next bunch the Church sent, in another ten years, might have some of the brains that God surely had intended to give them!

We formed up at dawn on the morning of March first, the training completed. A hundred fifty thousand men stood at attention on the great concrete parade ground.

I nodded to a priest, who said a quick mass without a sermon. Few of the men could have heard him, anyway. Then I nodded to Baron Vladimir, Hetman of the Army, and he led the troops in the oath that I had cribbed years ago from that of the Boy Scouts. It was fitting. Many of these troops weren't much older than Boy Scouts.

We raised our right arms to the rising sun, and a sixth of a million men chanted with me:

"On my honor, I will do my best to do my duty to God and to the Army. I will obey the Warrior's Code, and I will keep myself physically fit, mentally alert, and morally straight.

"The Warrior's Code:

"A warrior is: Trustworthy, Loyal, and Reverent. Courteous, Kind, and Fatherly. Obedient, Cheerful, and Efficient. Brave, Clean, and Deadly."

Hearing that many men chant it, well, there was quite a difference from that first class of thirty-six men we graduated four years ago.

"Hetman," I said, "advance the army!"

Vladimir raised his voice and shouted to his three kolomels, "Kolumns, advance!"

And the three kolomels, the Banki brothers, turned to their eighteen barons and shouted, "Battalions, advance!"

And eighteen barons turned to a hundred komanders and shouted, "Komands, advance!"

And a hundred komanders turned to six hundred captains and shouted, "Companies, advance!"

And six hundred captains turned to thirty-six hundred banners and shouted, "Platoons, advance!"

And thirty-six hundred banners turned to twenty-one thousand knights and shouted, "Lances, advance!"

And twenty-one thousand knights turned to a hundred twenty-six thousand warriors and shouted, "Warriors, advance!"

And a hundred twenty-six thousand warriors shouted, "Yes, sir!"

It made a nice ceremony with a good crescendo effect. It would have been nicer if we could all have swung out right then and there, but of course there were the war carts. The men marched out to them, and the first few hundred were already on the tracks, but it was almost noon before the last cart went out the gate. Not that the departure was disorganized, far from it. We were double-tracked and the men moved out at a quick march, but it takes time for thirty-six hundred big carts to move down a pair of tracks. The column was sixteen miles long.

Yet once moving, they didn't stop. Early on, we had found that eighteen armored men could easily tow a war cart filled with their arms and supplies, and with the rest of the platoon riding on it, so long as it was a railroad track. A cook stove was slung from the back of the cart, and three cooks could keep the men fed. There was room for the other half of the platoon to sack out on top of the cart or to be slung from hammocks below it. Working three hours marching and three hours resting, they could go on indefinitely, making six dozen miles a day without ever breaking into double-time. Most caravans were happy to do two dozen miles, and few conventional military columns could do that! Actually, providing we could stay on the rails, we could probably outrun the Mongols. Providing.

I sat on Anna, watching them go out the gate. There was a big crowd outside cheering them on, dependents and refugees who were waiting to move into Hell as we left. Odds were that they were cheering more because we had vacated the premises than because we were going out against the enemy. Some of those people had been out there in the snow for days.

But there were others whose job it was to worry about those left behind. My job was with the riverboats. I was about to leave for it when a strange company of troops came up. I say strange because they were out of uniform. They had turbans wrapped around their helmets. Then I spotted Zoltan sitting on one of the carts. I went up to him and rode by his side.

"Zoltan, what the hell are you doing here?"

"Doing, sir? Why, I am riding off to war against my ancient enemies, the Mongols! We have many old scores to settle with them as you would say. And you must not call me Zoltan, sir. Not here. Now I am Captain Varanian of the two-tendy-eighth."

"But I never said that you could join the army! This is a Christian army!"

"True, my lord, but you never said that we couldn't, either. As to the Christians, we are not prejudiced, and we keep to our own company in any event."

"There's a whole company of you? How is that possible? Eight years ago there were only fifty men in your band, and no children. How can there be two hundred fifty of you now?"

"Oh, the word spread of your generosity and our security under your protection, my lord. Others of my people who were scattered over the world came to us in ones and twos and what could we do? Could we send them back to the cold and cruel world? So we took them in, even as you took us in. And now they repay you, with their lives, perhaps."

"I thought that there were only a hundred families of you."

"From Urgench yes, my lord. But there were many other cities in Khareshmia that is no more. Is it not enough that we join you in this Holy War?"

"Yes, I suppose it is, Captain. Carry on." I just hoped the Church never got wind of it.

The last company in line were specialists in cart repair, set up to get stragglers back on the road. Once they went by, Anna and I rode the trail beside the track and the men cheered us the whole way. I smiled and waved at them until my arm got sore, then switched arms. Good. Morale couldn't be better.

Halfway to East Gate, we passed the first of them, and Anna went over to the track. She said it was easier to run on the wood than on the ground. Springier.

I got there to find the RB1 *Muddling Through* just rounding the bend with the RB14 *Hotspur* right beyond her. There were also three companies of troops waiting to board them. They hadn't heard about the loss of the RB23 *The Pride of Bytom*, so I told the captain of the company that had been assigned to it that he would have to join up with the regular army. His boat ride was gone.

I turned to Anna.

"Well, girl, this is where we part company for a while."

She gave me an "I don't like this" posture.

"Now don't start that again! We talked this over weeks ago. There wouldn't be anything you could do on a boat but take up space. Baron Vladimir needs your help. You like Vladimir, don't you?"

She nodded YES, but sulkily.

"I know you don't want to leave me. I don't want to leave you either, but this is the sensible thing to do. Look, give me a hug."

I hugged her neck, her chin pressed firmly to my back.

"Anna, you know I've loved you since we first met. You've always been my best friend, and no matter what happens, you always will be."

She signaled "ME TOO." I felt a tear forming.

"Good. Now be off with you, love, and take good care of Vladimir! I love you!"

She galloped back west.

Captainette Lubinski, the woman commanding East Gate, came out to report to me.

"We have over twenty thousand people in there, sir. I tell you that they're stacked up to the stone rafters! We can't possibly take any more!"

"Then don't," I said. "There's plenty of room in Hell. Send all the newcomers there."

"But everybody wants to be in here!" she said. "They've all heard that this fort is invincible."

"It just might be. But there is a limit as to how many people it can hold. You'll just have to shut your gates and tell them to walk another day to Hell. It's the only thing you can do! Oh, give them some food and water, of course, but send them on their way!"

"Yes, sir, but some of them—"

"But nothing, Captainette! It's not what *they* want that counts! It's what *we* can possibly do! You have your orders. Dismissed."

She was crumbling already, and the battle hadn't even started. I wondered if I should replace her, but I didn't know any of the other women here well enough to pick her replacement. Maybe she'd be all right.

The boats pulled up to the dock and their front drawbridges went down. They must have been carrying a thousand refugees each.

"Send those people on their way to the Warrior's School!" I shouted to the troops standing around. "There's no room for them here!"

Baron Piotr had gotten there before me, and he had his crew organized. He was to run Tartar Control, our command and control center, acting as my chief of staff. He only had two dozen radio operators and clerks under him, but in fact he would be running the Battle for the Vistula—under my occasional direction, of course.

The RB1 *Muddling Through* was a command boat, the only one we had. It had six radios instead of the usual one, so we could cover all the frequencies that we used without retuning. It had an operations center with a big situation map, plus bedroom space for all the extra people. Aside from that, it was just another steamboat.

It was late afternoon by the time the boats had taken on more coal and supplies, loaded the troops, and headed downstream. As we left, two other boats were coming up to replenish their coal. I gave their masters a chewing out over the radio for being so bunched up.

RB1 EG TO RB18 EG AND RB26 EG. WHAT ARE YOU? TWO WOMEN WHO MUST HOLD HANDS ON THE WAY TO THE POTTY? THE NEXT TIME I SEE YOU SO CLOSE TO-GETHER, I WILL PERSONALLY DRESS BOTH OF YOUR BOAT'S MASTERS IN BUNNY SUITS! CONRAD. OUT.

Our range being as short as it was, the rules were that any boat between the sender and the receiver should relay the message onward. In this case, where all units concerned were at the same location, it shouldn't have been relayed at all, but the substance of the message was such that I knew the radio operators would send it the full length of the line, which is what I wanted.

Doctrine was that the boats should be evenly spaced. We had three-gross miles of river to patrol, upstream and down, with three dozen boats. They should have been two dozen miles apart!

We got on the radios and had all boats report their positions and headings. If they bunched up, that meant long stretches of the river weren't being patrolled. It also meant that boats might be so far apart that radio messages between them might not be received, and that could cut our communication lines in half. We put markers on a map and started getting things organized. By midnight, we had schedules for all of them, where they should be at what time, assuming they weren't involved with refugees or Mongols. Even then, they were supposed to try to make up the time, since the schedule had them moving at only half speed.

At dawn, the RB9 *Lady of Cracow* reported a heavy enemy concentration across the river from Sandomierz. I told them to make a three-mile switchback, letting them hit the concentration three times. They complained vigorously when I ordered them to continue the patrol, but the RB20 *Wastrel* would be on station in minutes to take over the load.

The next four boats by there did the same, while we saw only scattered patrols. I wasn't going to let a bunch

of boatmasters, excited at their first contact with the
enemy, upset our schedules! As long as we could keep
the bastards on the west side of the river, we'd get them
all eventually.

But when we got near Sandomierz, I saw that they
hadn't been exaggerating a bit. Through my telescope, I
could see the Mongols had troops thirty deep along the
shoreline. More importantly, at the shoreline men and
horses were piled five and six high, and dead! There
must have been twenty thousand dead along that sector
of river, but they kept on coming. The riverboats were
earning their pay!

Chapter Fifteen

I RAN below decks and told Piotr to order the closest dozen boats to join the fun. We could just cruise up and down, raking them with everything we had except the flamethrowers, which had to be reserved for bridges.

That done, I opened the hatch to go back up on deck. A dozen Mongol arrows flew in at me! Four stuck in my armor and by the time I had them pulled out, I had been hit two more times. But I wasn't hurt. That armor really worked! So I ignored the arrows and pressed on.

On deck, the men looked like pincushions and were laughing about it. The deck itself was so filled with arrows that you couldn't take a single step without breaking some. Tadaos had the boat running a few dozen yards from shore, letting them hit us but making sure that we couldn't miss!

I saw a warrior go down with an arrow in his eyeslit; and another man take his place at the gun before the first had hit the floor. But the medics were right there and there wasn't anything I could do. Men running up ammunition moved with a skating motion that broke off the arrows so they wouldn't have to step on them.

The noise was deafening. Both starboard peashooters were firing without letup, throwing six hundred rounds a minute into an almost solid mass of Mongol troops. Those iron balls had about the ballistics of a carbine bullet. When they hit a man, he was wounded or dead, armor or no armor. Shooting into that tangled mass, I don't see how any of them could possibly have missed.

The sides of the boat were two and a half stories high, with smooth surfaces so they couldn't be climbed. But I saw a Mongol try to get in by grabbing on to the paddle wheel. I got my sword out, but before I could swing, the man was killed by one of the arrows flying at us. His body continued around and back into the water. I sent a runner to get a dozen men with pikes to guard the rear railing, and watched it until they arrived.

The Halmans were chunking away, and Tadaos was aiming one himself, laughing and shouting with every round that exploded above the mass. It was good shooting and better loading, because the loader had to time the fuse so that it exploded just above the heads of the enemy. Too high or too low and much of the effect was lost. The millions of rounds expended in training were paying dividends. Mongols were dying in droves.

The gunners from our boat's company of troops had their three dozen swivel guns set up on deck, adding joyfully to the carnage. Their rounds were far more powerful than those of the peashooters. You could see rows of three and four horsemen go down, all killed by the same bullet!

I'd heard that in modern battles, a quarter-million rounds are fired for every enemy killed. We were averaging considerably better! In fact, I never saw anybody miss!

And everything we were doing was soon multiplied by twelve, since the men in the other boats weren't acting like old maids either!

Any sane army would have run away from us, but these people weren't that sane. A modern army might have dug in, but that hadn't occurred to these horsemen, and with luck, it never would.

I could imagine Mongol commanders in the rear hearing about the slaughter and not believing it! I could imagine them sending observer after observer forward and not having any come back. Or better yet, going forward to see for themselves what the racket was and doing a bit of dying of their own!

It was likely, since our gunners always went after anyone who wore a fancy outfit or looked like he was giving orders. Besides a loader, each gunner had an observer whose job it was to point out good targets, and a boat gunner's helmet had "ears" on it pointing backward so he could hear what was being shouted at him.

After a few miles of this, we started running out of Mongols, so Tadaos had the boat turned around and we went upstream for some more gleeful mayhem. The troops quickly remounted their swivel guns on the port railing and reloaded. There were so many arrows stuck to the inside of the port parapet that they had to get out their axes and clear away the gun ports before they could mount their weapons! The men on the port peashooters, who had been dying of frustration up to this point, got ready to get their inning in.

The RB7 *Invincible* was coming downstream at us, followed closely by the RB12 *Insufferable*, so we had to stay a little farther out in the channel and try not to shoot holes in them.

The sun was well up now, and shining in our eyes, but we didn't need accurate shooting at this point, we just needed shooting! Even at a gross yards, we could hardly miss that mass of enemy troops.

I went to the starboard side and looked over. Since it was only sheet metal over wood, there were thousands of arrows stuck in the ship's armor. But I guess we had judged the metal gauge right, since none of them penetrated all the way.

On the opposite shore, people on the walls of Sandomierz were waving at us, cheering us on. But sightseeing, I wasn't doing my job. I turned to go back down to the control room when a plane flew over. One of the oversized message arrows thunked into the deck. I picked it up myself and waved at the pilot. He wagged his wings and flew off.

Downstairs, I read the message.

"Praty gud!" it read. "Bot they mak a bridge 7 mil downstream of U. Lambert." So Count Lambert was finally learning how to read and write! A pity about his spelling, though.

I checked the situation board and found that we had no boats between Sieciechow and Sandomierz. There should have been, but nobody nearby wanted to miss out on the action here. I sent a message to Tadaos to turn downstream again and radioed RB17 *The Ghost of St. Joseph* to follow us.

The RB21 *Calypso* reported that another concentration of Mongols west of Brzesko had been spotted by a plane, and wanted to turn back and investigate. With the planes flying, we really didn't have to keep up a steady watch for breakthroughs from the boats. Permission granted.

As we proceeded downriver, it was soon obvious what Lambert had seen. Along the shore, a long line of small boats was being lashed together, gunwale to gunwale, and ropes and logs were being fastened on top of them to form a roadway. All the boats on the west bank were supposed to have been destroyed, but I guess that hadn't happened. Once completed, they would swing that pontoon bridge into the current and fasten it to the opposite shore. At least that looked to be their plan.

I called for Captain Targ, who commanded the company of troops we had on board.

"I need three platoons with axes," I said.

"Good, sir. The boys down below have been looking for something to do. It's no fun for them, sitting there while everybody else gets to play," he said, grinning.

"Such a rough life. Bow landing, you know the drill. And move some of your gunners up to the bow."

"Aye, aye, sir."

Piotr sent a message to RB17 *The Ghost of St. Joseph* to get their troops ready to take out the downstream half of the bridge. I went to Tadaos, who was pulling Mongol arrows from his deck and saving them.

"Most of these are long enough for me to shoot," he said. "I suppose you'll be wanting the flamethrower warmed up."

"No, we do this one with axes," I said. "We'll give it one pass to soften them up, then we put some troops ashore at the middle and cover them as we go upstream. The *Ghost* will take the first half of it."

"You sure about that, sir? I think now's the time for the flamethrowers."

"It's a little late to change things. I've already given orders to the *Ghost*."

"As you will, sir."

We'd drilled this maneuver last summer, but most of the men were new. The knights had been through it, though, and that should be enough.

We went into them with our escort right on our tail. This bunch of Mongols hadn't been fired on before, I think, because they didn't seem to take us very seriously until we opened fire. Then it was a little late for them.

The river embankment was twenty yards from the shore and pretty high just here, higher than the boat, actually, and not too many of the Mongols made it over the top. A few tried to outrun us, and we were going pretty slow, but not quite *that* slow. There wasn't much for the *Ghost* to clean up.

We made a U-turn and headed back to the middle. Of course, playing administrator was about as frustrating as sitting below, waiting for something to happen. As we approached our touchdown point, I decided *what the hell!* and ran down to join the landing party. It had been years since I had swung a sword in earnest, and rank hath its privileges.

I slipped the lanyard of my sword over my wrist as I approached Captain Targ.

"Do you have room for an extra man?" I said.

"Always room for one more! Or eighty more, for that matter."

"I see. All six platoons, huh?"

"I left the gunners up top, but we're so low on ammunition that they don't need loaders or spotters. They can take their time because they don't have enough bullets to shoot fast anyway."

"But surely you had the standard thirty-six thousand rounds in your carts," I said.

"Maybe a mite more than that, sir, but we just did one hell of a lot of shooting. We're down to a gross rounds per gun right now, and that's counting the boat's stores besides our own."

"I didn't realize consumption was that high. We should have conserved ammunition."

"What for, sir? We couldn't have used it better than we did! When every round kills an enemy or three, they're doing what they were made for!"

Before I could reply, the boat touched the shore and the front drawbridge dropped. We all rushed out and through the knee-deep freezing mud. What with my goose-down padding and all the excitement, I'd forgotten how cold it was. We started chopping up boats, lashings and any Mongols that showed signs of wanting to be alive.

The guns above were ready to give us covering fire, but it wasn't needed. Those few of the enemy who had gone over the hill were still going.

The captain and I were at the end of the line going out, and there wasn't much for us to do as we walked slowly along the riverbank, keeping even with the paddle

wheel of the boat. The two hundred men in front of us
were chopping everything up into tooth picks and ham-
burger. One of the troops ahead of us stopped to cut the
purse off one of the Mongol dead, and this annoyed Captain Targ.

"Hey, you asshole! You know the doctrine! We don't
pick up loot until the battle's over!"

As a general thing, he was right, of course. Countless
medieval battles had been lost because the troops had
stopped to loot instead of staying in formation. Our rules
were that we didn't loot until afterward, and then all loot
was divided up evenly, no matter who did the looting.
But first you had to win, dammit!

But just now, there wasn't any enemy opposition and
we really didn't have enough to do.

"Captain, maybe he's right. Detail a platoon to take
the Mongol purses. Tell them not to bother with weapons
and jewelry, but let's see what we get," I said.

"Done, sir. Blue platoon only! Start looting! Purses
only! Pass the word!"

While he was giving orders, I picked up one of the
purses myself. It was full of silver and gold, almost half
and half, and must have weighed four pounds! I was
holding everything this bastard had been able to steal in
three years of looting Russia! Yet in a way, it made
sense. While he was pillaging, he had to carry everything
he gained with him. It wasn't as though there was a bank
he could have deposited it in.

Doing some crude mental calculations, we must have
killed a half-million Mongols this morning! If every one
of them had two pounds of gold on him, that was . . .
well, given a fifty-to-one exchange rate, silver to gold,
and a six-to-one rate, zinc to silver, that was . . . more
than I could work out in my head. But maybe I shouldn't
have worried so much about the deflated currency. If
something wasn't done, we were about to see one bodacious inflation!

I picked up eight more purses and was musing on this
when all hell shut down for payday.

Chapter Sixteen

I SAW my error as soon as it happened. The riverbank being taller than the boat, our gunners couldn't see over it. They didn't see the horde that was coming until it was on top of us. I should have put observers up there. To add to our problems, while our helmets offered excellent protection, you couldn't tilt your head back in them. The helmet and beaver clamped into a ring around the collar of the breast and back plates. The helmet could turn sideways, but not up and down. The only way to look up was to tilt your whole body. Most people rarely look up in any event.

I think the reason that we weren't all killed was that the Mongols stopped at the top of the embankment to let off a flight of arrows. This got our attention.

It also got me an arrow in the eye.

I staggered back, scattering the gold and silver I'd picked up, tripping over the wreckage of the pontoon bridge and falling into the freezing mud. For a moment, I couldn't figure out what happened, except that I couldn't see out of my right eye, and my left was blurry. The pain came a bit later.

I struggled to get up, but kept falling back into the slippery wreckage. I could hear the shouting and fighting around me, the peashooters and the swivel guns firing, but I couldn't seem to get untangled. I broke off the damn arrow and could see with my left eye. I guess it was only that the shaft was in the way.

I was on my left side, and suddenly I was surrounded by legs and boots. But those weren't army uniforms! I tried again to get up and something unseen bashed into me, knocking me down again into deeper water and mud. I fumbled for my pistol, brought it up and aimed at a huge gold belt buckle a yard away. The gun fired, but what with the slippery mud and all, it flew from my hand. There wasn't time to reload it anyway.

Someone slammed into my side and we went down in a heap. I managed to get hold of my sword, which was still tied to my wrist, rolled over onto my knees and jabbed someone with red pants in the groin. He went down, but I got another bash on the back of the head from somewhere. But while that helmet restricted visibility, it sure protected you! I don't know how many times that ring around my collar saved my life.

Then I heard an army rallying cry! I saw three pairs of red pants go down as a group and then suddenly I was being lifted up into the air by strong arms under each of my armpits.

"Can you walk, sir?" It was Captain Targ.

"I think so. How goes the battle?"

"Time for a strategic withdrawal, sir. Or in nonmilitary parlance, let's run away!"

"Okay. But don't leave any of our men behind! Not even if you know they're dead!"

"Right sir. Standard doctrine. Fall back to the boat! Don't leave our own men! Pick up our dead! Pass the word!"

The gunners above us were keeping most of the enemy from getting to us, but there wasn't anything they could do about those already on top of us. We were hard-pressed to keep up any sort of line, and in that damned mud, a saber had the advantage over a rapier. You couldn't get enough traction to lunge!

Fortunately, most of our men had axes and I had my sword. It was only the captain and his knights who had serious problems.

With only one eye, I still did my share. I think I must have killed a half dozen of the bastards, taking a dozen hits that would have killed me had I been wearing lesser armor. The stuff got in the way, but it was worth it.

In minutes, we weren't fighting in the mud anymore. We were fighting on top of the enemy dead, and that's treacherous footing. The Mongol sabers bounced off our armor, but many of them were armed with a spear that had a long, thin, triangular point, and that thing was a killer! Carried by a man on the run, or thrown at short range, they could punch right through our armor, and most of our serious casualties were caused by them.

Yet discipline and training held true for us. Our lines tightened up, our dead and wounded were put aboard and soon we were safe. I was next to the last man off the shore, and I would have been the last, except for the captain.

"My honors, sir. This is my company, and I'll be the last man off!"

He'd earned it, so I clambered aboard and let him follow me.

As Tadaos pulled the boat away from the shore, a medic took me inside and I was the last man to be hustled up to sick bay, even though I wanted to see what was going on topside. Medics have no respect for the wishes of a wounded man. They're all mother hens who are convinced that they know best.

He got my helmet off and *tsk-tsk*ed at my right eye.

"Have I lost it?" I said.

"No, sir, it missed the eyeball. But it stuck in the bone just to the right of it. You're going to have a scar, I'm afraid, but you'll see again. You were lucky."

"I would have been a damn sight luckier if the arrow had missed!"

"There is that, sir."

"Well, open that surgeon's kit! Get the arrowhead out, clean the wound, and sew it up! Didn't they teach you anything in medic's school?"

"I never sewed up an eye before, sir. In fact, I've never sewn up anything but dead animals in training."

"Well, boy, now's your chance to learn! First, wash your hands in white lightning, and then wash around the wound as best you can."

"Yes, sir."

After a bit, I said, "You got that done? Then get the pliers out of your kit and pull the arrowhead out. Better get somebody to hold my head still. It'll hurt, and I might flinch."

"You, sir? Never!"

"I said get somebody to hold my head and stop acting like I'm God! That's an order!"

"Yes, sir. You're not God. Hey, Lezek! Give me a hand! Hold his head!"

"Now the pliers," I said.

I don't know if I yelled or not, but I saw the most

incredible visual display and I think I might have blacked out for a few moments.

"It's out, sir," he said, holding the bloody thing so I could see it with my good eye. The right one still wasn't working, somehow.

"Good. Throw it away. That kind of souvenir I don't need. Now get a pair of tweezers and feel around in the wound for any bits of broken bone or any foreign matter."

This time, I know I screamed. Having somebody feeling around inside of your head without anesthetics is no fun at all!

But he took his time at it and seemed to take out a few chunks of something. I wanted to tell him to leave *some* of the skull behind, but I thought better of it. I couldn't see what was happening and so I had to trust to the kid's judgment.

"I think that's all of it, sir."

"Thank God! Now, clean it all out again with white lightning. Pour it right in."

By now, the area was getting numb, and I didn't scream. I wanted to, you understand, but I could hold it in.

"Okay. Now get out your sterile needle and thread and sew it up. Use nice neat little stitches, because if my wife doesn't like the job you did, she will make your life not worth living. Believe me. I know the woman."

"Yes, sir. Try not to wince so much. It makes it hard to line the edges up."

"I'll try."

He put nine stitches in there. I counted.

"That's it, sir."

"Well, bandage it up then, with some peat-bog moss next to the wound!"

"Yes, sir."

Without adhesive tape, the thing had to be held on by wrapping gauze around my head and under my chin.

When he was done, I sat up.

"Well. Good job, I hope. Thank you, but now you better get around to the other men who were wounded."

He looked around the room. "No sir, I think the surgeons have taken care of everybody."

"The surgeons!" I yelled. "Then what the hell are you?"

"Me, sir? I'm an assistant corpsman."

"Then what the hell were you doing operating on my head?"

"But, you ordered me to, sir! It was a direct order from my commanding officer! What was I supposed to do? Disobey you?"

"Then what were you doing with a surgeon's kit?"

"Oh, they had extra of those at the warehouse, sir, so they handed them out to some of the corpsmen, just in case."

"They just handed it to you?"

"Yes, sir. It's nice to know what some of these things are for."

I found I couldn't wear my arming hat over the bandage, but I could get the helmet on.

Before I could leave the sick bay, the chief surgeon came up to me, his armor hacked in a dozen places. I could see by the insignia and the fact that he carried a mace rather than a sword that the equally battered man standing next to the chief surgeon was the company chaplain. In any modern army, both of these positions would have been given noncombatant status, but in ours, every man was a warrior. This Sir Majinski was banner of the orange platoon, besides his medical duties.

"The butcher's bill, sir," he said.

I looked at it. Eleven dead. Twenty-ten seriously wounded, and I wasn't on that list. Fifty-one with minor wounds. Had I done it Tadaos's way, with flamethrowers, these men would all be alive and sound.

"Sorry about the incident with the corpsman, sir. I kept an eye on him while he was working on you, but I had a man with a sucking chest wound on my table, and I thought I might be able to save him. But the corpsman meant well, and he did a fair job."

"Well, give the corpsman my apologies. The man with the chest wound, could you save him?"

"No."

I checked in with Tartar Control. The battle near Brzesko was up to three boats now, and the battle across from Sandomierz was still raging, with a dozen boats still butchering Mongols. But it wasn't the same dozen. That group, out of ammunition, was heading back upstream to East Gate to rearm. I knew the supplies we had there and it wasn't going to be enough.

In the history books I read when I was a boy, some said that the Mongols had invaded with a million men. Others said that this was impossible, that the logistics of the time couldn't have supported more than fifty thousand. But if the estimates that I'd made and those I was getting from the other boats were anything like correct, we had killed more than a half a million Mongols in the first morning of the attack! Furthermore, they showed no signs of thinning out! In any event, the numbers involved were so much higher than I had expected that I had vastly underestimated the ammunition requirements.

On the other hand, they were showing absolutely none of the tactical brilliance that they were supposedly famous for and that I had feared. So far, they were easier to kill than dumb animals. Not that they could be expected to stay that dumb.

Then too, some of my actions had been pretty dumb as well, and it was my duty to see that my last set of stupid mistakes was not repeated.

RB1 TO ALL UNITS. WE HAVE ENGAGED THE ENEMY IN HAND-TO-HAND COMBAT AND LEARNED THE FOLLOWING:

1. WHEN PATROLLING A RIVERSHORE ON FOOT, PLACE MEN AS OBSERVERS ON TOP OF THE RIVERBANK TO WATCH FOR ENEMY COUNTERATTACKS.

2. ENEMY HAND WEAPONS ARE LARGELY INEFFECTIVE EXCEPT FOR A SPEAR WITH A LONG, THIN, TRIANGULAR POINT. THIS WEAPON IS CAPABLE OF PENETRATING OUR ARMOR WHEN CARRIED AT A RUN OR THROWN.

3. WHEN FIGHTING ON RIVER MUD, THE RAPIER IS NOT EFFECTIVE DUE TO THE LACK OF TRACTION DURING A LUNGE. OFFICERS ARE ADVISED TO ARM THEMSELVES WITH AXES UNDER THESE CIRCUMSTANCES.

4. WHEN TAKING OUT A PONTOON BRIDGE BEING CONSTRUCTED ON A RIVERSHORE, FLAMETHROWERS ARE MORE EFFECTIVE THAN AXES.

GOOD HUNTING—CONRAD.

OUT.

Was that worth the deaths of eleven men? Or the maiming of dozens others? I swear that I was never meant to be a battle commander.

But something had to be done about the ammunition situation, and there was only one place to get more ammo. Our other units. We sent out radio messages ordering all units to send one-sixth of their swivel gun ammunition to East Gate, and for the Odra boats to send three-quarters of their peashooter and Halman ammunition in addition to this. I hated to strip the other units, but as the captain said, the ammunition couldn't possibly be spent better than it was right here.

I also ordered that all reloading equipment and supplies be transported from Three Walls to East Gate, along with any ladies who knew how to operate it.

I went back up on deck. We were heading upstream again to the fighting at Sandomierz.

"How did the battle go, Baron Tadaos?"

"Well, sir, since we was out to destroy the bridge, I guess you have to say we won. It's gone."

"We got the whole thing chopped up?"

"The *Ghost* did all right, but it wasn't attacked. We only got about half of our half done. But after we pulled out, the *Ghost* took out the last quarter with a flamethrower. That bridge burned real good. So did the Mongols."

Captain Targ came up. "It was quite a show, sir. Mongols don't like burning to death. A lot of them jumped into the water and drowned in preference to it."

"A good thing to know. Captain Targ, you saved my life today. If you hadn't killed the Mongols around me and pulled me out of that wreckage, I'd be a dead man. I owe you."

"No sir, you don't. I was just paying an old debt."

"Debt? What debt? Should I know you from somewhere?"

"I didn't expect you to recognize me, sir. You only saw me once and that was in the dark, plus I was only ten years old at the time. But I'd hoped you would remember my name."

"I'm sorry, but I still draw a blank."

"My father told me that if I could do you some personal service, I should tell you that once you threw bread on the waters, and that it has come back to you tenfold. Well, it isn't really tenfold. If I've saved your life, well, you once saved the lives of my entire family."

"I remember now. When I first got to this country, I

was lost in a snowstorm, and your father let me in to the warmth of his fire. Doing that saved my life, I think."

"Perhaps, sir. But the next summer, my father's fields were flattened by a hailstorm. We would have starved to death that next winter except you came by and gave him a purse of silver. So now perhaps that debt is paid."

"In full, with compound interest, Captain. There were two of you boys, weren't there?"

"Yes, sir. Wladyclaw is a banner with the elevendy-third."

"And the rest of your family. Are they well?"

"Yes, sir, or at least they were as of a month ago. But my father wouldn't evacuate and that region is probably overrun by the Mongols now. There's no telling what's happened."

"I'll pray for them." It was all I could say.

Chapter Seventeen

▚▚▚▚▚▚▚▚▚▚▚▚▚▚▚▚▚▚▚▚▚▚

"WHAT ARE those things?" Tadaos said, as we cruised by the fighting near Sandomierz. What with the restrictions on ammunition, we were shooting now only on the closer, downstream leg of the circuit. We had ammunition left for one pass, so we wanted to spend it well.

"Darned if I know," I said. There were four of them, and they looked sort of like big door frames without the doors or the walls, either. They were maybe three storeys tall, and had a sort of teeter-totter mounted on the cross beam. Ropes seemed to be coming from where each seat should have been.

"Maybe they make a playground for giants," Captain Targ joked.

We got our answer shortly when fully two gross men picked up ropes that were hanging from the near end of one of the teeter-totters and pulled, all at once. A rock bigger than a man flew in an incredibly high arc, and landed a few dozen yards upstream of us, kicking up a cold, drenching spray.

"It's some kind of Mongol trebuchet," the captain said.

"They could be big trouble if they get the range right," Tadaos said.

"True," I said. "Captain, have your men target on those catapults, once we get in close."

"Right, sir."

Another rock came flying, and another. The rate of fire on those catapults was remarkable. They were shooting as fast as they could drag up rocks!

They were set up on a hill for better elevation, and they were shooting at us from three gross yards away without difficulty. I had the feeling that their ultimate range might be a good deal more.

A second one got into action as we turned in to make our run.

Then a huge rock crashed into RB4 *The River Belle*, directly in front of us. Three more fell into the beach area right on top of the Mongol troops, but that didn't slow their rate of fire. It was as though they didn't care if they took casualties!

Tadaos and I were on the foredeck as I watched through my telescope. He was out of Halman bombs, and there wasn't a good target for his Molotov cocktails, so he had his bow out. He'd scrounged hundreds of Mongol arrows and was politely returning them to their rightful owners.

Our troops opened fire on the catapults about the time that the other boats started to take them seriously. The Mongols had to be close together to pull simultaneously, and bunched up like that they were dog meat for the swivel guns. Chunks of wood went flying from the uprights as well.

"It looks like it was a paper tiger," I said.

"Yeah, until they get brains enough to mount them things on the other side of the hill," Tadaos said. "Oh, shit."

"What?" I said, still looking through my telescope.

There was a huge crash and the deck bounced under me, throwing me off balance, tumbling me to the deck. I looked to my left and there was a yard-wide hole in the deck right next to me, right where Tadaos had been standing.

"Tadaos!" I shouted.

"Yes, sir?" he said from my right.

"My God! I thought you were dead."

"I saw it coming in time."

"Then why didn't you warn me?"

"There wasn't much time, and you was safe enough where you was. Could of been trouble if you moved."

Then a grappling hook with a leather rope attached came flying at me. It caught on the parapet, between two merlons. I got my sword out in time to lean over and slash open the face of a man who was climbing up the side of the boat.

"Captain! Get all your men on deck!"

"They're learning," Tadaos shouted as he drew his sword from over his left shoulder. "They're maybe a little slow, but they're learning."

Four platoons of troops ran up on deck and fended off what turned out to be a concerted boarding attempt. Once, the Mongols actually made it on deck, and had to be expelled with a pike charge. Things were interesting for a while, but then Tadaos came to me.

"We can handle things up here, sir, but I'm worried about that hole in the bottom. That rock went right through, you know."

"Well, I guess I am the best man for that job," I said. After all, I'd designed these boats. Who better to fix one? So I changed hats from battle commander to steamboat repairman.

That rock had gone through the top deck, through a double bunk on the middle deck, through the middle deck, through the cargo deck and through the bottom a half yard below that! I had the feeling that if it had hit me on the way, I wouldn't even have slowed it down!

The most serious damage was to the bottom, of course, and even that wasn't catastrophic. The volume between the cargo deck and the bottom was cut into dozens of watertight compartments, and only one of them was flooded. It would have been a different story had we been hit in the paddle wheel or the boiler. But there was no way to armor against two-ton rocks, so there was no point in worrying about it.

Except for the ones in the bow, the watertight compartments were all identical. The boat's dining room had three trestle tables that were just the right size to fit in the bottom of these. One of my better ideas. I got together a couple of crewmen and we lifted the floorboards, sank a table, and nailed it in place with all of us standing in the knee-deep water to hold down the table.

We put a portable pump down there and one man was left working it. It leaked some, but he could keep up with it. We stopped a moment to admire a job well done, when another rock came crashing through not four yards away, taking the corner off a war cart before it went through the bottom. Blood dripped through the ragged hole from the deck above.

"Do you remember what we did here," I said to the man next to me. He said he did.

"Well, do it again over there."

I went up to Tartar Control and discovered that we had a third killing ground going north of Czersk. Four boats were on it and the one near Brzesko now had six. All the rest were in transit to or from East Gate, to get more coal and ammunition.

The Mongols were completely inexperienced in dealing with us and our weapons, and paid heavily for the lessons they learned. Yet it was equally true that we were inexperienced with them. But with the radios, we could pass fighting tips around, while fighting in three separate groups; the Mongols had to go through each learning experience three times. And we charged full tuition to each and every one of them.

I got back on deck just in time to see the RB10 *Not For Hire* take a rock square on her paddle wheel. She was dead ahead of us and even as she slowed, Tadaos was getting a towing line ready. Using one of the Mongol grapnels as a monkey's fist, a line was tossed to her by one of the experienced boatmen in the crew just as we stopped alongside. Within a minute, Tadaos was calling for full-speed ahead and we resumed our way to East Gate. As we towed her home, I caught glimpses of the *Hire*'s crew dismantling the wreckage, preparing to re-build. We were taking casualties, but we weren't giving the bastards any trophies.

RB1 TO ALL RIVER UNITS. THE ENEMY HAS A CATA-PULT THAT LOOKS LIKE A TEETER-TOTTER MADE FOR GIANTS. IT CAN THROW A HUGE ROCK FOUR GROSS YARDS, WHICH CAN DAMAGE A BOAT. IF YOU SEE ONE, DO NOT ATTACK UNTIL YOU HAVE TWO OTHER BOATS TO BACK YOU UP. THEY NEED A LARGE NUMBER OF MEN WORKING CLOSE TOGETHER TO OPERATE THEM, SO THEY ARE EASILY SLAUGHTERED BY OUR SWIVEL GUNS WHEN THEY ARE MOUNTED ON A HILL. THE PROBLEM IS THAT THEY ARE WILLING TO REPLACE MEN AS FAST AS WE BUTCHER THEM. IF THEY GET SMART ENOUGH TO MOUNT THEM ON THE OTHER SIDE OF A HILL, WE WILL BE ABLE TO REACH THEM ONLY WITH HALMAN BOMBS AND RIFLE GRENADES. ANY OTHER USE OF BOMBS IS NOW FORBIDDEN, TO SAVE AMMUNI-TION. IF THEY ARE HIDDEN BY A HILL, THEY MUST

HAVE SOMEONE ON TOP OF THE HILL TO AIM THE CATA-
PULT. TARGET THIS MAN. CONRAD. OUT.

Of course, I wasn't the only one handing out advice,
not by a long shot. Some ideas were brilliant, some were
dumb. But a cumulative learning process was taking
place.

Darkness fell as we passed Cracow, still safe on the
west bank of the Vistula. Piotr's crew was radioing the
boats, reminding them that we had now lost our air
cover, and we would have to go back to patrolling until
dawn. Fortunately, the Mongols seemed to have had
enough for one day and were breaking contact. We
couldn't follow them, so it was a quiet night.

There was only a platoon of boatwrights at East Gate,
but they were our *best* boatwrights, and they had plenty
of eager if unskilled help. Because we had called ahead,
an entire paddle-wheel assembly was waiting for the
Hire, and a crane swung it into position even as the
troops were running on more ammo, food, and coal.

The patches in the bottom of the *Muddling Through*
were inspected and secured with lag bolts. Linen caulk-
ing was pounded in the cracks and we were pronounced
good enough. They gave us some boards and nails, and
we were told to patch the upper decks on our way back
to the fighting. Just then the boatwrights had better
things to do.

Our badly wounded and dead were taken to an impro-
vised hospital and morgue in the boat factory. I should
have had something better planned, but I hadn't expected such heavy losses. I'd thought that our boats
would be invincible!

We were almost ready to leave when I saw a Big People come galloping in hauling a cart full of swivel gun
ammo and four terrified troops. The carts were three
yards tall and lacked brakes, springs, and a suspension
system; they were never intended to move at the speeds
that a Big Person was capable of. But she stopped it in
time and gave me a "Hi there!" posture.

"Hi there, yourself!" I said. "Are you Anna?"

She said YES, so I gave her a big hug.

"You see? I told you they needed you! But I've got to
run, love. See you in a few days. Don't scare these boys

too badly!" I ran to my boat and went back to the war. I hoped she hadn't noticed my wounded eye.

I sent a message to Duke Henryk that night, telling him that we were holding the Mongols at the Vistula, but we could not do it forever. I begged him to advance now with whatever forces he had. He did not answer.

FROM THE AUTOBIOGRAPHY OF SIR VLADIMIR CHARNETSKI

Count Conrad's instructions had been quite clear. Duke Henryk was at Legnica with his own men, including my father and brothers. Count Conrad had sent him a written apology for not being there, along with six crews of radio operators who worked out of those little seven-man Night-Fighter carts. Duke Henryk was not pleased with us.

Duke Boleslaw was a fifteen-year-old knight who had resolved to defend eastern Poland. He was not on good terms with our liege lord Henryk.

If we dropped back to Legnica, as Duke Henryk wanted, we would be abandoning all of our factories and forts to the enemy. Our women would have to try to save themselves without our help, and the Mongols had long experience taking cities that were defended by both men and women. With women alone, well, I had to side with Count Conrad.

Yet if we fought alone, we would be a third separate force defending Poland. It was necessary that we make contact with Duke Boleslaw and join forces with him. But it was also necessary that we do so in such a manner that he supported our efforts as well as we supported his.

A combined strategy was necessary, and the young fool had rebuffed our earlier attempts at diplomacy. He had heard too many stories about knightly prowess and heroic deeds, and he could see no advantage in saddling himself with a "band of peasant footmen," no matter how large.

Myself, I think Conrad a fool for not using Countess Francine as his emissary, at least on the second try. That woman could talk a hungry dog away from a dead pig. But a young husband is often a fool when it comes to his new wife.

As it was, I left Hell with the biggest Christian army

in all of history at my command, and I didn't know where I was going. All I knew was that Duke Boleslaw was somewhere between Plock and Sandomierz, and that somehow I had to join forces with him and work out some sort of strategy.

I had over two dozen of Anna's daughters, and I put a dozen of them with good riders to search for Boleslaw, men who were scions of the old nobility, men who Duke Boleslaw would not dare scoff at.

The other Big People were needed to run messages along my sixteen-mile-long train, and to lightly screen our flanks. We went on without stopping, and normal horses could never have kept up with us. My old Witchfire, now long in the tooth, was safely in the barns at Three Walls, and my love Annastashia was with our children not far away from him.

I had pulled a few strings and seen to it that my mother, my sisters, and sisters-in-law, along with all our peasants, were also at Three Walls, since I judged it to be our strongest fortification. Rank has its privileges, and I meant my family to be as safe as they could be.

We had practiced this business of continual motion last winter with six dozen carts, and had continued in circles for a month without mishap. Of course, that was with better trained men, men that had been winnowed out to remove the weak and the stupid. With this last class, well, they had been given only four months' training and we hadn't washed out anybody, except for those who had died. Still, their officers had been well trained, and we'd hoped that this would be enough.

Supplies of wood had been waiting for us along the roads since last summer with remarkably little pilferage. Supplies of water were provided. Crews of greasers went down the lines of moving carts, greasing the ball bearings in the wheels. The rails were new, the bridges intact, and we made six dozmiles a day on foot.

Some of the men had a hard time sleeping on the move, but experience had taught us that when they got tired enough, they would sleep.

By dawn of the second day we had passed Cracow, and still I had no word of Boleslaw.

Chapter Eighteen

▲▲▲▲▲▲▲▲▲▲▲▲▲▲▲▲▲▲▲▲▲▲▲

FROM THE DIARY OF CONRAD STARGARD

The battle was not going as well as it had at first. As Tadaos said, they were learning.

They took out their first riverboat with a tree. During the night, they had chopped almost through the trunk of a huge pine tree right on the riverbank, then made a demonstration around it. When the RB14 *Hotspur* attacked, they dropped that tree right across her deck, which nearly smashed her in half. Then they swarmed up the trunk and overpowered the crew.

By the time the RB12 *Insufferable* got there, the Mongols were learning how to use the swivel guns. After an exchange of gunfire, I ordered the *Insufferable* to burn the *Hotspur* with its flamethrower, and she went up quick. I pray to God in Heaven that all our men were dead before that happened.

They had mostly stopped using arrows on us, but they were still using the catapults, and still mounting them on hilltops. We kept on mowing down their crews and they kept on replacing them with a seemingly complete disregard for the lives of their men.

The RB21 *Calypso* got snagged on an underwater obstruction directly in front of one of the catapults. She took more than a dozen direct hits before her crew was taken off by the RB10 *Not for Hire*. By that time, the *Calypso* was completely out of ammunition, and her crew burned her before they left.

We got to avoiding the catapults as much as possible, and at full speed, zigzagging, it wasn't likely for a boat to be hit. It took a very tempting target to get one of our boats to slow down and stay near one spot, a temptation like a concentration of twenty thousand Mongols.

And seeing this, the enemy provided us with targets just to sucker us in! They were willing to spend ten or twenty thousand men just to kill one of our boats with less than three hundred men aboard! Madness!

Then they learned the best way to take out a riverboat, and we lost six boats in front of Sandomierz in less than an hour. Instead of rocks, they started throwing sewn-up ox hides filled with burning oil. The seasoned wood of our boats went up quickly, and usually we weren't able to save many of the crew. They were hurting us.

Yet we killed as many of them that day as we had on the first. I knew the ammunition we were using up, and I knew the conditions under which we were using it, mostly firing into packed crowds at pointblank range! Even the most conservative estimates still came out that we had killed over a million enemy troops! Yet they still kept coming!

We got to spraying our boats with water, inside and out, and this helped some. Wet wood burned more slowly and sometimes it took three or four fire bombs to destroy one of our boats. Fighting an oil fire with water is the wrong thing to do, but we didn't have any alternative. Sometimes enough oil could be flushed off the deck to save a boat. Sometimes not.

But the battle was on, and nobody ever suggested that we should quit. Even if we lost the Vistula, if we could kill enough of them, the rest of the army might have a chance.

By midnight of the fifth day, we were down to nineteen boats.

We couldn't patrol much that night. All of the boats had to go back to East Gate to replenish supplies, and our crews were exhausted, physically and emotionally. At dawn, we found three bridges more than half completed across the river, and we lost four more boats taking them out. The enemy had found a target that we couldn't refuse.

But after that, they were back to throwing rocks at us. Our best guess was that they had simply run out of oil.

Yet there seemed to be as many Mongols as ever, despite the fact that there were long stretches of riverbank strewn with their dead. Near Sandomierz, the enemy dead were more than ten yards deep in some places, and still they kept coming, like lemmings to their deaths.

We were hardly patrolling north of Czersk at all, since our boats were generally more than half out of ammunition by the time they got there. Our strategy, if it could be called that, was no longer to hold the Vistula. We knew we couldn't. It was simply to kill as many of the enemy as possible, and that was easier to do near our base.

Every night, I sent a message to Duke Henryk, begging him to advance with whatever men he had available. And every day, I waited for his reply, in vain.

Interlude Four

I HIT the STOP button.

"Tom, I just can't believe the numbers of Mongols he's fighting."

"Believe it. At the time, those tribes of herdsmen had a population of over eight million, of which three million counted as fighting men. It wasn't as if they had to leave most of their men home to run the factories. Many of the Mongol warriors were on garrison duty, but they got most of their front-line troops from their conquered subjects. Most of those men Conrad was killing weren't Mongols. They were Iranians, Bactrians, Chinese, Russians, and what have you. Conrad mentions that they didn't seem to care if they lost men. They didn't. The troops they were losing were subject populations that were just surplus to them. Throwing them at the Poles was just another way of killing them off. Conrad's estimates were too conservative. All told, he killed over two million men at the Vistula.

"Those Chinese catapults had crews made up of prisoners, many of them Polish peasants. I suppose it's a good thing that Conrad didn't know the truth. He couldn't have done anything but what he did, but it would have been rough on his conscience."

"Wow. I'd always thought that the Mongols won so often because of superior tactics and strategy."

"It didn't take much to have tactics superior to those of the Europeans of the time. Like the Japanese of the same period, Westerners simply never trained as groups. It was all part of the mystique of knighthood. All their training was purely individual training, and one to one, the Europeans were inferior to no one. But their only group tactic was to get in a line and run at the enemy, mostly all at the same time.

"Also, it's a normal human thing to praise your enemy to the skies. It makes you look better if you win and not so bad when you lose.

"I don't know how many times I've heard Americans praise the fighting ability of Germans, for example, despite the fact that in all the time that there was a country named Germany, the Germans won only one small war, fighting little France alone, while losing a lot of big ones that they were foolish enough to start. In fact, the Germans were lousy fighters and their strategy was always absurd. It just feels better to say that you conquered a race of heroes than to admit that you blew away a bunch of damn fools."

"Huh. Another thing. Why didn't the Mongol delegation look Mongolian?" I said.

"Because the Mongolians were originally a Caucasian people, not an Oriental one. They only became Oriental after the conquest of China, thirty years after the time of this story, in our timeline, when for a hundred years, five or six generations, every Mongolian man came home with a dozen Chinese wives. A thing like that changes the blood lines pretty thoroughly. The Mongol of later centuries was racially and culturally a totally different animal. Devout pacifists, most of them."

"Oh."

I hit the START button.

Chapter Nineteen

▲▲▲▲▲▲▲▲▲▲▲▲▲▲▲▲▲▲▲▲▲

FROM THE AUTOBIOGRAPHY OF
SIR VLADIMIR CHARNETSKI

Finally, we know where we are going! My riders didn't find Duke Boleslaw's army, but Count Lambert's flyers did. They were proceeding up the Vistula from the north, and it looked as if we could meet up with them near Sandomierz.

When we were within a day of getting there, I collected a dozen of the Big People and set out ahead of my troops to talk to the duke. We got there at dusk, and were eventually escorted in to see the young man.

"Who were you, again?" Duke Boleslaw said.

"I am Baron Vladimir Charnetski, your grace. We haven't met, but we are related. Two of my aunts married two of your uncles, and one of my second cousins married two of your aunts, once removed, one on your father's side and one on your mother's, after the first one died. Surely you remember your Aunt Sophy and your Aunt Agnes. Well, they're my aunts as well."

Reminding him of our family ties seemed like a good idea. Actually, it was no big thing. I occasionally think that I must be related to everybody. Coming from a vast family helps, sometimes.

"You are the nephew of my Aunt Sophy? I haven't seen the old girl in years! How is she? And what of my Uncle Albert?"

"Just fine when I saw them last, a few months ago. They have thirteen children now, with another on the way."

"Thirteen! How is that possible? Two years ago, they had only nine!"

"Twins, your grace. Two pairs of them."

"No! That's amazing! And my Aunt Agnes?"

"Not so good, your grace. She's had a bad cough for almost a year now, and we're all worried about her."

"I shall include her in my prayers. But look, things are rushed just now, Vladimir. What can I do for you?"

"I think it's more what I can do for you, your grace. I am Hetman of Count Conrad's army. I have a hundred and fifty thousand men coming to join your forces."

"That was true, then? It wasn't some kind of silly joke? He really does have that many men?"

"Of course, your grace! Who could joke about such a thing? Anyway, they'll be here in a day and you can see for yourself."

"Here in a day? That's disaster!"

"How can that be, your grace? We're on your side, after all."

"It's disaster because I can't feed the men I've got now! The food merchants have not come! The cowards have all run away! Even the peasants have gone, and they've taken most of the food with them! I can't feed the twenty-five thousand men I have now! How am I going to feed a hundred fifty thousand more?"

"Oh, don't worry about that, your grace. We have food for a month with us, and all the grain we could ever need at the granaries in the Bledowska Desert. In fact, I can easily feed your entire army. I can have tons of grain here in a few days. Until then, we can feed your men and horses with what we have with us, but more food can be on its way here in an hour."

"How is this possible?"

"Easy. I brought a radio and a radio operator with me. We can send a message in a few minutes to the granary. They have mules and carts there. Why, four dozen carts a day can feed all your men and animals well. It has to come by rail instead of by boat because the boats are busy right now." I sent one of my men out to attend to it.

"Yes, I'd heard there was a battle going on at the Vistula. That's Conrad's riverboats, isn't it?"

"Yes, your grace, and Count Conrad is with them. They are slaughtering incredible numbers of the enemy, but it doesn't look as though they can hold out much longer. They say that tomorrow or the next day, the enemy will break through. Already, more than half of our men on the rivers are dead."

"Half dead? And still they fight?"

"Yes, your grace. They'll fight until they are all gone, every last man of them. I know. I trained them."

"On boats, perhaps. But what can footmen accomplish on a battlefield? Everybody knows that battles are won by men on horses! A footman can do nothing but get trampled."

"Wrong, your grace. Horsemen can do nothing against a mass of trained men with pikes! A pike is six yards long and can knock a knight out of the saddle before his lance can touch the footman. Believe me! We've practiced the very thing many times in the last five years. Furthermore, I have more than twenty thousand guns coming with my troops, and they can kill an enemy at a mile! What I don't have is a force of horsemen, but you do. If we can work together, we cannot be beaten!"

"Vladimir, we'll have to talk more on this. For now, do you swear that food supplies will be here by this time tomorrow?"

"I swear it by all that's holy, your grace."

"Then I'll believe that much at least. I must go and give orders that the last of the food reserves are to be handed out and eaten. That will give the men one good meal, and after that we are at your mercy."

Chapter Twenty

Of all the mistakes I've made, the most serious was to set the number of riverboats at only three dozen. We needed six times that number!

Of course, at the time, I wasn't sure if we would be able to use them at all. The river might have been frozen over, the water level could have been too low to get by some of the rapids, or any one of a number of things could have gone wrong. I don't know. I needed sleep, and there wasn't much of that to be had.

There came a time when we were the only boat north of Sieciechow, on a sector that hadn't been patrolled in days, and we found that the Mongols had completed a bridge across the Vistula. Thousands of enemy troops were rushing across it.

"Baron Tadaos, we've got to take that bridge out."

"Sir, we're out of Molotov cocktails and Halman bombs. We're out of peashooter balls. The flamethrower is exhausted. We have maybe a thousand rounds of swivel gun ammunition left and those troops outnumber ours by hundreds to one. How are we going to do it?"

"We're going to ram it. Captain Targ! Prepare to offload your men and your war carts!"

The captain gave a few orders that had his men scurrying, then ran up to me.

"We're going to attack that bridge, sir?"

"We are, but you are not. We're going to ram that bridge, and doing that will likely sink us. There is no point in your company going down with the boat. It would accomplish nothing, and you are needed elsewhere. You will get your men ashore and fight your way

162

south to Sandomierz. Once there, you will join the garrison and help defend the city."

He stared at me for a long minute.

"Yes, sir. What about my wounded?"

"Take the walking wounded with you. The others will have to be left behind. There's nothing else we can do."

"Yes, sir."

I could see that he wanted to say more, a lot more, but he turned and went to obey his orders.

"Tadaos, I can handle the helm alone, but I'll need one man in the engine room. See if you can find a volunteer, a good swimmer. Then get the rest of your men ready to join Captain Targ."

He looked me straight in the eye and said, "Pig shit!"

Then he spat on my boots.

"Nine years I've been working for you and you don't know me any better than that? You might have taken command of this battle, and done some dumbshit things, but I am still master of this boat and baron of the whole damn River Battalion, or what's left of it anyway! Three-quarters of my men are dead now, and you expect me to turn around and run away? This is *my* damned boat and this is *my* damned duty station and I will damn well stay here until we've won or we're dead! And if you think that any man of mine feels any different, you can damn well ask them yourself!"

Then he turned his back to me and put a new string on his bow, his hand shaking with anger.

I stood there, not knowing what to do. Then I turned to the helmsman, a young kid who looked to be fourteen.

"Get out of here, boy."

"No, sir." His face shield was open and he was crying, tears running down his cheeks. "No, sir," he repeated and continued to stand his post, though the tears must have blinded him.

I turned and went below.

"Baron Piotr, get your men together. I'm going to take out a bridge by ramming. You and your men are going ashore with Captain Targ."

He didn't get up from the map board.

"Yes, sir. We heard something about that. But the fact is that we really don't know whether the boat will sink or not. Ashore, well, we wouldn't be able to do that much good for Sandomierz, since most of us here have been sitting at desks and radio sets for years. We are way out of training. But if the boat does stay afloat, we're going to be needed here to continue coordinating our efforts. We still have eleven boats on the river, after all. So, begging your pardon, sir, but we're staying."

"Damn you, Piotr, that was a direct order!"

"Sir. I am a Radiant Warrior, blessed by God to do His holy work. I am not going to run away now."

I looked around the room. All of the men were trying to look busy.

"This is mutiny!" I shouted.

"Yes, sir, I suppose it is," a mousey-looking radio operator said. "But it's really for the best, sir. Our place is here."

"Damn you all," I shouted and went down to the cargo deck.

One of the crew was flooding the odd-numbered watertight tanks, to give the boat more weight, he explained, and never mind about the buoyancy. He wanted to make sure that we hit the bridge as hard as possible.

"It'd be a shame to waste our last blow at the bastards, wouldn't it, sir?"

The troops were jamming the war carts up against the forward drawbridge, again to increase the impact.

Captain Targ came up to me.

"I regret that I have to report a mutiny, sir. I was afraid that this might happen, but the men won't leave. We're down to less than four full platoons now, and they've seen too many friends die to run away at this point. It would be like dishonoring the dead. Anyway, if the boat hangs up on the bridge, you'll need us to repel boarders, so it's for the best."

"God damn you all to hell! But that bridge still has to go!"

"Of course, sir. Speaking of which, we'd better all get up on deck or we'll miss the show. Tadaos won't be waiting for orders, you know. All platoons! Report on deck! Pass the word!"

"You are all crazy people!" I shouted.

"Yes, sir," a warrior said as he brushed by me, heading for the stairs. "I suppose we are."

I got on deck when we were less than three-gross yards from the bridge. We were going full-speed downriver and the helmsman had us aimed dead center.

The bridge was built rather high for such a temporary thing, and the top of the roadway was higher than the deck of the boat. It was built on wooden tetrahedrons made of oversized telephone poles that looked to be simply set on the river bottom, with the roadway strung on ropes above them.

There were thousands of men and horses on it, rushing across, and while some of them were shouting and pointing at us, they still kept coming. There were men getting on the bridge the moment we hit.

The impact was enough to knock us all over, and we all went skidding across the splintered deck. As I got up, I saw that we had not punched a hole through the bridge, as I had expected. We had actually tipped it over!

The part of it that was right in front of us was already in the river, and the roadway was caught by the current. On both sides of us, like water breaking over a dam, the long flexible bridge was pulled slowly over on its side.

The water was filled with thrashing horses, but with fewer men than you would expect. Not that many of the desert-bred Mongols could swim. Those few that did make it to shore didn't live long. The captain already had the swivel guns in action.

But the bridge was still in one piece and we hadn't gone through it. Tadaos got us into reverse and we backed off the wreckage.

A crewman ran up from below and reported to Tadaos, who turned to me and said, "The bow is smashed up, but we're still afloat. Maybe you ought to see about repairing the damage, sir."

So I went down to play steamboat repairman, again. On the way, I stopped to tell Piotr to radio the other boats that a bridge could be taken out by ramming. He had already done so.

The next morning, after the other boats had taken out four other bridges and lost two of their number doing it, it became strangely quiet, all along the Vistula. Some men thought that we had actually won and the enemy had given up. Others were sure that it was some kind of a trick. The planes reported that the Mongols were concentrating in a dozen groups, each a few miles east of the river, but not going back any farther. It was eerie and quiet for the first time in a week. Even the catapults were unmanned.

Then, the morning after that, an even stranger thing happened. All at once, along the whole river as far as we could tell, enemy troops led their horses down to the frozen banks of the river. Holding on to the horse's tail, they got the animals swimming across the icy waters of the Vistula, pulling the rider behind them.

We steamed through them, drowning hundreds, but they were like lemmings and we couldn't begin to stop them all.

Tadaos looked at it in disbelief.

"If they could do that, why didn't they do it a week ago?"

"There's your answer," Captain Targ said, pointing to the west bank. "Every horse had a man behind it when it went into the water. Only maybe half of those men are still there when they come out."

"Good God in Heaven, you're right! They are deliberately throwing away half of their army just to get across! Who could order such a thing? Why do they do it? Don't they realize that we no longer have anything to fight with?"

We all shook our heads and watched half of the enemy army die.

I don't know. Maybe they ran out of food. Maybe they just got impatient. It's likely they never realized how close to the wire we were. The only thing sure was that the Battle for the Vistula was over and the Battle for Poland had begun.

FROM THE AUTOBIOGRAPHY OF SIR VLADIMIR CHARNETSKI

We set up a system where each platoon "adopted" up to ten of Duke Boleslaw's troops, at least for dining purposes. Later we had to up it to twelve. More of them were coming in every day, and many had had a hard time finding us.

The printshop in Cracow made up thousands of little signs that said where our camp was; one of the Big People ran them to Eagle Nest and the planes were soon dropping them on friendly troops who looked lost. It helped, but as it turned out, it also told the Mongols where to find us. Maybe that wasn't so bad. We wanted to find them.

Grain was arriving daily from the granary, the first batch brought in by a dozen Big People the first day. They'd gone out and taken over the first dozen carts from the slow moving mules, mostly to show Duke Boleslaw that there was nothing to worry about.

Yet for three days there was nothing to do but wait. Patrols were sent out, but they found little. The area was evacuated, since the refugees that had been through a week ago had finally convinced almost every noncombatant to leave.

In hours, we'd set up what amounted to a very large city. Carts were hauled a set distance apart and tarps were zippered over and between them for roofs, just like in a training exercise. Hammocks were slung both under the carts and between them. Cookstoves all had their proper place by the streets, and latrines were dug as per the manual. Oh, everything was covered with freezing mud, but that was only to be expected. After the training we'd put our men through, it was hardly noticed.

Everything was just perfect except for Duke Boleslaw, who couldn't comprehend any sort of tactics except for charging at the enemy and killing them all gloriously.

After days of discussion, persuasion, and pleading, I finally had to threaten to cut off his food supply if he didn't let us take part in the fight. Couching it that way, where he was doing a favor for the people who were feeding him, he came around a little.

The plan we came up with, and after vast trouble got our knightly horsemen to agree with, was that they would locate the enemy and entice them into a trap.

They would charge gloriously in, slaughter droves of the enemy and then pretend to run away. They would lead the Tartars into a huge V-shaped formation of war carts, who would open up on the enemy with their guns. After twenty minutes, the horsemen would come back and finish the Mongols off. Thus, Boleslaw's knights would get both first blood and the kill, while we foot soldiers would be content with an assist. I had to use hunting terms with them because their hunting was organized, even if their warfare wasn't.

One problem with this, as far as the knights were concerned, was that it involved running away from the enemy. I had to convince them that it was a legitimate ruse of war and really a very clever thing for them to do.

I even promised them a beer while we were shooting up Mongols. Actually, I thought that there was a fair chance that they would *have* to run away, since all reports from the Vistula said that we would be vastly outnumbered, but I couldn't tell them that. I just wanted to make sure that they ran in the right direction.

Another problem was in being able to identify friend from foe. This was difficult enough in a hand-to-hand combat, especially since the riverboats had reported that the Mongols had drawn troops from all of their vast realm, and some dressed not too differently from Polish knights. At a distance, from the perspective of a gunner a half mile away, the problem was serious. Foreseeing this difficulty a year ago, I had caused to be made fifty thousand surcoats, each white with a broad red vertical stripe running up both the front and the back. They were easily identifiable at a great distance, and quite nicely made, since our knights insisted on going into battle looking their best.

The knights all admitted to the advantages of wearing identifiable clothing. The trouble was that they all had their own family devises and colors, and these were a particular point of pride with them. Many had taken vows to never fight without their family colors, and so felt honor-bound to refuse to wear the surcoats I'd given them. Days were spent squabbling over this point, until the duke at last ordered all his men to wear the red-and-white surcoats, *over* their own surcoats if necessary, but to wear them or leave the battle. At that, a few of our Knights actually went home, but not many.

Then we got word that the Mongols had crossed the Vistula, and two days after that, that they were camped five miles away.

Chapter Twenty-one

LATE IN the afternoon on the day before the battle, Duke Boleslaw called together all of his leaders, barons and above. This meant that my army was grossly underrepresented, because a conventional baron often had as few as half a dozen knights whereas mine each commanded a battalion of nine thousand men. But there was nothing I could do about it, so we went.

I'd had a big map made up of the area, and after the duke made a short, boisterous speech, I was surprised that he let me come up and give a presentation outlining the situation. Many of these men were not good with maps, but most of them had been on patrols throughout the area and were able to understand the situation.

I showed them how to get from here to there, where our ambush would be set up, what their "retreat" route should be. I stressed the importance of a good night's sleep, and a hot meal in the morning. And I repeated my promise of a beer if the ambush worked out well, having shipped in forty thousand gallons of beer for the purpose. These men had been dry for over a week and I think the beer was a serious inducement.

A priest said mass and we all went to communion. I think every man of mine went into battle in a State of Grace. There are no atheists on the battle lines.

It was dark when Baron Ilya came to me. The weather that had been perfect for the past week, a rare thing at this time of year, was turning bad. Thunder and lightning were crashing in the distance and it looked likely that we would be fighting tomorrow in a cold spring rain. The lightning had been raising hell with the radios since the day before, but fortunately, they had already done their jobs.

I was with the duke and a few of his friends, boys as
young as he was, telling them the story of how Count
Conrad and I had once chopped up a caravan of Teutonic
Knights and rescued a gross of children that otherwise
would have been sold into Moslem slavery. The story
went over well, since despite the fact that the Teutonic
Knights were nominally the vassals of Duke Boleslaw,
they had not come to the battle, saying that they had to
defend the northern borders, which was bullshit. The
duke vowed that if we beat the Mongols, we would fight
the Teutonic Order next. I had the boys in high spirits by
the time the last Crossman raced over the hills with shit
on his breeches. Two against seven, and they were van-
quished without putting a mark on us!

"Sir, may I speak to you for a moment?" Baron Ilya
said.

"Certainly. Is it something that can be discussed before these fine knights?" These boys were more proud of
their knighthood than they were of their higher titles.
Knighthood, after all, had to be earned, while their bar-
onies and all had been inherited.

"I don't see why not, sir, since it's about the invasion.
You know that I lead the battalion of Night Fighters. For
four years, we have been training and learning to fight at
night, in the dark. Well, it's a dark and stormy night out
there, and now's the time to put that training to use! Let
me take my battalion out there and shake them up a bit!
Me and the boys can be back in time to help out with the
battle tomorrow, but give us our chance tonight."

I was about to say, "Certainly, go see what you can
do," but the duke was talking before I could get my
mouth open.

"Just what is it that you plan to do, Baron?"

"Well, your grace, we'll probably surround them in
the dark, send in creepers to take out their sentries, then
roll grenades under their tents and so on. After that,
we'll give them a good shelling to cover our men as they
come out, and maybe slaughter their horses while we're
at it. We'll get some of the bastards and cost them a
night's sleep if nothing better."

The young duke was getting progressively more horri-
fied as Ilya spoke, but Ilya wasn't sharp enough to realize it. Or maybe he was just too bull-headed to care.

"What a disgusting thing to even talk about! Do you

think for a moment that I would allow such a dishonorable thing to be done under my command? I absolutely forbid this cowardly act you propose, and I tell you that you better see a priest and confess again if you want to be in a State of Grace for tomorrow's battle!"

"A State of Grace! I tell you that I am a Radiant Warrior and personally blessed by God!" Ilya exploded. "And cowardly? I want to go alone with only nine thousand men against half a million and you call that cowardly?"

I had to stand up between them to make sure they didn't come to blows. "Ilya, you damn fool! Shut up!" I pushed him toward the door of the tent.

"Forgive him, your grace. He's normally a good man. He's just overwrought. I'll take care of this." I followed Ilya out.

As soon as we were out the door, he said, "Sir—"

"Shut up! Keep your damn face closed until we get back to our camp!"

Thunder was crashing overhead and the rains had started.

Once there, I said, "Don't you have brains enough to not shout at a duke, for God's sake! And especially a duke who could wreck the whole battle plan if he gets a hair up his arse? Didn't your mother teach you anything?"

"I never had a mother. They said the stork brought me."

"I can believe that, judging from your manners! I've worked for almost a week convincing that kid that we're not a bunch of crude peasants and you had to prove otherwise in half a minute!"

"Sorry, sir. What about the raid on the Mongol camp tonight?"

I took a deep breath, letting my anger subside. "Can you do it so that no one from this camp sees you leave and come back?"

"In this weather, sir? Easy! The duke's sentries will never see us."

"Then do it. But don't get caught, or the duke will hang us both!"

"Don't worry, sir. It's just like stealing a pig."

AS TOLD BY BARON ILYA THE BLACKSMITH

"So like I was saying, we got us permission to make a little night raid, even if it was sort of an underhanded one. I got the boys out of the sack, fed, and called together. We'd been sleeping during the day to stay in shape, and doing night guard duty until we'd done more than our share by the night before. I'd timed the thing just right.

"The camp was quiet when we left, pulling our small night-fighter carts. See, most of the troops fight out of big, forty-three man platoon carts, but in the dark, there's no way that you can keep track of that many men around you. The most is about six, and you've got to know who your own men are, because everybody else is likely the enemy! So we use a small lance-sized cart, and right then they was unloaded of everything but the gun, ammunition, and grenades that each one carried. We don't use pikes or halberds. In the dark, them weapons ain't worth firewood! But we was pretty good with the knife, the garrote, and the grenade.

"I thought we was clear of the camp when we came on an outlying sentry, and you know it had to be one of Boleslaw's men.

"'Hold! Who goes there?'

"'Baron Ilya,' I says. 'Beer run.' It was the first thing that came into my head. Never mind that I had nine thousand men coming up behind me.

"'Beer? There's two dozen big carts of beer in the camp!'

"'Yeah, but that's what our hetman promised you horse jockeys. Now we're going out to get enough for the foot soldiers, too.'

"'What, all that beer for us alone? Well, carry on then.'

"I don't figure that man ever knew he had a creeper right behind him and a garrote over his head. I sure would have hated to do him in, but I did promise Vladimir that nobody would see us leave. If he reported that I went on a beer run, well, wouldn't nobody take it seriously.

"We had scouts ahead planting markers in the ground, sticks split so the white side showed toward us. There

wasn't no problem finding the Mongol camp. The only
surprise was how big that sucker was! It was fully four
miles across and they had fires going all around it. No
way we could surround this thing the way I told the
duke.

"'Fire line, two yards apart, a gross yards from the
pickets, pass it on.' I says that would put us a quarter
way around the camp, and the carts split off by companies to either side of me, forming wings a mile and a half
long. The carts were tipped up on their sides and the
guns mounted. They wouldn't be needed for a while, but
it's always a good idea to be ready. The signal strings
were strung up along both wings, and I waited.

"I got my telescope out and looked over the enemy
sentries. Dumbshits, the lot of them! They was sitting
around the fires, staring at the fires and talking. A captain with any brains posts his men so the fires show in
the enemy's eyes, not your own. Those men were about
to get a very expensive education in night-fighting.

"'Plan eight, red and white flares. Pass the word,' I
whispered to both wings and to the sentry behind me
who was sorting out the companies.

"It was a while before we got settled into position, but
I wasn't worried none. The thunder and rain covered
most everything. We was being quiet mostly out of habit.
Them sentries weren't looking for trouble, but that
wasn't going to help them none. Trouble had just come
looking for them!

"It would have been nice if I could have gone in with
most of the other men, but we'd proved time and again
that the leader had best stay back and direct things, so
that's the way I had to play it. That's one of Count
Conrad's big problems. He always has to do everything
hisself, and there ain't nobody can do everything, not
and do it right.

"I got four tugs on the right-hand string, saying that
the right wing was ready, and a few minutes later, the
left-hand string pulled four times.

"I gave both strings three long, slow pulls and
watched as the first-string creepers went out. These
were the one best lance from each platoon, and we had a
lot of contests to see who that lance was. They figured it
was an honor to be the ones that went out ahead of the
others and killed the sentries real quiet like.

"I saw the men in front of me in position, but I gave it a few more minutes to make sure that everybody else was ready. Then I lit off a small, red rocket. Count Conrad had made these things as a festival toy, but once I saw one, I knew it was just the thing to signal men in the dark.

"If any of the Mongol sentries saw it, they were looking at the rocket and not the men behind them. Just like a machine, six of my men came up behind six of theirs and slipped garrotes over their heads. The wires were pulled tight and most of them heathens didn't hardly even kick around. Those that did got knifed, but most of them got to die without getting their clothes bloodied. The sentry fires were smothered, usually by piling dead Mongols on them and stuffing the edges with mud and dirt, and it was time for phase two.

"I pulled the signal strings again and five more lances from each platoon went out, leaving only the gunners behind. I put a big white rocket in the launcher to be ready in case of any commotion, but I rested back with my telescope for about an hour and let the men do what they were trained for. They were going through the enemy camp, wreaking any silent mayhem they could do, and that was a lot. Those boys went out with six garrotes each, and they all complained later that they could have used more.

"There was a lot of knife work, too. You take sleeping troops a tent at a time, cut every throat at the same instant without a sound, then go on to the next tent. The trick is to get men on their stomachs laying all around the tent, ready to go under it. Then one man walks in the front door, calm as he can, and lights a pocket lighter. Before the sleepers know what's happening, they all have an extra mouth and the light goes out. It takes training and practice, but any job worth doing is worth doing right. I could see quick flashes as tents lit up for a moment and then were dark.

"There were enemy troops up and around, but our men was all walking natural and they weren't much noticed. Those Mongols must have had fifty different kinds of people there, and didn't none of them speak the same language. They all figured that if you was in the camp, you must be on their side, so they each had to learn different on their own. It stayed quiet for the longest time.

"One of the rules was that the most important men in the camp usually had the biggest tents, and these were usually in the center of the camp. When there are more than a dozen in a tent, it gets pretty hard to kill them all without somebody on one side or another making a noise, so doctrine was to frag the big tents. Course, the big ones often had sentries of their own, a sure tip-off that you was in officer country, so the sentries had to be taken out first, but we were pretty good at that sort of thing. When a man's upright, a garrote's the thing to use.

"You could always roll a grenade under a tent, but the effect was better if it was up off the ground. The best way was to slit the tent, put in the grenade dangling from a string with a fish hook on the end and with the wick hanging outside, and then light it with your pocket lighter when the signal went up.

"It was still awfully quiet down there and I checked the traveling clock we had with us. Yeah, it had been over an hour, and it was one of Conrad's double-sized hours at that. Some of the boys would be getting real antsy about now, so it was time for the fireworks.

"I lit off the big white rocket flare, which exploded pretty white streamers over the enemy camp so nobody could miss it.

"In a few seconds, there were explosions all over the Mongol camp, and most especially in the center of it, I was pleased to note.

"I sat back for another two-twelfths of an hour watching the mayhem through my telescope. The boys were really ripping them up. Each man had had two small four-pound grenades in his pack, as well as a big twelve-pounder, and didn't none of that ordinance get carried back to our firing line.

"As the first of our men got back, puffing and running with the big white crosses they'd opened up on their chests so our gunners would know not to shoot them, I started pulling on the signal strings again.

"The gunners generally let loose with a few rifle grenades first, in part to start some additional fires to shoot by, but mostly because they didn't get to shoot them very often, except for dummies, and they're kind of fun.

"A few fires were started near a horse park and that

attracted some gunfire until the surviving horses stampeded through the Mongol camp and out of sight.

"More and more of our men were making it back, but the Mongols themselves hadn't acted like we was here yet. One of my worst nightmares had the enemy and our men running out all mixed together, and the gunners having to shoot them all down or be killed themselves. But that didn't happen. The enemy was real slow on the uptake. Me, I figure that was caused by the way we killed most of their officers, but there ain't no way to prove it. Only it figures, you know?

"We were almost all back, those that were coming back, anyway, before the invaders got together enough to attack us. There was thousands of them on horseback, all yelling and screaming and running into each other, since they had the muzzle flashes coming in at them and that will blind a man or beast in the dark.

"Then we started doing jerk-fire shooting. That's where each gunner fires just after the man to his left does. This lets him aim by the muzzle flashes of the guns that just went off, so the field is almost perfectly lit up. But the men out there that you're shooting at look like they're jumping and jerking around real funny. Conrad explained it to me once, but I never did figure out what he was talking about.

"From out in front of it, when you're being shot at, it's just plain scary. It looks like there's these big bright moving things streaking from your right to your left, and there isn't a horse that will stay around it. Them that wasn't dead took off and their riders went with them.

"After that, they tried charging us on foot, but we shot that one up just as bad or even a little worse. There was dead bodies as thick as a carpet from their camp to almost our lines. I tell you that a man could have walked on dead Mongols the whole way and never stepped on the ground, they was that thick.

"But we were getting low on ammunition and dawn wasn't that far away. If they knew how few of us there was, they could have walked all over us, and anyhow, I told the hetman that nobody would see us coming back. I signaled a pullout.

"Slow burning flares were stuck into the ground in front of our positions, to maybe make them think we was still there. Then we pulled out in the reverse order that we came, and some of the gunners kept on firing right up to the end. We were halfway back, walking in the rain, when I got the butcher's bill. Four hundred fifty-five missing and likely dead, and damn few wounded. Well, in that kind of a fight, if you were hurt bad, you just didn't get out. We lost a whole lot less than I thought we would, but even so, odds were that a lot of those men still out there were friends of mine.

"That same sentry was there when we got back near camp. I guess the duke's men weren't much on relieving the night guard.

"'You didn't get the beer!' he says.

"'Naw, the place was closed.'

"'Damn shame. Maybe we'll have some left over for you.'

"'You'd better.' What a dumbshit, I thought."

Chapter Twenty-two

^^^^^^^^^^^^^^^^^^^^^^^^^^^^^^^^

FROM THE AUTOBIOGRAPHY OF SIR
VLADIMIR CHARNETSKI

I talked to Baron Ilya in the cold rain at dawn. He reported a successful mission and requested more ammunition, most of his being exhausted. I put his little carts in back of the north line as a backup in case we were attacked there on the wrong side. He could scrounge ammunition from the carts near him, but I didn't want to do anything official about replenishing him, not when I had just disobeyed a direct order from the duke.

The radios were still picking up nothing but static, so I had all but two of them packed away, and their crews put on the battle line. I didn't know what was happening on the Vistula or in the rest of the country, but I told myself that it wasn't important now. This day's business could be done with horns and signal flags. The worth of all that I had done in the last five years would be decided today in the time of a few hours and the space of a few square miles.

We ate a hot breakfast in the dark, and the camp city was quickly taken down. Everything not essential to combat was packed neatly on the ground. The carts were empty except for arms, ammunition, and a light lunch.

I led the men in the sunrise service, even though we couldn't see the sun, and we moved out.

I'd picked the spot for the ambush carefully. It was a long, low valley with a small creek running down the center. The hills were gentle enough so that our war carts could be easily pulled over them, but they provided enough of a backdrop so that the carts would not be too

obvious against a skyline. The valley averaged a mile
wide and was ten miles long.

As each war cart got into position, the top was taken
off, spare pike shafts were set into the armored side of
the cart, and the yard-and-a-half wide-armored top was
slung out to one side as a shield for the pikers. The four
great, caster-mounted wheels were unlocked from their
fore and aft traveling position and locked spread out to
the sideways moving combat position. Pikes and halberds were broken out and distributed. Six gunners
climbed in each cart and mounted their weapons. The
thirty-six pikers and axemen snapped into their pulling
harnesses and tugged the cart into its final position. Well
coordinated, this took less than a minute. Then they
stood and waited in the rain.

Our war carts stretched more than six miles along on
each side of the valley and flared out at the end like a
funnel mouth, two miles across. Sentries were posted
behind us and the Big People were scouting to insure
that we wouldn't be taken unawares. We were all in position by midmorning, and then there was nothing to do
but wait.

Duke Boleslaw's horsemen had left at dawn, and I
was worried about them. They were such a disorganized
mass that I wasn't sure whether they could all stay together enough to get a decent charge at the enemy. But
there was nothing I could do but wait and worry.

I was worried about Count Conrad as well. I hadn't
heard from him in days, what with the problems with the
radios, and in this rain, the planes couldn't fly safely, so
I lacked that source of information as well. Until the day
before, I had always known what was happening. Now,
just as all things were coming to a climax, I was suddenly all alone. It seems strange to say that, since I had
about me the finest and largest army in Christendom, but
it was true.

After an hour of tense waiting, I saw one of our planes
flying low toward us from the north, and then I saw another right behind it. Soon, there were twenty of them,
and they circled low over the valley. Then they proceeded to land!

This was crazy! Planes landed only at Eagle Nest!
Anywhere else and they couldn't take off again! Not unless we built a catapult on the spot. Furthermore, they

had landed in the very place where we were expecting a horde of Mongols to come charging in at any moment! Those planes were a big sign that said "Mongol, run away!"

I had my Big Person, Betty, run me down to the first plane that had landed, its propeller still spinning and its engine making enough noise to scare away a saint.

"What the Hell are you doing here?" I shouted.

The engine stopped and Count Lambert got out, wearing his gold-plated armor.

"Baron Vladimir, fortunately I couldn't hear that, but you must learn to speak more politely to your betters," he said.

"But my lord, you have landed right in the middle of an ambush! The Mongols could be coming in any time now!"

"No, it will be another half-hour at the least. We saw them fighting Duke Boleslaw's men three or four miles from here. But have your men move these planes if they are in the way. Don't worry about hurting them, they'll never fly again. Be careful of the engines. They're expensive and they can be salvaged."

All of this made no sense to me, but I galloped to our lines and gave the necessary orders to get those planes hidden. By the time I got back to the count, a squire had ridden out leading two dozen war horses, all saddled and ready for combat. This crazy stunt had been planned!

"My lord, what is all this about?" I said.

Lambert put on a red-and-white surcoat and swung into the saddle. "About? Well, you could hardly expect us to miss the final battle, could you? For over a week now, we've been in the air, watching you and Conrad garner all the glory while we could only look on! We have taken some heavy losses doing it, too! You see those twenty planes there? Well, there were forty-six of them to start!"

"That many? What happened to them?"

"Three crashed on landing at Eagle Nest. Two were seen flying too low over the enemy and were brought down by arrows. One flew into a thundercloud and we found the pieces later. The rest, we don't know. They just didn't come back."

"My God. I didn't realize it was that bad, my lord.

But why leave the rest of them here? Surely you can't fly them out of here!"

"No, of course not. But don't you see? They're not needed anymore! They've done their job! The Mongols are all here. The army is here. The whole affair will be settled right here! If we are to get our share of the glory, we have to get it now! As to the planes, well, we have wood, glue, and cloth in abundance. We can build more later."

"But, but does Count Conrad know of this?"

"Who gives a damn about Conrad? Look, boy, Conrad is sworn to me, not me to him! But just now there's a battle to get to. The plan's still the same? Lead them through here, then come back in a bit for the kill?"

"Yes, my lord."

"Good!" He waved to his mounted aviators. "Let's go! *To war!*"

And they rode out of the valley.

Maybe the planes weren't needed, but as I saw it, things were still very much afloat. Who could tell what we would need and what we would not! I was almost glad that the radios weren't working. I would have hated to have to report *this* piece of insanity to Count Conrad!

We got the planes cleared away and hidden, and then it was wait and worry time again.

It was approaching noon, and I was wondering if I should feed the men when an outrider on one of the Big People came and reported that the battle was coming our way. I signaled "Ready" and "Hide," and could see the lines tighten up, the pikes drop, and the flag poles go down as soon as the message was relayed.

After a while, I could see our horsemen coming in exactly as planned, if a little late. They were in surprisingly good order, all things considered, and Duke Boleslaw himself was at their head, surrounded by his youthful group of friends. He was going a bit slower than a full frightened gallop, I suppose to insure that all of his men could keep up. A few Mongols had gotten out in front of him, but he wisely ignored them.

He came right down the middle of the valley, splashing over the little half-frozen creek twice just to keep going in a straight line. The kid was doing good! And after him came the vast horde of the enemy, which outnumbered Boleslaw's forces by at least twenty-to-one, galloping in a ragged mob and not noticing in the least the army waiting for them! It was working!

My station was at the mouth of the funnel, and as soon as the last of the Mongols went through, I advanced both our wings to seal it off. As soon as the duke's men were out of the trap at the other end, my second in command, Baron Gregor Banki, would close the small end and open fire, which would signal us to do the same, and the war would be nearly won!

The ends of the wings had more than a mile to go to close the gap, so this took a while. As I followed them in, another outrider reported that Count Conrad was arriving with what was left of the river battalion, forty-one war carts out of the two hundred sixteen he'd started with! I sent the man back with an invitation for Conrad to plug the gap in the center. After all that they had done, those men deserved the honor.

This delayed things a bit, but there wasn't an enemy in sight and I knew we could afford the time. I mounted Betty and rode around to my liege lord. I could safely leave my post because now there wasn't a single thing for me to do! When the shooting started, everybody would join in. I was no longer needed.

Count Conrad had a dirty bandage over his right eye and he looked horribly tired and old!

"My lord, it's good to see you! You look like you need this!" I threw him my wine skin. It wasn't exactly a regulation part of the uniform, but rank has a few privileges.

"Thank you." He took a long pull. "Things go as planned?"

"Perfectly, my lord. We're only waiting for Gregor to close his end and start shooting. It should be any time now."

"Good. We're out of ammunition. Can you supply some?"

"Of course, my lord!"

I gave the orders and runners started coming in with crates of swivel gun rounds. As we waited, I told my liege about Baron Ilya's night raid, and about Duke Boleslaw's reaction to it.

"You did right," he said. "At least, that's what I would have done."

Then I had to tell the count about his air force, or rather his lack of one.

"Damn," he said, looking more weary than ever. "If we live through this, I swear either I'm going to get control of Eagle Nest, or I'm going to build another one."

When Conrad's forces were supplied, we still hadn't heard from the small end of the funnel. Then horsemen started coming at us, but they weren't all Mongols! There were Polish knights mixed in with them, and soon a vast, slashing and hacking free-for-all was going on right before our eyes! Something had gone very, very wrong.

The signal flags started wagging, sending the same message to us around both sides of the ambush:

> BOLESLAW HAS NOT LEFT THE TRAP, IT SAID. ONE OF HIS YOUNG FRIENDS FELL TO A MONGOL ARROW. BOLESLAW TURNED BACK AT THE LAST INSTANT AND WENT TO AID HIS FRIEND. THE DUKE'S HORSEMEN ALL FOLLOWED THEIR LIEGE BACK INTO THE MONGOL FORCES. THEY ARE NOW ALL MIXED TOGETHER. WE HAVE CLOSED THIS END BUT WE CANNOT SHOOT WITH-OUT KILLING OUR OWN MEN. BULLETS GO RIGHT THROUGH ENEMY AND THEN CONTINUE THROUGH OUR MEN WHO ARE BEHIND THEM. WHAT SHOULD I DO? GREGOR BANKI.

"That's a good question he asks, my lord. What should we do?" I said.

"I don't know. What can we do? Nothing, that's what! We just have to let those crazy knights get themselves killed."

"Do you want to take command, my lord?"

"Me? No. This is your show. You do what you think is best. I screwed things up enough on the river. Now it's your turn."

"But I had heard that you had killed vast numbers of the enemy," I said.

"Perhaps, but look around you. Of the men I led into battle, not one in five is still fit to march. How can that be called a victory? I made mistakes, many mistakes. You have command here, Vladimir. Try to do better than I did."

"Yes, sir."

I signaled "Defend Yourself," "Give Aid," and "Stand

By," which meant they should not let themselves be hurt, they should help out where they could, and then they should wait for further orders. What else could I tell them?

A half-hour later, I told them to break out lunch and eat in rotation, one lance per platoon at a time.

FROM THE DIARY OF CONRAD STARGARD

In front of us, like on a movie screen, the Polish nobility was slugging it out with the Mongol horsemen. Our men were hopelessly outnumbered, but they were giving a good account of themselves. They had some advantages.

They were generally bigger and stronger than their adversaries, and had much better arms and armor than the enemy. Most of them had been equipped out of my factories, and the poorest page had at least a full set of chain mail, doubtlessly a hand-me-down, but better than what many knights wore ten years ago. The Mongols, on the other hand, were wearing whatever they could steal or scavenge off of various battlefields, and many of them had no armor at all.

The Polish horses were considerably larger and more powerful than those of their adversaries, and in shock combat, this counted for a lot.

But mostly, the western knight was trained to fight as an individual, both on the tourney field and in battle. This was often to their disadvantage in combat with the more sophisticated easterners, but it wasn't that way today. The Mongols were showing none of their vaunted organization and discipline. If anything, they seemed more disorganized than we were. Perhaps Ilya's men really had fragged every Mongol officer.

Furthermore, our men could come to our lines when tired or thirsty or wounded. Any Mongol who got close enough to offer a clear shot was killed.

Our men had some advantages, but they weren't enough to offset a numerical disadvantage of twenty-to-one.

One by one, the pride of the Polish nobility was dying.

Chapter Twenty-three

▲▲▲▲▲▲▲▲▲▲▲▲▲▲▲▲▲▲▲▲▲▲▲▲▲▲▲▲▲▲▲

THE SLAUGHTER in the cold rain went on for hours, and watching it and not being able to do anything to help was one of the most frustrating things that I have ever done. It was equally rough on the men of the army who were looking helplessly on.

A group of women came by driving mules that were pulling a standard army tank cart filled with beer. They filled all our cooking pots with it.

"Compliments of the Sandomierz Whoremasters Guild," one saucy wench said. "Just be sure and save half of it for them fine young knights out there doing all the fighting!"

"What is the Whoremasters Guild doing with an army tank cart?" I asked.

"Oh, they was just sitting around, going to waste, when all them handsome knights was thirsty," she said. "We figured we'd do us a public service, being in that business, you know. Servicing the public, that's our job!"

"They? How many of my tank carts did you take?"

"Oh, there was maybe two dozen of them, and the mules wasn't being used either. But *your* carts? Then you must be that Count Conrad they talk about. You're the size they tell. Say, you ain't mad about this beer, are you? I mean, it ain't like we stole it to sell or something."

"No, I guess I'm not mad, and I suppose the men need a drink. But look, once you share out the beer, come back with that thing filled with water, all right?"

"Right-o, your lordship. Say, why don't we never see you around any? A man your size would be a fun one!"

"I'm happily married. But by the same token, what

are you doing being a prostitute? You know the army is always hiring women as well as men. You could get a good job and maybe find a real knight of your own."

"What? Leave the guild? Say, my master'd whup me for even thinking about it!"

"You don't have to put up with that sort of thing! No whoremaster ever dared beat a member of the army!"

"What? Not whup me? Then how'd I know he still cared about me? Whoops! The cart's four places down already! Got to run, your lordship! *Ta-taaa!*"

And with that, she waved and ran away. I don't think I'll ever understand some people.

Well, at least I could understand the men around me. They wanted to go out there and kill somebody! Some of them had been training for this day for years, and now there was nothing they could do! We had over twenty thousand swivel guns pointed at the enemy, and they were useless! A bullet fired would go right through the Mongol it was aimed at, and kill some Christian who happened to be fighting behind him! It was all my fault, too. I made those guns too powerful! I'd had visions of Mongols charging at us six ranks deep, and our guns ploughing furrows through them. I never imagined anything like this!

One of my men looked up at me from the ranks in front of my cart and shouted, "Dammit! Do something!"

He was as insubordinate as hell, yet he had expressed the common feeling, and I had to answer him.

"Do what? What can we do? If we advance, we'd only squeeze them closer together, and our knights need room to fight in! If we shoot, we kill our own men as well as the enemy!"

"They're dying anyway!" another man yelled.

"Then better they should die at Mongol hands and not ours! If the knights would just get out of there, we could end this in minutes! This is their decision! There's nothing we can do!"

That didn't satisfy anybody, but there was nothing they could answer. I looked away from the slaughter and saw a strange thing.

A knight rode along the backs of our carts, not in the trap at all. He wore gold-washed chain mail of good quality but of the old-style. His barrel-type helmet was gold-washed as well, with trim that looked to be solid gold.

He was staring at the war carts and guns like a country peasant visiting the city for the first time. But what really caught my notice was his horse. It was pure white, but aside from that, it was absolutely identical to my mount Anna! The same gait, the same facial features, the same everything!

I had my face plate open when I said, "Can I help you, sir?"

He looked at me and I thought for a moment that he was going to fall off his horse! After a bit, he said in very broken Polish, "What . . . what this all is? Guns and plate armor! Here? Now! How?"

Now it was my turn to be startled, for he spoke with a strong *American English accent*!

"Just who are you?" I asked.

"I am Sir Manuel la Falla," he said.

"In a pig's eye!" I said to him in Modern English.

He almost fell over again, but a commotion out on the battlefield distracted me from talking further with the man.

Count Lambert was coming toward me with the battle behind him. There was a Mongol spear in his gut, one of those sharp, thin, triangular things that could pierce our armor. He was swaying in the saddle, and his horse was staggering as well. As I watched, horse and man collapsed to the ground not a hundred yards in front of me.

I jumped down from the war cart and pushed my way through the pikers. Tapping two of the front-rank axemen and motioning them to follow me, I vaulted over the big shield and ran to Lambert's aid.

I swear that my only intention was to drag my liege lord back to safety. I never meant to cause what happened. But that strange, crazy foreign knight, whatever he was, ran out after me, waving at the lines to advance and shouting *in English*!

"Come on you apes! Over the top! Up and at 'em! Chaaaarrrrrge!"

Somehow, the man had gotten one of our red-and-white surcoats. I suppose they thought he was obeying my orders, for I was out in front of him. They couldn't have understood a word of what he said, but his meaning was clear and *it was what they all had wanted to do for hours*!

From a hundred thousand voices came a roar!

"FOR GOD AND POLAND!"

All along the lines, a hundred and twenty thousand pikers and axemen went up and over the shields and staged an impromptu infantry charge on three times their number of cavalry!

Interlude Five

▲▲▲▲▲▲▲▲▲▲▲▲▲▲▲▲

TOM HIT the STOP button.

"Yeah, that was me! I think I led the biggest infantry charge in history, right there!"

"To me it looked like a damn fool thing to do!" I said. "An infantry charge on cavalry? That's unheard of!"

"It was when I did it, but it happened another time maybe three hundred years later, during one of the wars between the English and the Scots, for about the same reason and with about the same outcome.

"You see, it was getting late in the day, and if the thing wasn't settled by sunset, those Mongols might have broken out. All those horsemen on both sides had been fighting for at least eight hours without a break, and the Mongols hadn't gotten much sleep the night before. And a horseman has it all over a footman, *providing the horse can move*! Once those pikers got them pushed back and jammed together, they were dog meat!"

"Hey, if you'd just gotten there, how did you have the time to figure all that out?"

"Well, I got there late. That was obvious, so I did a one day switchback so I could be involved in the whole battle. I was with Duke Boleslaw when he rode out that morning! I was there for the whole thing! Of course, I was taking stim pills to keep up with those youngsters, but that doesn't count. I *am* over eight hundred years old, after all. Then when Conrad went over the shield, I was back by his lines. I dismounted and led the charge."

"So you're pretty proud of yourself, huh?"

"I saved the day! There's only one thing wrong, though. The background scenery isn't right. That place doesn't look like Chmielnick at all. I know that area!

189

That looks like it's about twenty miles west of Sandomierz, and the battle wasn't fought there!"

"Well, it was fought there now!"

I hit the START button.

Chapter Twenty-four

FROM THE DIARY OF CONRAD STARGARD

I stared in horror at the men running past me. The Mongols still vastly outnumbered us, and what had started so well would now end in absolute disaster! All because of Duke Boleslaw's stupidity and that crazy foreigner, our army would be destroyed, our country overrun, and our families all murdered! I yelled, I shouted but no one paid any attention. With all the noise and every man shouting, I doubt if any of them heard me. There was nothing I could do, and again, I was helpless.

But there was something I could do for Lambert, so I did it. I went over to him.

In falling from his horse, he had rolled clear of the animal, but that was the most expensive roll in his life.

"Ah, Conrad. I see that you have your medical kit with you as always. It seems that I need it for a change. Damnable thing! The first time in ten years I get a chance to get into a fight and this has to happen!" Lambert gestured toward the spear in him.

"See? You should have left the fighting to me. I only got an arrow in the eye." I ripped open and laid aside his red-and-white surcoat, unlatched his breastplate, and pulled it off. The Mongol spear came with it, dripping with blood and gore. Then I opened his gambezon and shirt, and surveyed the mess. There was a gash in his stomach as wide as both my hands, and deep.

"What? That little hole in my armor and that mighty slash in my gut? How can that be?"

"It was when you fell, Lambert. The spear spun around in there. The edges on those damned things are sharp."

"Well, that's it, then, and a sad ending it is! Done in by my own horse and my own peasant!"

"My lord? How so? I know your horse was wounded. I saw it stagger."

"He wasn't wounded. He was drunk! A half hour ago, I went to our lines for a drink. One of my own peasants, only he's a knight now, came out and gave me a well needed beer. When I asked for some water for my horse, he said they had none, though they had plenty of beer. I hated to see Shadowfax suffering, for he had served me well this day. I was in too much of a hurry to take him down to the stream, so I bid the man give my horse some beer, and he did, using his own helmet as a horse bucket. It was strong beer, and that was my downfall."

"My lord, this wound . . ."

"I know. I can see it. There's shit mixed in with the blood, so my gut is cut open. It will fester and I'm a dead man. Still, it's not a bad way to die, on a battlefield. Better than growing feeble and blind and impotent with old age, and that's all I had to look forward to. It was getting so sometimes I could only take one wench a day, and the virgins were getting hard to service. No, this is for the best."

"Shall I find you a priest, my lord?"

"In a while, in a while. I have some time left. I can feel it. I'm glad you're here. There are some things I want to talk to you about. I was right about your origins, wasn't I? You really were sent here by Prester John to save us from the Mongol invasion, weren't you?"

What could I say? "Of course, my lord. You alone had it figured out from the beginning." I lied, but it was a good lie.

"I knew it! But tell me, why did he only send one man?"

"Well, my lord, there was only the one invasion."

"What! Oh, ha-ha! Ooooh!" Suddenly his face went white. "Oh. It's like the old joke. It only hurts when I laugh. Well. Then there's my estate. I'm minded to give my daughter my lands in Hungary, which are twice as large as those in Poland, and richer, though not so well run, but I don't want you to be saddled with a liege lord who is whoever she marries. I haven't had time to pick the man! He might not treat my peasants properly or even service the girls at the cloth factory as they deserve, and that would be a shame and a waste! So I'm giving my Polish lands to you. Don't look so surprised or say anything. I've thought this out and that's the way that I want it. I've had it written all up and Duke Henryk himself has approved it."

"Thank you, my lord," Even though it didn't mean anything, it was a nice thought. I'd never inherit that land. As soon as the Mongols broke through our footmen, I'd die right here next to Lambert. Still, it was a nice thought.

"Just take good care of my vassals and my peasants, and see to it that the girls are well loved. They need that."

"We all do, my lord."

"That's God's truth! But do you swear it?"

"On my honor by all that is holy, my lord."

"Good. Well, be off with you, then. You've got a battle to fight. And if you see a priest, send him by. I'll spend my time getting my soul together. Be off now. No. Wait. You better take these. I won't be needing them anymore." He gave me back the binoculars I had given him on the first day we met. I took them. It would have been rude to do otherwise.

"Good-bye, my lord Count Lambert Piast, and may God bless you and love you."

I stood up, tears in my one eye, and looked out at the battlefield. The fight was a good ways away, more than a mile, and I started walking toward it. I heard a familiar whinny behind me and turned around.

"Anna?"

She nodded YES. She was looking at my wounded eye.

"Yes, I got hurt a bit, but it's all right. I'm glad you're here! But come on, girl, there's work to be done!"

I mounted and we rode to battle.

A half-mile later, I saw the strange, gold-clad knight back on his white horse, fighting two Mongol horsemen who had somehow slipped through the line of Polish footmen. I didn't know who or what he was, but he was wearing one of our surcoats now and he seemed to be on our side. I drew my sword and we galloped to his aid.

I was almost there when one of the Mongols threw one of those deadly spears at him. At a dozen yards, it flew straight through his eyeslit and the point punched its way out the back of his helmet!

I caught one Mongol unawares and chopped his head off before the other saw me. The second was just recovering from his deadly throw, and I got in a blow on his horse's neck. One does not have to fight fair with one's social inferiors.

He spilled on the ground and I took his right arm off at the shoulder on the next round. That was enough. Let the bastard bleed to death.

I dismounted near the strange knight. I was sure he was dead, but head wounds are sometimes surprising. People have recovered from the damndest things. I had to pull out the spear before I could remove his helmet and I had to put my foot on that helmet to pull the spear out.

There was no breathing, no pulse. The spear had made a ghastly hole where his left eye had been and I think it had severed the spinal column as well. He was dead. There was something familiar about the man, but I couldn't place him. The weird thing was his haircut. He was completely bald back to the top of his head. Even his eyebrows and eyelashes were gone, yet there were little cut-off hairs laying loose all over his face.

The white horse was acting shocked and nervous. From down here, it was obvious that she was a mare. "Are you one of Anna's people, like this girl here?" I said. She didn't respond, but then I remembered her rider speaking English. I repeated my question in that language, and she nodded YES, exactly as Anna does.

"Then I think it would be best if you came along with us. Your friend here is dead. There is nothing we can do for him," I said in my rusty English.

She nodded YES.

Interlude Six

I HIT the STOP button.

"Tom, are you all right?" I said. He was staring fixedly at the screen, his eyes bulging, and he was making gurgling sounds.

"What? No. I'm not all right, you idiot! I'm dead! Don't you realize that we just saw me die?"

"But you know that this is some kind of alternate reality. It's not exactly real."

"It's exactly as real as the reality around us! Is that some *third* me who died out there? Or am I going to go back there later, subjectively, and die there in my own future?"

"Damned if I know, but if I were you, I'd never go to thirteenth-century Poland again!"

His hand was shaking as he pushed the COMM button and ordered a double martini. A naked serving wench brought it in instantly and he gulped it down. Then he sent her back for another, and she was out of the room and back in so fast that she must have passed herself in the hallway. Of course, that sort of thing happens all the time around here. I ordered a beer and she made a third trip.

"It didn't really happen that way," he said, staring at a blank wall. "That spear only glanced off my helmet. I saw it coming and I ducked!"

"It looks like this time you forgot to duck. Tom, why weren't you better protected than that?"

"I was! I always am! I wear a bio-engineered fungus coating called a TufSkin."

I was familiar with the stuff. I wear it myself, like

most people. It's not only a cheap insurance policy but it makes shaving a breeze.

The stuff isn't noticeable, but it has these billions of tiny interlocking plates made of crosslinked tubular graphite, the toughest substance known. If you are hit from the outside, on impact and in microseconds, tiny muscles interlock those plates and give you an armor equivalent to a quarter inch of tool steel. Of course, when it does that, it shears off your hair in the process, but that's a small price to pay!

Tom was still talking in a dazed sort of way. "The only place it can't cover is the eyes, but the helmet I was wearing should have sensed that spear coming and slammed shut the eyeslits! Or I could have blinked! I should have been completely safe!"

"I guess this time there was some sort of mechanical failure."

His face was still white as he said, "But there wasn't one! My God, is the whole universe shredding apart?"

He hit the START button.

Chapter Twenty-five

FROM THE AUTOBIOGRAPHY OF SIR
VLADIMIR CHARNETSKI

Looking through my telescope, I saw a knight who I
think was Count Lambert fall on the field, and another
man who I am sure was Count Conrad run out to aid
him. Surely there could be no other knight of his size!

But then I saw that Count Conrad was leading a
charge against the Mongols, and doing it without my
orders! He had, after all, left me in charge, and one of his
first rules of leadership was unity of command! If he
wished to take command, that was his perogative, but he
had no right to do so without notifying me!

And why in the name of all that is holy had he left the
carts and gunners behind? It made absolutely no sense!
Even if the pikers could encircle the Mongol horsemen,
what could they do to harm them? They might skewer
the first few ranks, but by that time, the enemy formation would be hundreds of yards thick! And completely
unharmed! This was madness!

But there it was, and there was no way to call those
men back now. If I countermanded his order, the results
would be pure chaos! Some pikers would be out in the
field and some of the carts would have no one but gunners to defend them. There would be gaps in our lines of
footmen, and the Mongols could bypass them, cut
through those unsupported gunners with ease and escape
our trap. Already, I saw two Mongols riding behind our
footmen, and a single conventional knight charging at
both of them. My people have sometimes been called
fools, but no one has ever dared question our courage.

There was nothing for it but to back my liege lord up,

and hope that there was some reason for this insanity. I
ordered "All Footmen Charge," and mounted Betty to
follow them out.

FROM THE DIARY OF CONRAD STARGARD

When I got to the battle lines, I was astounded! We
weren't losing at all! Our lines had been six men deep
when we started, but as we closed with the enemy, the
circumference naturally got smaller, and since we had
started out in a long thin oval, the ends were naturally
thicker with men than the sides, which pushed the mass
of horsemen inside into something of a circle.

As I got there, our men were twelve to eighteen ranks
deep, and as pressed together as a Macedonian phalanx!
I think that if it were not for their clamshell armor, many
of our front rank men would have smothered to death.
Certainly, most of the horses died that way. They were
squeezed so hard together that they could not breathe.

The enemy horsemen were packed so closely together
that they could not get out of the saddle! Their legs were
pinned in! Who could have imagined such a thing!

There were men with halberds and short axes milling
around the periphery, wanting to get at the Mongols, but
not knowing how.

Then one man wearing a turban wrapped around his
helmet and wielding a short axe screamed and ran right
up the backs of the outside row of pikers! He climbed to
the top of the men and then actually ran down on the
tops of the packed rows of pikes at the enemy! Shouting
a war cry that sounded like the howling of a wolf, he
leaped to the back of a Mongol horse that was so penned
in that it could not move.

"*El Allah il Allah!*" he screamed again, in vengeance
fifteen years delayed.

He stretched high as if he was chopping firewood and
hacked into the neck of the rider. He swung a second
time, though it surely wasn't necessary, and the Mongol's head flew loose. Then he stepped to the haunch of
the next horse and repeated the performance!

Seeing this told our men what to do! A human wave of
axemen ran up on top of the pikers, then across their
shoulders and heads to get at the enemy! A lot of pikers
might have had bruised backs, but I never heard any

complaints. In minutes, ten thousand axemen and swordsmen were *running on top of* five hundred thousand Mongol horsemen, butchering them without thought of mercy.

It was over in less than a dozen minutes, and none but the Christian horsemen were left alive. A half-million of the enemy had been killed in this battle and the army's losses were almost nonexistent, a few broken legs and sprained ankles, plus one case of what looked like a heart attack.

Then it was over and a strange silence came over the battlefield. The pikers were still pushing forward, since they knew nothing better to do. The axemen on top of the enemy just looked around dumbfounded, seeing nothing else to kill and awestruck at the carnage that they had created. And they all stood there, breathing.

Then someone started singing one of the army songs, the one that one day would be the Polish national anthem.

"Poland is not yet dead!

"Not while we yet live!"

Then the song was over and someone started in on *"Te Deum."* The men backed off and the Mongol horses slumped to the ground, asphyxiated or exhausted. Most of our warriors went to their knees as well, and gave thanks to God.

The war was over.

Hetman Vladimir came by and we discussed the cleanup. Our wounded to go to one place, our dead to another. Some men were detailed to collect booty, others to get supper going.

"And the Mongols?" he asked.

"Put their money and jewelry over here, their weapons and anything else valuable over there," I said, pointing. "Their bodies on that rise for burning, and their heads on that hill. I want a real head count, so stack them neatly."

"Yes sir. What about the Mongol wounded?"

"Once you've put all their heads on that hill and their bodies on that rise, you can give medical attention to any that request it."

"Right sir, no prisoners. I just wanted to make sure."

"Well, what could we do with a Mongol prisoner?

They have no secrets to tell us. We can't keep them, guarding and feeding them forever. If we let them go, they'd have no choice but to rob and murder their way home, so that's out. The horde would never trade Christians for them. They look on one of their men who was taken prisoner as one who has failed in his duty! They want him killed! Best to just kill them now and be done with it."

"Yes, sir. I doubt if there are any of them left alive, anyway." He started giving efficient orders and I wandered on.

I saw by his mace that a priest was standing near me and I remembered Count Lambert. At first he was hesitant to go two miles away when there were so many who needed his services right here, but I dismounted and offered him Anna to get him there in a hurry.

She gave me a "I don't like this" pose.

"Look, girl, the war is over and Lambert needs a priest. I'll be okay. I have your white sister over here and she can take care of me as well as you can. But I'm the only one who can speak her language, so I can't lend her out. You understand, don't you?"

She was still sulking when she rode off with the priest. I mounted the white Big Person and rode about the field. There was a vast silence about all of us, as if a mass were being said and we must not speak. Men were working diligently at the tasks assigned to them, but they spoke only when absolutely necessary, and then in whispers. Something had happened that was vaster than all of us, something great and, somehow, holy.

The gunners had not participated in the final kill. A gunner stood to his gun no matter what happened. I told them to stand down and report to the field for duty. They passed the word and soon were helping get things in shape.

Beyond the north line, I came upon our battalion of Night Fighters, with sentries posted but most of them fast asleep in the rain and mud. I looked up Baron Ilya and got him out of his hammock.

"Ilya, you slept right through the battle."

"Our orders was to guard this flank, sir. We done that."

"You missed quite a show."

"Yes, sir, but so did they, last night. We did our part."

"Maybe more than that. But get your men ready to move. I want you to go back to the Mongol camp and see if you can secure it, since you have the only well rested men we've got."

"Yes, sir. That's an odd horse you're riding."

"Odder than you think. I've found another Big Person."

"There were *two* of them? Amazing. But for now, sir, I need your permission to strip ammunition out of these abandoned carts if I'm going to see about that camp."

"Granted." God, but I was tired.

Then I went back to my own cart, set up my old dome tent, and got my first full night's sleep in a week.

The next morning, after a breakfast of fresh horse meat, I found that the radios still weren't working, but I got the battle report. The amount of booty taken was fabulous. Every single man in my army was rich, and there was doubtless far more to be had once we cleaned up the killing grounds on the east bank of the Vistula. Some accounting would be necessary, but I think that the danger of inflation was very real.

Somehow, I would have to make sure that, while the troops were well rewarded, the economy was not ruined. I did not want to happen to us what happened to Spain after the conquest of the New World. There, so much gold poured in that even the lowliest Spaniard saw no reason to work. Farms and orchards were abandoned because if you were rich, why should you go out and do grunt labor? But within a few years, they discovered that there was nothing left for their money to buy and that the land had been wasted. Spain never did recover.

Our losses were surprisingly light. Out of the whole land army, there were only some six hundred dead or missing. Half of the Night-Fighter casualties were still alive in the Mongol camp when Ilya's battalion returned. Some had retreated in the wrong direction in the dark and some had been knocked unconscious by their own grenades and what not.

But after the Mongols pulled out in the morning, our stragglers had taken over the Mongol camp themselves! The Mongols had left behind only their most severely wounded and the surviving Polish girls they had captured on the way in.

The stories the girls told our men were so brutal that all the Mongol wounded were killed, despite the fact that most of the girls had actually been killed by us, in the course of the fragging. It had never occurred to us that the Mongol officers would have slave girls with them. In our ignorance, we had slaughtered more than three hundred young ladies, our own people.

But while the army's losses were small, the traditional forces were another matter. Duke Boleslaw of Mazovia was dead, as was the Duke of Sandomierz. Out of the estimated thirty-one thousand men that followed them, less than four hundred were left alive, and most of those were severely wounded. Virtually every nobleman from the duchies of Mazovia, Little Poland, and Sandomierz was dead!

A new age was coming to my country, but the flower of the past was gone.

The next morning, some of my depression had worn off and I was feeling a bit better. I saddled Anna and went to have a look around, with the white Big Person tagging along. That was another problem that would have to be worked out somehow. Anna wouldn't leave me and the new mount had no one that could talk to her but me. Yet it seemed a shame to waste the services of a Big Person.

Baron Vladimir had ordered Count Lambert's aircraft sent back to Eagle Nest. When I got there, the last of them was pulling out, strapped to the top of a war cart with the wing dismounted and roped next to the fuselage. The pilots who had flown them were dead, every last foolish one of them.

The Christian knights were being buried, each in his own grave, with a dog tag on each wooden cross and another on his arms and armor, neatly bundled for return to his family. Someday, we'd send a crew of stonecutters here and have proper tombstones made.

It was too wet to get a decent fire going, so the Mongol dead were being piled naked in a huge common trench, along with the dead horses. Even the horses had been stripped. Baron Vladimir had apparently felt that a half million horsehides was a prize well worth taking. If he could get them salted down in time, they'd keep the army in boots for many years. I doubt if we had salt enough to do the job, even at Three Walls. Likely, we'd have to send men to the mines and get the mines going besides.

The heads of the Mongols were stacked separately, as I had ordered. A crew was putting them up on stakes made of old lances, in neat squares a gross heads to the side, for easy counting. Good. I wanted to make sure that no one ever doubted what we had accomplished here. Those heads were a fitting monument to this battle.

In a day or two, the cleanup would be done, and we could go home. Well, some of us. A contingent would have to be sent to loot and clean up the mess we'd made on the east bank of the Vistula. Likely, Baron Tadaos was starting that already. If only the weather would clear up so we could use the radios again. But the thunder and lightning went on and showed no signs of stopping. It seemed unfitting, somehow. Victories should happen in fine weather.

Finally, we found Baron Vladimir.

"Good morning, my lord. The sleep seems to have done you good. You're looking better. Have you had a medic examine your eye lately?"

"No, but I suppose I should, at least to change the bandage."

"Most of them are down at the field hospital, at our old campsite, my lord."

"I'll go there next. But for now, I want you to set up a meeting for me with the troops, captains and above, for late this afternoon, at six. There are some things I have to tell them."

"Done, my lord."

"Is anything coming through on the radios, yet?"

"I'm afraid not, my lord."

"Then perhaps you should put a dozen men on Big People and have them spread the word of our victory. Our wives are doubtless worried and Duke Henryk should be informed. Tell the duke that I advise sending at least his foreign troops south to King Bela."

"I'll see to it, my lord."

"Good. Then I'll see you at six, if not before."

The medic said that my wound was healing well, and it looked like the eye was uninjured. The only problem was that when he removed the bandage, I couldn't tell the difference. My right eye was blind.

Perhaps it's odd, but somehow it didn't bother me.

After all the death I had seen and caused, well, maybe losing the eye was some sort of penance.

The day wound on and it was time for my talk.

I stepped up on the makeshift podium in front of my captains, komanders, and barons.

"Brothers!" I said. "I wish that I could address the entire army, and not just the officers, but you all know that it would be impossible. Talking to the almost eight hundred of you is about all my lungs can handle. I am therefore going to ask you captains to each give a similar talk to your men, so I'll thank you to take notes."

Notebooks and real lead pencils dutifully came out.

"Thank you. First, I want you all to know that riders have been sent to tell your families that you are safe, so they can stop worrying about you.

"Next, I want to praise you all for the magnificent victory you have won. For the first time in all of history, the Mongols have been beaten. In the last fifty years, those murdering bastards have defeated over fifty armies, and most of those armies outnumbered the Mongol invaders. But we went at them outnumbered twenty to one, and we killed them to a man!"

"Over a hundred major cities in China, Asia, and Russia have fallen to their rape, murder, and plunder, but not one major city in Poland has been lost, and all because of you men! The slaughter you worked has saved the lives of millions of your countrymen, and millions of other Christians, besides, for had we lost, the Mongols would not have stopped with Poland. They would have gone on to take Germany, France, and even England, Spain, and Italy. By stopping the Mongols here, you have saved all of Christendom! Your children and grandchildren and their descendants will be singing your praises for a thousand years!

"To honor you for this mighty deed, we are changing the name of our organization. No longer will we be simply 'the army.' From this day onward, we will be known as the 'Christian Army,' the defenders of all Christendom!

"The Mongol plan was to hit King Bela of Hungary at the same time as they invaded us. We don't know yet if they planned to take the Hungarians from the east, or from the north through Poland. If the second, you have saved Hungary along with Poland. If the first, if the

Mongols actually had enough men to make both invasions at the same time, we have at least saved the many thousands of Christian Knights who are still with my liege lord Duke Henryk at Legnica. I have this day sent a message to my liege urging him to release those fighters to help King Bela. It may yet be that a victory to the south will happen, and part of the credit for that victory will be due to you.

"Then there is the matter of the booty you have earned. You all know that it is fabulous! Though it will be awhile before it can all be properly accounted and a fair distribution made, I think I'm safe in promising every man below the rank of knight at least a thousand pence! The knights will get twice that, and captains eight times that amount! So you are all rich!

"But you won't get a chance to start spending it immediately. There's still work to be done. The River Battalion killed far more of the enemy than were killed here on this plain, and there are too few of them left to do the looting, let alone the cleanup. But there at least we won't have the sad job of burying our own men!

"And now I want to talk a bit about the future.

"We have won a great victory here, but don't think for a minute that the Mongols have gone away forever. These marauders that we have killed had descendants, and if we don't do something about it, in twenty years our own children will have to try and repeat what we have done here. And next time maybe the Mongols won't act as stupidly as they have in the last few weeks.

"Yes, I said that we have defeated a stupid enemy! They lined themselves up on the east bank of the Vistula and let us cut them down like a farmer cuts down hay! They set up a stupid night guard on their camp, and let Baron Ilya's battalion of Night Fighters go in and kill fifty thousand of them, including most of their officers! And without those officers, the Mongol troops rode stupidly into a trap that got the rest of them slaughtered.

"Well, next time, they won't be so stupid! Next time, they will have learned something from the hard lesson we gave them, and next time they might win!

"Next time, we have to be far stronger than we were here. Next time we must have more troops, better weapons, and better defenses!

"So don't think that you can retire from the army and

go back to whatever it was that you were doing before the Mongols and I came along. You can't! There's work to be done!

"I have bought up most of the land for five miles on both banks of the Vistula. We are going to build a fort like the one at East Gate every five miles along the river, all the way down to the Baltic, and on both sides! And after that, we'll build them up the Bug as well! Every one of those forts will be manned by a company of our men, so the army will not be disbanding. We will continue to grow, and you all can continue to look forward to promotions, for not only will we have to build and man the forts, we will have to vastly expand our manufacturing facilities to equip them.

"The Christian Army that we all belong to will be a permanent organization. In the same manner that the Church defends the souls of all Christians, we will defend their bodies. We will do our work in the realm of the physical just as the Church does its work in the realm of the spiritual. We will be doing God's work, and every one of you will be needed.

"Yet no man will be forced to stay in the army. Once we have finished with the cleanup, any man who wishes to leave may do so. I simply promise any man who leaves that he will regret it later, when he is a peasant and his old friends are knights and barons!

"In times to come, we will not only be defending Christendom, but we will eventually be able to take the war to the enemy. Millions of souls in the Russias and elsewhere are now living under the Mongol's brutal tread. We are going to go out there and free them, and make proper Christians out of them besides!

"I promise you all interesting times!

"That's about it. Have a talk with your men and then get a good night's sleep. Like I said, there's work to do!"

Interlude Seven

^^^^^^^^^^^^^^^^^^^^^^^

THE TAPE wound to a stop.

"That's it? There?" Tom said.

"What do you mean?" I asked.

"But it didn't end there! Not when I was alive!"

"Tom, I know that this thing has been quite a shock to you. You need to unwind, to relax for a while. Then things will be clearer for you. Look, let's have a few more drinks, then take a steambath and maybe invite in a few of the wenches. After that a good rubdown and some more girls and I know you'll feel better."

"You think I'm crazy, don't you? I'm not! Something Conrad has done, or something about him has shattered the temporal continuity of all creation! Can't you understand that *I* built the first time machine and *I* don't understand what is happening!"

"Tom, I don't understand what's happening either, but I do know that a drink and a wench never hurt anybody. Come on." I took him by the hand and led him out of the room.

Appendix to
The Flying Warlord

^^^^^^^^^^^^^^^^^^^^^^^^^^^^^^^^^

Conrad's Army

ORGANIZATIONAL STRUCTURE OF A
TYPICAL COMPANY

      1 Captain
      6 Knight Banners, called "banners"
     36 Knight Bachelors, called "knights"
    216 Warriors, in three grades
             72 Squires
             72 Pages
             72 Warriors, called "grunts" when in basic

This was the plan, but such things rarely work out. Always there were people in school, people on indefinite leave, extra people temporarily assigned. The above represented a never-to-be-attained ideal.

In addition there were the wives and children. Warriors were encouraged to marry, and often met their wives in basic training. On being knighted, a man had the right, with his wife's permission, to have a "servant," a euphemism for a second wife. This was as permanent a relationship as marriage, and was attended by similar ceremonies, though it was not sanctified by the Church. A servant had all of the rights, privileges, and duties of a wife, and her children were considered to be fully legitimate, but she was slightly inferior to the first wife socially.

A banner could have two servants, and a captain three. Higher ranks could have more in proportion, although relatively few took full advantage of this privilege.

As with any primitive people recently receiving proper sanitation and medicine, the population exploded. Families of nine were the average, and a certain Captain Sliwa was famed for having thirty-nine children and four happy wives. Aside from the rhythm method, contraceptives were unknown. Conrad was unconcerned. The population of thirteenth-century Poland was only three million. The land could easily support fifty million. Furthermore, there were vast tracts in Russia and the Ukraine that had been denuded of people by the Mongols, and after that there was always North America, Argentina, South Africa, Australia, and New Zealand; areas with climates suitable to North Europeans. And of course, the problem would eventually take care of itself. Education and a higher standard of living always cut the birth rate.

In addition to the above-listed line personnel, the typical company was supported by a number of auxiliary organizations, with the following typical staffing. They are listed as so many "men," but most positions could be held by either male or female personnel:

Chaplain's Corps—three men

Usually a pastor with two assistants, these priests were responsible for the Church, the library, and the school. School teachers were often qualified line personnel who taught on a part-time basis.

Communication Corps—six men

Responsible for the radios, the telegraph, and the mail within the company and all cartage and shipping outside of it.

Accounting Corps—three men

Responsible for all financial transactions between companies, outside suppliers, etc. Also handled payroll and kept individuals' bank accounts.

Medical Corps—one man

Medical Officer also had 12 trained part-time Corpsmen for emergencies. Responsible for the general health of the company, and also for sanitation inspection.

Commercial Corps—four men

Operated a general store that sold all sorts of products to anyone who came in. They also had a catalog sales operation and would handle the sale of farm produce from neighboring, nonarmy farms on a commission basis.

The Inn—twelve men

Personally owned by Conrad and the basis of his personal fortune. These inns were generally a smaller version of the Pink Dragon Inn.

Observers—fourteen little old ladies

These were a group of older people whose job was to sit in the towers and to keep a lookout in case anything bad happened. Equipped with telescopes and intercoms, each was usually somebody's grandmother. It gave them something useful to do, a place to live, and a modest income, while freeing up warriors for more strenuous duties. They usually had two-person cottages on top of the towers and spent their days and nights gossiping. But those towers were also equipped with machine guns, and on certain rare occasions these people were known to use them.

Many of the above positions were filled by women, and throughout the army there was no limitation as to how far a woman could rise. Women received combat training of a less vigorous nature and their armor was much lighter. However, women were excluded from combat except for guarding castle walls when the men were away. Also, women were forbidden to do strenuous work for the four months prior to childbirth and the two after it. Because of this last and because most women were pregnant half the time, few of them rose high in the hierarchy. As in most countries, a woman's status was largely determined by her husband's.

The family was vitally important to the army and was kept together at almost all costs. If shift work was necessary, then husband and wife were kept on the same shift regardless of the needs of the army. Further, their children went to school on that shift. If one spouse was assigned to a school, the other was also assigned to the complementary school. Vacations were always assigned to the entire family at the same time. Retirement was always announced for the family as a whole. This last was true even when it conflicted with the wishes of the individual.

One of the results of this policy was that single individuals were often promoted faster than their married counterparts. It was simply easier to move them around and promotion often comes with motion. Single ladies sometimes rose quickly and high.

Pregnant women and those with minor (under five years old) children worked fewer hours than normal and they were paid at half the usual daily rate.

The typical company had its own castle or buildings and was the basic unit of the Christian army. A person's company was his home, and except for promotions or when new companies were being formed, a person was rarely transferred out.

Even then, new companies were usually formed by a process of "budding." A banner, six knights, and thirty-six squires would be sent from a single company to three-month-long schools for promotion. Then in the following four months they acted as drill instructors for two hundred sixteen basics who had survived the first part of their training. Training completed, the basics and their instructors became a new company and left as a group for their new assignment.

Even in basic, where the attrition rate was high, a serious effort was made to break up groups as little as possible. Support personnel were generally assigned to a company on a permanent basis.

Other things were done to generate a team feeling. Everyone ate the same food in the same dining hall. Except for insignia, their military clothing was the same. Housing was allotted on a square yard basis proportional to the number of people in the family, although higher ranks were stationed higher up in the building.

The unit was a company in the commercial as well as the military sense. Each company usually had agricultural, commercial, and manufacturing interests as well as military duties, and each company was treated as a profit center, for accounting purposes. Economically, they competed freely with each other and with nonarmy organizations. In addition to their pay, individuals received a quarterly bonus proportional to their rank and the company's profits. Profits were determined in the usual manner and were split between the army's general fund and the company's personnel. Each company was thus externally a capitalist entity in a free enterprise system, although internally it was a socialist institution.

The company, then, was the home of about three hundred families, or about three thousand people, living in a set of buildings that looked like a castle, but was in fact an apartment house with a church, a school, a store, an inn, factories, and usually farms. They tried to make it a nice place to live.

As in a modern navy, every adult had both a combat occupation and a noncombat occupation. Rank was often but not always the same in both. When they were different, pay and status went according to whichever was higher. One lived with or near one's combat unit, no matter where one worked. Uniforms had a large arm insignia for combat rank and a small collar design for noncombat rank.

The banners often had several noncombat occupations. Companies often required an executive officer, purchasing agent, sales officer, military training officer, agricultural officer, manufacturing officer, etc. And anything else that the captain felt was best. He did not actually command the support personnel attached to his unit. These corps each had their own separate hierarchies. However, the radio operator who did not take a captain seriously was a fool. The captain's job was to decide what was to be done and who was to do it, and he had limited judicial functions, but it was intended that a good captain should spend most of his time idly observing the operations of his company.

FIELD GRADE OFFICERS

A Komander	ran a	Komand of	6 companies	with	1,500 Men
A Baron	ran a	Battalion of	6 Komands	with	9,000 Men
A Kolomel	ran a	Kolumn of	6 Battalions	with	54,000 Men
A Count	ran a	County of	6 Kolumns	with	324,000 Men
A Hetman	ran a	Division of	6 Counties	with	1,944,000 Men
A Duke	ran an	Army of	6 Divisions	with	11,664,000 Men

Of course, it was never anything like this neat. While the companies were remarkably stable, the upper command was in a constant state of flux. During its first thirty years of existence, the Christian Army expanded from nothing to over twelve million fighting men, plus their wives and an ungodly number of children. Countless changes were made as the structure tried to accommodate new technology and rapid expansion. It got so that warriors often did not know who their field officers were, but then, it was not important that they know. Their captains knew and that was enough.

But despite the growing pains, there were never more than six ranks above captain and an officer rarely had fewer than four or more than ten subordinates.

Except in time of war, komanders rarely took direct control of their komands. Instead, they functioned as staff officers for their barons. These seven officers, with a rump company, generally had a castle, but spent most of their time touring their thirty-six odd companies, either in a riverboat (if all of their battalion was on a river, as many of the earlier ones were), or a set of traveling cars pulled by the Big People (as Anna's progeny were called). Each komander had a specialty (agriculture, military training, etc.) and acted as a counselor to the banner in charge of that function within a company. The baron counseled the captain. The emphasis was on training rather than on reprimands, although ass-chewings occurred.

These visits lasted a day or two, happened to a company four to eight times a year (at the discretion of the baron, who was supposed to allot more time to problem children), and were always on a surprise basis. On rare occasions, the baron might take direct control of a troublesome company and spend a month there with his komanders straightening things out. The usual technique was to have the unfortunate captain and banners stand silently by while their stand-ins directed their subordinates. I mean a banner literally had to stand beside a komander, keep his mouth shut and take notes. That evening, he was permitted to ask questions. An embarrassing procedure, it rarely had to be repeated on a company.

This constant traveling encouraged the use of multiple wives. The members of an inspection team each took one or two of their wives with them on their endless tours, leaving other wives home to take care of the children. The wives provided companionship of course, but most of them were skilled managers in their own right and helped to spread knowledge and new techniques within the battalion.

When an organization was sufficiently large that a kolomel was not in charge, the counts and kolomels functioned in a similar manner to the barons and komanders, visiting their counties on a regular basis.

The head of an organization (be it the Chaplain's Corps, the Regular Army, the Wolves, the Eagles, or whatever), always had a large staff with sections in charge of inspection, engineering, auditing, etc. Each organization published a magazine, usually monthly.

THE CHAPLAIN'S CORPS

The Chaplain's Corps was in an awkward position in that it was subordinate to both the Pope and to the army. It survived by turning a blind eye to various army practices, such as the custom of multiple wives and not taking prisoners in combat. It maintained a college for novitiates in the Sudeten Mountains and did not accept candidates unless they had survived basic training. In combat, chaplains fought along side the men of their company, although they used a mace rather than an edged weapon since the Church forbade the shedding of blood.

THE TRAINING CORPS

The Training Corps was the only organization that did not maintain stable companies. Instructors were constantly being cycled back into the field and were normally there on a temporary duty basis only. However, the upper echelons were stable and kolomels acted as if they were captains. The Training Corps had a huge base near Three Walls, popularly called "Hell." It maintained the following schools:

BASIC TRAINING

This school accepted anyone aged fourteen to thirty who presented themselves at the door, and army policy was to provide free transportation to anyone who wanted to enlist. Enlistment was not for a fixed term of years. Any member of the army could quit at any time, except in a combat situation. Well, you could quit during combat, but your superior was then required to shoot you.

Women were accepted for training as well as men and more girls applied than boys. Perhaps this was because girls are more adventurous, or that this was a place where one could find a husband who would become a knight, or that here was where a woman could develop her own self, without having to be a peasant or a rich man's toy. Or a combination of the above. In truth, it is impossible to properly raise children and maintain a career in any culture. Many doubtless intended to travel single careers, but Mother Nature generally won out.

Basic training was extremely rigorous, with only about half of the male candidates surviving the first eight months, after which things eased up. Many candidates washed out for physical, emotional, or intellectual reasons, but eight percent actually died in training. Female training was less demanding physically, but equally rough on mind and spirit. About two-thirds of the girls graduated and actual deaths were rare.

These factors resulted in a sexual imbalance within the entire army, women outnumbering men by even more than could be accounted for by the knight's multiple wives. Yet to correct the problem, the army would have had to either reject some female candidates for arbitrary reasons, which seemed unfair, or to make the girl's course more demanding, which seemed impossible. Then, too, many men claimed that there was no problem at all and that the surplus of ladies was a good thing.

A candidate washing out was generally permitted to retake the course after waiting a year.

KNIGHT'S SCHOOL

This was a three-month-long course that prepared people for the first level of command. When a man attended, his wife attended the parallel school for women, while the kids were being taken care of by their home company. The emphasis was on training rather than on weeding out the unfit. Virtually everyone graduated, but one's grades counted toward one's next promotion.

BANNER'S SCHOOL

Like the knight's school, one grade up.

CAPTAIN'S SCHOOL, KOMANDER'S SCHOOL, BARON'S SCHOOL, KOLOMEL'S SCHOOL, COUNT'S SCHOOL

Each step up the ladder had its three-month-long course and was required for permanent promotion. There were no schools above those listed, though, as there were never enough candidates to maintain permanent classes. And anyway, who would teach in them?

THE REGULAR ARMY

This was the largest full army organization. Its combat-mission was to defend the country in the event of invasion and to maintain a vast number of forts strung along the borders, rivers, and other strategic (and not so strategic) positions. These forts usually housed a full company, were generally placed about five miles apart, and were connected by railroads. Each commanded about twenty-five square miles, which land was owned by the army and farmed extensively. Also, each fort contained some light-to-medium industry. Depending on the season, people worked at farms or factories. Except for military training, which occupied one day a week, army personnel stayed productive. There were never any of the time-wasting activities that predominate in the usual modern army.

THE CONSTRUCTION CORPS

This large organization was responsible for building the countless forts, bridges, dams, canals, and whole cities that the army required. Since much of the work was repetitious (the forts were all virtually identical), whole companies were specialized in the various phases of the construction of a single type of building. Once the legal department had acquired the land, and engineering had approved the site, a company of railroad builders would extend a line out to it. Then a site-preparation company might spend a week there and move on. On their heels would come a company of foundation layers who would move in and do their job in another week. In this manner, forts would pop up along a river on a weekly basis, each to be manned by a new company of Regulars fresh out of Hell.

Although the Construction Corps had no direct combat role (aside from its own defense), it was actually the most aggressive unit in the army. When invading enemy territory, army policy was to move slowly and build forts as they went. Territory taken was taken permanently.

Construction Corps companies lived in hundreds of rail-mounted mobile homes, which were set up in precisely the same way each week, to give some feeling of continuity. They could knock down their installation, move it five miles and rebuild it, complete with a dining hall, a church, a school, a store, and an inn, all within half a day.

Winters were often spent logging, not so much because of the need for lumber (most construction was in concrete), but for land clearance. In the twentieth century, forests have become precious, but in the thirteenth, eighty-five percent of the known world was forested. The wilderness was the enemy. The army needed vast amounts of agricultural land to feed its growing population, and a Mongol can't hide in a potato field.

THE WOLVES

The Wolves were the army's only full-time combat unit. Composed almost entirely of the sons and daughters of the old nobility, their role was to guard the construction corps when it operated in enemy territory and to raid the enemy, keeping him off balance.

The lowest rank in the Wolves was a knight and companies were led by a komander. Wolf bases were few and large, with six companies of Wolves and a support company of regular army.

This support duty was hated and the Regular Army tended to use it as a punishment detail.

THE EAGLES

The Eagles were the air force and were the most prestigious unit in the army. Flying wood-and-canvas planes for over a century, until aluminum was available, their casualty rate was high. Yet always there was competition to get in.

The Eagles recruited young people (fifteen was the maximum age of entry) who had completed the first eight months of basic training. They maintained their own schools and had their own aircraft factories. Although most of them spent most of their time in building and repairing aircraft, it was a point of pride with them that every Eagle, man or woman, was a pilot and flew regularly.

Their combat role was to patrol the borders and to work with the Wolves in harassing the enemy.

TRANSPORTATION AND COMMUNICATION CORPS

This was the most profitable unit in the army, as its services were unique and available to civilians as well as military users. It maintained steamboat lines on all navigable rivers, even on many outside of Poland. It maintained the railroads and supplied most of the transportation in the entire country. It maintained a complete postal system. It took care of the telegraph system as well as the radio system. Radio was strictly a communication device until after Conrad's death. Conrad felt that home radios, televisions, telephones, and private automobiles were detrimental to civilization and refused to let them be developed.

The Transportation and Communication Corps maintained ocean ships and eventually developed and totally controlled world shipping. It also made a bundle publishing the reports of its Explorer Force, which often made for fascinating reading.

LEGAL CORPS

The Legal Corps was concerned primarily with criminal law within army jurisdiction, but it did handle civil matters occasionally. It had its own school and publishing house. It provided circuit-court teams consisting of a judge, four lawyer-prosecutors (they took turns), a recorder, and a bailiff. These teams stopped at each company about once a month and heard any serious cases.

(Captains had the authority to handle minor offenses.) Higher courts handled appeals.

The usual sentence was a bad conduct discharge and a term of years in a prison coal mine, which was run by the Legal Corps.

Attached to the Legal Corps, but largely independent, was the Detective Force. Each detective was paired with one of the Big People, and their arrest rate was excellent. The Big People's sense of smell was particularly important in this work. They made a bloodhound look like a dog. Warsaw and Katowice had their own uniformed police forces, but there were no other police forces in Poland.

MEDICAL CORPS

Besides providing a medical officer to every company in the army, the Medical Corps maintained a number of company-sized hospitals and a major teaching facility.

COMMERCIAL CORPS

Maintained stores at every army installation, as well as some in major civilian cities. It also ran a catalog sales operation out of its single huge warehouse. It bought and sold commodities, maintained the huge granaries in the Bledowska Desert, and eventually maintained trading posts around the world.

WARSAW CORPS

In our timeline, Warsaw was not built until the sixteenth century. But like every modern Pole, Conrad had to have a Warsaw, so he built one. This was a city of almost half a million people, larger than any city of the time outside of China.

Its primary function was political, though few people living there would have believed that. Conrad wanted to so impress the sovereigns of Europe that they would be eager to join his planned Federation of Christendom. What he built would have impressed even a jaded twentieth-century American. It was part university, part palace, and all World's Fair.

The city had no manufacturing facilities and little direct trade. Tourism was the biggest industry, with education running a close second.

The transport system consisted of eight moving slide-walks, seven of which were circles a third of a mile in diameter. The eighth was a mile across, enclosing the others. Each of these walks consisted of many bands, each a yard wide, each of which moved three miles an hour faster than the one before it. The center band of the longest walk moved at thirty-six miles an hour, was eight yards wide and was equipped with benches and food-vending kiosks. Vertical transport was handled by elevators of the *pater nostra* variety.

With this system, it was possible to go from any point in the city to any other point in less than twelve minutes.

The transportation deck was covered by a sixteen-yard-high ceiling and amounted to a vast mall, with stores, restaurants, and theaters.

Above the mall was an outdoor park and garden.

Outside of the big walk were a gross of company-sized buildings, each two gross yards long and seventeen stories tall, arranged like cooling fins, where most of the inhabitants lived. Each had its own dining facilities, church, and school. Young children did not have to be exposed to a big city environment. Many of these companies were home companies. Some were for transients.

Each of the smaller circles contained a single large building. The center one held the tallest, the cathedral. This was twice as high inside as the recently completed Notre Dame, and contained eight times the volume. You couldn't hear a sermon beyond the tenth row, but the place sure was impressive.

The palace had room for a senate and legislature, the private chambers of King Henryk the Pius, office space, and lots of room for visiting firemen.

Three of the circles contained institutes of higher learning. The University taught the usual subjects of the time—law, theology, the classics, etc. The Institute taught sciences and engineering. The Academy taught art, music, and drama. Soon, this was where the nobility of Europe came to be educated.

One circle contained a sports arena that was covered once structural steel became available, and the last circle had a major hotel.

Surrounding the city and subordinate to it was a

power plant and nine company-sized forts. These companies were primarily engaged in providing fresh foodstuffs and included a huge bakery and a bodacious dairy. Tunnels connected these installations to the city proper.

South of the city was a modern zoo, with lions and tigers and bears, and attached to it was an international village, with Chinese pagodas and Burmese stupas and Javanese temple dancers and Indians and Batu warriors.

All told, Warsaw was an incredible place.

THE MANUFACTURING CORPS

With a greater population than any other unit in the army, the Manufacturing Corps was not really a military organization. After the Battle of Chmielnick, early in the army's history, it was never once called to active duty. Furthermore, more than half of their workers were not actually members of the army, but were civilian employees. These employees got the same pay and benefits as their military counterparts and they did not have to participate in basic training and military exercises. On the other hand, they did not receive the twelve-year bonus, and promotion was faster for army personnel.

The Manufacturing Corps was responsible for mining, heavy industry, and a fair amount of medium industry, the borders with the Regular Army being pretty vague as to who could do what. There were many Regular Army companies that had their own coal mines and one Manufacturing Corps company produced musical instruments.

Much of the Manufacturing Corp's facilities were located in a mile-wide strip over the Upper Sileasian coal basin. This amounted to a city of over six million people that was over four dozen miles long and under one roof. Sprawling and brawling, Katowice was considered by many to be a greater wonder than Warsaw.

Others thought it a vision of Hell.

THE MILITIA

There was a major bonus, equal to all the money that a person had received up to that time, paid after twelve years of honorable service in the army. A man's wife(s) was also given a bonus at that time. At this point, certain less-than-acceptable personnel were eased out. Most had the option of remaining in and letting their eventual bonus increase.

A person accepting his twelve-year bonus was effectively retiring from the army. Since many people joined at the age of fourteen, this often happened when they were only twenty-six and a second career was expected. But a person never totally left the army. He could be called back in the event of an emergency, in theory at least. Oh, he could always quit, but that would mean giving up the prestige of his rank (it was customary to bump a man a grade on retirement), giving up his eventual rights to an army old folks' home, giving up his right to return to the army if things didn't work out, and possibly giving up the friendship and use of his favorite Big Person. And, in fact, the Militia was almost never actually called up.

The army had various offers to relieve a retiree of his money. Whole towns and small cities were built, all of them with public utilities like sewage systems. A man could buy a farm or a condo and office or shares in a factory. Many men left as a group to work on some commercial venture. If a knight bought into Militia property, he knew that his children would have schools and churches. Since his wife(s)'s money was also involved, be assured that most men stayed in the Militia.

In order to pay for essential services, Militia towns charged their residents certain taxes and fees. These were the only taxes that existed within the entire system.

THE PINK DRAGON INNS

Throughout Conrad's lifetime, the Pink Dragon Inns were not exactly part of the army, but rather were Conrad's personal property. They were the basis of his considerable private fortune. Every army installation of any decent size had one attached to it and thus they had a large captive audience. But in their defense, it must be said that they were extremely clean, cheerful, and inexpensive. Waitresses were always attractive and single, although the requirement for virginity was dropped after the first decade, and they were remarkably well paid. Permanent personnel had pay and benefits identical to those in the army and when the inns were transferred to the army on Conrad's retirement, the transition was hardly noticed.

THE WORK DAY

In the Middle Ages, the normal work day was dawn to dusk, which in a Polish summer could be eighteen hours. As soon as clocks became available, Conrad cut this to twelve, but with artificial light, the twelve-hour day, six-day week became the standard. The day started at dawn with a short, obligatory sunrise service. The Regular army stayed as much as possible with a day shift only, but many units worked around the clock, especially those with expensive capital equipment. The entire city of Warsaw ran nonstop, even the universities, and night was like day in Katowice.

RECREATION

The army was by no means all work and no play. Every company had an inn. There were bands of traveling entertainers, some under army contract but most operating independently. Athletic competition was strongly encouraged, especially when it was related to military training. Whole companies fought mock battles with each other and the betting on these was so heavy that the battles themselves sometimes got out of hand.

Less vigorous competitions also took place, with chess and music being the most popular. The ability to play a musical instrument was considered to be a standard accomplishment, and only a clod couldn't play at least a recorder.

Children's needs were carefully attended to, with nurseries, playgrounds, and youth centers. Scouting was popular.

All personnel got a paid two-week yearly vacation. Once there were enough Big People to go around, it was possible to rent a railroad car set up as family living quarters and go touring. Many companies operated as tourist traps.

THE ARMY'S BETTER HALF

All of the above really describes the activity of only half the army. The army was composed of two distinct intelligent species. Anna's progeny, the Big People, were a breed of genetically engineered horses. The products of a technology vastly beyond Conrad's Poland, these beings were in many ways superior to humans.

Their eyesight, hearing, and sense of smell were phenomenal and they possessed full use of a magnetic direction-finding sense that humans have but can't use. They didn't need sleep. They could eat anything organic, up to and including coal. They could run at thirty miles an hour all day long. They were immune to all diseases and seemed to have no fixed life span, apparently living forever.

They were all female and could reproduce voluntarily by parthenogenesis. It was only necessary to ask one to have babies and she would do it. A litter was always four. They were sexually mature and full-sized in four years. They could understand Polish, but not speak it.

Most astoundingly, they possessed a sort of racial memory. At around three, they started to remember everything their mother knew up to the time of their conception. The process was completed in about six months.

The Big People were less intelligent than the average human and were completely unable to handle higher mathematics or other systems of abstract thought. Given a concrete problem, on the other hand, they would often do as well as humans. Their ability to travel from point to point was near perfect, and their memory seems to have been eidetic.

They had a very amiable, placid temperament, except in combat, where they were absolutely deadly. Ordinarily, they were happy to go along with just about anything, although they expected to be treated politely. They were gregarious and they liked being around humans even more than their own kind. They liked being talked to and for this reason got along very well with children.

Anna was very taken with a sermon she heard and became extremely religious. Her daughters, being her identical twins in both mind and body, followed suit. Among the other trials and problems faced by the Chaplain's Corps was the necessity of baptizing, confirming, and giving sermons to beings who looked like horses. They gave silent prayers of thanks for the fact that no

Big Person was ever observed to sin, so it was not necessary to confess them in pantomime.

The Big People were considered full members of the army, with all privileges. They were paid as warrior basics and when they spent their pay at all, it went mostly on sweets and jewelry. They had full legal rights and their testimony was admitted in court.

There were too few Big People at the time of Chmielnick to have much impact on the battle, but in the years that followed they became increasingly important. The Wolves had first priority to their services and then the Transportation and Communication Corps, who used them to carry the mails and pull railroad cars. Once they knew the route, a rider or driver was unnecessary. Because of their night vision and ability to see into the infrared, they were used as pilots on boats and ships. Big People showed no interest in aircraft and refused to board them. Some Little People claimed that this was obvious proof of their wisdom.

Eventually, there were enough Big People so that some could be spared for agriculture. Within a few years they had taken over ninety-five percent of all farmwork, which they preferred. Pulling a plow was no different than pulling a railroad car and you got home every night. Spending all night weeding? Hey, that's grass, our favorite food. Humans had little to do but make the decisions, keep the machinery fixed, and help out with the harvest.

When the Big People population approximately equalled that of adult Little People, they were asked to stop reproducing. Thereafter, the two populations were kept about equal and a one-on-one relationship was the most satisfying to all concerned. Big People were often "adopted" into human families, attending church and amusements with them, and taking vacations at the same time.

For fear that they might be mistreated, Conrad had asked the Big People to never leave the army and none of them ever did. Many followed their best friends into the quasicivilian Militia, but after the death of that person, they always returned home.

FINANCES

The army never taxed anyone and it refused to pay taxes. It supported itself by selling its products and services. Most of its production was consumed internally and most of its people spent most of their pay on army-supplied items, so there was little need for external money. Most of what was spent went to the purchase of land, and the army never sold any of the vast tracts it conquered from the Mongols.

Poland had large reserves of zinc ore, but zinc, as a separate metal, was unknown in Europe in the Middle Ages. Conrad developed a production process, but kept it an absolute secret, more tightly held than that of gunpowder. He cast a coinage out of it, used this coinage internally within his organization, and declared it to be equivalent to the existing silver coinage. Since he was always willing to trade it evenly for silver, people naturally believed him. This was brilliant from the standpoint of economics, but had the disadvantage of making zinc a rare metal. He had to keep secret the fact that brass was a zinc alloy and to charge absurd prices for galvanized iron.

Pay scales stayed absolutely constant throughout the period under discussion. All other prices fluctuated and generally went down, but not these. The army pay scale eventually became the "gold standard" of the world. Zinc coins with their actually increasing value became the standard coinage everywhere. This had the result of vastly increasing the army's wealth, since valuable goods could be purchased with cheaply produced coins. Furthermore, it was rarely necessary to redeem these coins with goods in return, since they often stayed circulating in the local economy. A similar thing happened to American paper money in 1945–60, when Europeans, desperate for a stable currency, took to using American dollars. Those "eurodollars" never were returned and the United States economy got a major boost. The amounts involved were several times those spent on the Marshall Plan.

Salaries were automatically banked on a bi-weekly basis. When you wanted your pay, you went to Accounting and got it.

DAILY PAY RATES

Warrior.....................1 penny
Page ....2 pence
Esquire....................4 pence

Knight Bachelor . . . . .8 pence
Knight Banner . . . . .16 pence
Captain . . . . .32 pence
Komander . . . . .64 pence
Baron . . . . .128 pence
Kolomel . . . . .256 pence
Count . . . . .512 pence
Hetman . . . . .1024 pence
Duke . . . . .2048 pence

By the standards of egalitarian twentieth-century America, where superiors are often paid only ten percent more than their subordinates, the rate of these increases might seem excessive, but remember that the Middle Ages were well convinced that rank hath its privileges. If an army baron was noticeably poorer than a traditional baron, the prestige of the army would suffer. Also, remember that these moneys represented "spending cash." One's necessities (food, clothing, housing, etc.) were provided free by the army. And lastly, Conrad never once drew his own pay. His personal expenses and his extensive charities were paid for out of his profits from the Pink Dragon Inns. Further, many higher officers imitated his comparatively modest style of living and did not draw their full salaries.

POLITICS

Democracy never developed in the army except in the Militia. At first, this was because Conrad felt that his countrymen weren't ready for democracy and later, after his retirement, because nobody really felt the need of it.

Militia towns were each governed by an elected counsel, although the elections were weighted. Warriors got one vote, knights got two, captains four, etc. These counsels eventually formed a Grand Counsel, but its decisions were purely advisory and it never was very powerful.

But there are other ways than elections for the will of the people to filter up to government, and the army used questionnaires. Twice a year, all personnel filled out an extensive form and answered questions about everything imaginable. The last one was always "What should we have asked about, but didn't?" These forms were tabulated quickly and taken seriously. The results were published in the *Army Magazine* in a few months along with Conrad's commentary. He never bound himself or his successors to follow the recommendations of his subordinates, but he always tried to justify his position when army policy was contrary to army opinion.

RELIGION

Most of the people in the army were Roman Catholics, and it often seemed that Catholics were promoted faster, but other religions were never forbidden. Jews were particularly welcome because they were happy to work on Sunday when everyone else wanted off.

Much to the annoyance of the Pope, the army refused his orders to slaughter a surviving pocket of Catheri heretics, but rather talked them into moving bodily to a protected area in the Ukraine, where they remained.

The army never ceased in its efforts to reunite the various branches of Christendom. On one occasion they hosted delegations from the Roman, Orthodox, and Coptic Churches at an isolated site where they could hopefully resolve their differences. With nothing accomplished after three years, the frustrated site komander put all of his charges on a diet of potatoes and water and refused to let them leave until such time as there was a uniform doctrine of faith. Even that didn't work and there was no end of flak from the Vatican.

TECHNOLOGY

Army technology was, by the standards of the main timeline, extremely spotty and inconsistent. Electronics was well developed because of Conrad's training in that field. They had radar before they had a reliable diesel engine, and their aircraft had solid-state computers while still made of wood and canvas. Astronomy was retarded and medicine was primitive, except for the universal cure given them by Conrad's uncle. Chemistry was behind but rationally organized so that progress was steady. Manufacturing techniques were superlative, with many factories being almost completely automated in Conrad's own lifetime. Agriculture too was well developed and as the Big People did most of the work, human input was limited to supervision, specialty harvesting, and research. Transport was both primitive and efficient. The Big People could only run at thirty miles per hour, but things ran smoothly day and night and except for intercontinental service, the mails traveled about as fast as they did in twentieth-century America. Physics was totally developed but completely Newtonian. The very existence of atomic power was unknown and research in that direction was discouraged. Conrad wrote a secret book on the horrors of atomic war and set up a tiny group of scientists to police the field. Their technique was to recruit any researcher who stumbled onto the forbidden knowledge.

INHERITANCE

The inheritance of position was not permitted in the army and even Conrad's legitimate children got nothing.

The inheritance of wealth was never actually forbidden in the army, but for several hundred years, Conrad's dislike of the system resulted in those with considerable inherited wealth being socially snubbed as those who "couldn't make it on their own." Eventually, this practice declined. So did the army.

THE STAR LINE

It eventually became obvious to Conrad that promotions within the army were being made largely on the basis of seniority. To a certain extent, this was good, since the average age of his men was so low. But it had the effect of keeping bright young people out of upper management and he feared a repetition of the Russian system, where only old men run the country. Also, there was the problem of eventually picking his own replacement.

His solution was to set up a secret organization whose function was to single out outstanding young people while they were in basic, and to observe and guide their careers.

Only about one person in two thousand got this special treatment, and that person never knew that he or she had been so honored. But a casual acquaintance would suggest that he apply for advanced training at Warsaw and, by golly, it would be approved. A star found himself transferred fairly often, to broaden his background. Promotions happened more quickly, even though his superiors didn't know what was happening.

Even his love life was molded and many were channeled out of inadvisable marriages, finding themselves in situations where the only available partners were of their own caliber.

Not everyone responded to this sort of nudging, but enough did to populate the upper echelons with some very competent people.

Conrad decided that he would retire at the age of sixty-five and that his successor should be between thirty and thirty-five. He should be technically competent, emotionally mature, and a born leader. Also, he had Krystyana, Cilicia, and Francine pass on his selection as well, since he knew that it was helpful to be handsome. At sixty, he settled on a vastly surprised twenty-nine-year-old komander, let it be known that the boy was anointed, and spent the next five years teaching him the ropes. The result was a remarkably smooth transition of power.

LIFE OUTSIDE THE ARMY

The Christian Army eventually became the largest organization in the world, and the only real fighting force, but by no means was it the *whole world*. Even at its peak, it never comprised more than ten percent of the population of Europe, nor more than three percent of the population of the planet.

Most civilian populations belonged to the army-sponsored Council of Peoples, originally called the Federation of Christendom. Any group of more than fifty thousand were allowed to join, providing that they guaranteed to support the army's three basic rights:

THE RIGHT OF DEPARTURE

Any person had the right to leave the country where he was living and go elsewhere. This effectively outlawed slavery and all other forms of involuntary servitude. A person could even run out on his debts. In the case of a criminal, that person had to be guilty of a crime by army law before the army would return him. It was only necessary for a refugee to set foot on army property to obtain army protection, and this was not just real property. Stepping on the shoe of an army knight was sufficient to invoke this right.

THE RIGHT OF TRANSIT

Both army personnel and civilians had the right to cross national borders for peaceful purposes. A country had the right to refuse people only on an individual basis, and only with cause.

THE RIGHT OF PURCHASE

The army had the right to purchase property in any country, after which that land was under army jurisdiction and no longer subject to the laws of the local country. The army paid no taxes.

In addition, the army often demanded of a country that was applying for membership a strip of territory around that country's borders that was typically five miles wide. This land was then turned over to the regular army, which fortified it and farmed it. Besides being profitable to the army, these border zones deterred aggression and, in the event of a war, made it obvious who the aggressor was.

In return for the above, the army guaranteed the national borders of any member state and would itself make war on any aggressor. It provided an arbitration service between member states that was also available to individuals. Aside from this, any country was allowed to do anything it wanted within its own borders, to have any sort of government and social institutions. But because of the right of departure, any government that was particularly oppressive found itself rapidly depopulated, soon losing its most energetic citizens.

In the thirteenth century, large nations did not exist in Europe. Few members had more than a million people. The army encouraged bilingualism, teaching Polish in the free schools available in every member country. The result was that many people were actually members of two cultures, their own local people and a worldwide civilization.

Conrad's historical branch never attained the bland homogeneity that the modern world is tending toward. There were interesting times.

About the Author

^^^^^^^^^^^^^^^^^^^^^^^^^^^^^^^^^^^^^

Leo Frankowski was born on February 13, 1943, in Detroit. He wandered through seven schools getting to the seventh grade and he's been wandering ever since. By the time he was forty-five, he had held more than a hundred different positions, ranging from "scientist" in an electro-optical research lab to gardener to airman to chief engineer to company president. Much of his work was in chemical and optical instrumentation, and earned him a number of U.S. patents.

His writing has earned him nominations for a Hugo, the John W. Campbell award, and a Nebula, but he hasn't won anything.

He still owns Sterling Manufacturing and Design, but got tired of design work several years ago and now spends much of his time writing and pursuing his various hobbies: i.e., reading, making mead, drinking mead, dancing girls, and cooking.

A lifelong bachelor, he lives in the wilds of Sterling Heights, Michigan.